CW01111886

THE BEGINNING OF CIVILIZATION
Mythologies Told True

Book One

TALLSTONE AND THE CITY

A New Heaven and Earth

Second Edition

Dennis Wammack

DCW PRESS
A Boutique Publishing Company

Birmingham, Alabama

The Beginning of Civilization: Mythologies Told True Series
Tallstone and the City: A New Heaven and Earth, Second Edition
© 2021, 2023 Dennis Wammack. All rights reserved.

Hardback: ISBN 979-8-9860246-8-4
Paperback: ISBN 979-8-9860246-6-0
eBook: ISBN 979-8-9860246-7-7

Characters, places, and events in this work are fictitious unless otherwise identified in the appendix. Any names, characters, companies, organizations, places, events, locales, and incidents are either used in a fictitious manner or are fictional. Unless identified in the appendix, any resemblance to actual persons, living or dead, actual organizations, or actual events is purely coincidental.

This is the Second Edition. Changes of consequence made to the First Edition of Tallstone and the City, ISBN 979-8-9860246-9-8, are detailed in the appendix.

Disclaimer: Within the six-book series, historical names are drawn from Greek, Egyptian, and Biblical references to protohistoric figures. Other names are derived from Sanskrit and Proto-Indo-European languages. Many characters, places, and events are inspired by well-known mythologies, but the narrative is not necessarily consistent with the myth. No effort has been made to provide historical accuracy of time or place or a scholarly development of technologies and themes. Histories spanning thousands of years have been compressed into hundreds to provide a single narrative across the series. Connections are made between characters who would realistically have lived in different epochs.

For rights and permissions,
contact Dennis Wammack,
denniswammack@gmail.com.
denniswammack.com

Cover design by the author using artificial intelligence resources.
Books are printed and distributed by IngramSpark, Nashville TN.
Published by DCW Press, Birmingham, Alabama, dcwpress.com.

HC240330

DCW PRESS
A Boutique Publishing Company

TABLE OF CONTENTS

The Appendix contains a Glossary of names and places.

1. In the Beginning
2. The Birth of Vanam — Year 0
3. The Birth of Kiya — Year 4, 4 years later
4. The Birth of Pumi — Year 10, 6 years later
5. The Birth of Valki — Year 13, 3 years later
6. Pumi, Apprentice Stonecutter — Year 16, 3 years later
7. Encounter with Chief Irakka — Year 18, 2 years later
8. The Liberation of Valki
9. Pumi — Year 25, 7 years later
10. Scouts Pumi and Kiya
11. Return to Pumi's Place — Year 26
12. The Rock Table and The Tall Stone
13. Encounter with Chief Nanatan
14. The Tall Stone and Nanatan
15. Pumi Returns to His Tribe
16. Tallstone and Saparu — Year 27
17. Winter Solstice Festival I
18. Valki of Urfa
19. Urfa and its People
20. Winter Solstice Festival II — Year 28
21. Valki's Great Experiment
22. Breathson and Wolfchief
23. Winter Solstice Festival III — Year 29
24. Valki and Kiya Go to Urfa
25. Wolves
26. The Scout
27. Winter Solstice Festival 11 — Year 37, 8 years later
28. Winter Solstice Festival 17 — Year 43, 6 years later
29. Pumi and Vanam
30. Valki and the Oceanids
31. Report from Tartarus
32. Valki Goes to Tartarus — Year 44
33. Return and Parting — Year 46, 2 years later
34. Winter Solstice Festival 34 — Year 60, 14 years later
35. The City — Year 65, 5 years later
36. Soliloquy
37. Tallstone — Year 87, 22 years later

APPENDIX

Author's Notes
Glossary of Names and Places
Second Edition Changes
Second Editions Publishing Schedule
Book One Publishing History

TALLSTONE AND THE CITY

A New Heaven and Earth

Second Edition

Book One. The Beginning of Civilization: Mythologies Told True

1. In the Beginning

Sunrise.

Ten thousand years ago, on the plains north of modern-day Sanliurfa, Turkey, a tribe of hunter-gatherers began their day as they had for over two hundred thousand years. But on this day, the first of four children is born. Driven by love, wisdom, ambition, and jealousy, these four will begin our transition from nomadic hunter-gatherers into stationary settlements—the beginning of human civilization.

The child is born.

So, it begins.

Vanam, Kiya, Pumi, Valki, Putt, Putt-pay, Breathson, Littlerock.

2. The Birth of Vanam

"His name is Vanam!" Chief Saparu shouted as he held his newborn son toward the heavens. "He will someday lead my tribe to riches and power beyond knowing. Vanam will be the greatest chief to ever live!"

The hunters were happy their chief was happy, but a butchered antelope would have made them happier. A son for the chief was fine but it was another mouth in a tribe with too many mouths and too little food.

The gatherers were happy to see the newborn, even if it meant losing another portion of food. The mother, Aman, was a young woman accepted into the tribe only nine seasons earlier.

Saparu's second-in-command, Ramum, had agreed to be the young woman's protector. This, however, did not include protection from Chief Saparu, whose self-established tradition was to be the first to mate with each new gatherer accepted into his tribe. After Saparu was tired of Aman, she was passed on to Ramum, two months pregnant. If she produced a male, Ramun would raise the boy as Saparu's son and heir apparent.

After allowing Aman almost a full morning to recover from giving birth, Saparu commanded his tribe to continue their northward run to the next campsite.

Chief Saparu was concerned. He thought, *This site had better have good hunting. At least better than our last two. We didn't see antelope or anything else. We are living on roots and plants.*

Saparu was beginning to doubt the expertise of his tribe's longtime moonwatcher, Nilla. *Nilla may be losing his good camp-predicting capabilities. He was never that great, anyway. Maybe it's time to start looking for another moonwatcher. Yes, I need a new moonwatcher. If I am to have a great tribe, I need a better moonwatcher.*

The tribe arrived at the location Nilla had chosen for this hunting season, and camp was made. The hunters and the chief's council sat around the campfire and discussed their situation.

Kattar, the elderly stonecutter, said, "We don't have enough spear points. At least here we have rocks to replenish our supply."

"Without game, spear points are useless," Ramum replied.

Saparu asked, "Tell me, Nilla, does anyone else know how to watch the moon, or are you the only one who knows how to do that?"

Saparu, Palai, Moonman. Nanatan, Vivekamulla, Vaniyal, Littlestar. Irakka, Mari, Irul.

Book One. The Beginning of Civilization: Mythologies Told True

"I am the only one capable of watching the moon and deciding where the next campsite should be," Nilla replied.

"Everyone agrees with that?" Saparu asked.

A respected hunter, Karan, offered, "I don't know about watching the moon, Chief. But I remember the last time we camped at this site hunting was miserable."

Saparu asked, "Then where would be a good site, Karan?"

Karan answered, "From what I remember and the feel of the weather, we are headed in the wrong direction. We should be many days south of here. I think at least three days south."

Saparu released an audible groan. "We would have to spend another day just to get back where we came from and then travel even farther south? That would mean even more hardship."

Saparu considered his options. *Nilla is finished. The tribe can no longer support him. Children see the moon. The skill is knowing which direction to go and how far to the next good hunting site. Karan is an excellent hunter and can read the terrain better than most.*

He asked, "Ramum? Kattar? Palai? Comments?"

Palai, the tribal elder woman, said, "The vegetation toward the south is adequate. We won't starve if we return that way."

Ramum said, "If there is no game to be found, it will be a greater hardship than not going back."

Kattar said, "I can collect rocks here and fashion them into spear points at a new camp, but I will need many uncut rocks and boys to carry them."

"I have decided!" Saparu roared. "Nilla, you led us here. You will hunt from here. This will be your Last Camp. Take extra spears and a full month of provisions. Don't return to my tribe."

He paused. "Kattar, at sunrise, collect the rocks you need. We will break camp and travel south as soon as you have your rocks. Karan, your name is now Moonman, and you had better be a good one. You will direct us to the best hunting sites. You are all dismissed." *We are on our way, Vanam. Your arrival is already changing things.*

Everyone except Saparu gathered around Nilla to wish him success and say goodbye. All knew that a lone hunter, whose greatest skill was as a moonwatcher, would, soon enough, be neither.

Vanam, Kiya, Pumi, Valki, Putt, Putt-pay, Breathson, Littlerock.

3. The Birth of Kiya

Four years later; ages 4, 0, 0, 0.

Sophia held her newborn daughter close. *You are beautiful, my daughter. As beautiful as the land and all that it grows. I shall name you Kiya. I shall be so proud of you. I shall raise you to be the wisest person to ever live. I shall find you a protector worthy of your great beauty and wise counsel. I will introduce you to your father in a while, but for now, you are mine. I will snuggle you until you are drowning in my love.*

The tribal chief, Irakka, awoke before sunrise. He felt by his side for his pregnant mate. She was not there.

He rose, looked into the distance, and saw the small fire. *Ahhh, Sophia. You did not wake me. How did you do this without my guidance?*

He chuckled. *Well, I suppose women know how to do these things.*

He dressed and walked toward the pre-dawn fire and the several women sitting around it. He saw Sophia, with a cloak over her head and shoulders, nursing the baby.

The women saw Irakka. All rose except Sophia.

As Irakka approached, the women clucked in delight:
"She is as beautiful as the night sky."
"Sophia did well with the birthing. She always does."
"You finally have a daughter to add to your collection of sons."
"She is a proud addition to our tribe, Great Chief."

He stood at the fire and looked at his beloved mate and their baby. Sophia looked up and said, "Great Chief Irakka, this is your daughter—Kiya."

"A simple name. A beautiful name worthy of your great wisdom. Thank you for this child, Sophia. We will raise her to be as wise as her mother."

"Yes," Sophia replied. "She will become a woman of great worth." Sophia then stood and gently handed Kiya to her father. "But for now, she needs someone to spit up on."

He placed his daughter on his shoulder and patted her back.

Kiya obediently spit up.

Saparu, Palai, Moonman. Nanatan, Vivekamulla, Vaniyal, Littlestar. Irakka, Mari, Irul.

< Vanam of Chief Saparu's Tribe >

Saparu and Vanam were always the first to rise.

Vanam had now lived through forty-eight hunting seasons—four years. He was barely old enough to keep up with the tribe when they migrated. Certainly, too young for a training hunt. But the boy was growing taller, stronger, and more determined. Ramum and Aman were doing an excellent job raising Vanam.

But it was always Saparu that the boy ran to see first. He enjoyed the roughhousing, the playfights, and the unending praise his biological father provided. "You're still too young for a training hunt, Vanam. But soon enough. You are going to take life by the tail and swing it around over your head. You are going to be the greatest chief to ever live."

Vanam, Kiya, Pumi, Valki, Putt, Putt-pay, Breathson, Littlerock.

4. The Birth of Pumi

Six years later; ages 10, 6, 0, 0.

The hunters were away on the hunt and the young woman's labor was not going well. Palai could not even remember her name. *What kind of elder woman does not even know the names of her tribe's women? Surely, she has a name, but I don't remember ever hearing it.*

This young woman, as Palai now painfully remembered, did not even have a "Protector." She was on her own in protecting herself. No young hunter would obligate himself to this girl. Her hair was too light—not like the nice black hair other gatherers had. She was too tall—as tall as a hunter. She was too skinny, too quiet, too reserved, "too" everything. And her mind was always somewhere else.

A suitable protector had been found for the young woman Palai was trading, but Palai could not reciprocate. Palai succumbed. "Very well. I will receive your woman into our tribe, but I offer her no protector. You will receive my well-trained young woman into your tribe, but she will be under the protection of your finest hunter. There are no other considerations. Are we in agreement?"

"We are," the other elder woman had replied. Then added, "Do the best you can with her. She is a sweet girl."

Palai had thought, *I lost an accomplished gatherer and gained a sweet gatherer of questionable worth. I did not do well. Chief Saparu will not be pleased.*

He wasn't. But still, Saparu mated with her as was his tradition. And now, the sweet young woman lay dying while giving birth.

Palai considered, *What will Chief Saparu want done with the baby? It has no mother and it's undersized. Better to make the decision now rather than wait and let the baby die later. But Chief Saparu is the father. He told me he wanted another son—that Vanam needed a little brother to command. My chief will have to decide the baby's fate when he returns.*

The hunters eventually returned. Saparu was exuberant. This had been Vanam's first training hunt and he had excelled. Also, they had slaughtered ample food. Life was good. Saparu ordered a feast for his tribe. He had not yet been told that which awaited him in the women's quarters.

The fires were built. The feast was completed. The chief gathered his council around the campfire. "Moonman was a great choice. I am pleased with myself for selecting him. He remembers the good hunting camps based on the weather and how long ago we were there. We have been

Saparu, Palai, Moonman. Nanatan, Vivekamulla, Vaniyal, Littlestar. Irakka, Mari, Irul.

Book One. The Beginning of Civilization: Mythologies Told True

camping in the wrong places for a long time. He said he could have told me, but I never asked. I predict our tribe will never go hungry again." Murmurs of excitement ran through the camp.

Kattar said, "I have replenished our supply of spear points. I'm trying to recruit one of our boys as an apprentice, but none will hear of it. They want to become a great hunter like Saparu."

"Keep looking," Saparu commanded. "You are getting old. I can't be without a good stonecutter."

Kattar laughed. No one else did.

Saparu asked Palai, "Any news from the women, Palai?"

"Well, yes. Great Chief. News that will require your decision."

"I'm good at making decisions. What needs deciding?"

Palai called in a loud voice, "Pen, bring the baby."

A girl stepped from the children's circle holding a wrapped object. She unwrapped the bundle to show Chief Saparu. It was the baby.

Palai explained, "This is your son, Great Chief. The mother died. I took what milk I could, but it was not a great deal. We have no nursing mothers to nourish it. None of the women wish to take it as their own. It was born small. I see no way I can raise it into a robust boy. There is a river nearby. What shall I do?"

Saparu inspected the baby. "Hmmm. He is rather small, isn't he? But he is my son. Hmmm."

Vanam walked to the child and poked its chest with his finger. The baby reflexively hit the finger. Vanam said, "I like it. I want to keep it. Aman will raise it as my little brother. How do you make a woman give milk? Find one to give it milk. I want a strong little brother. Can we keep it, Father?"

"Of course, we can keep it. Shall we name it Secondson?"

Vanam replied, "No. Give my little brother a proper name. Name him Pumi. I will teach him to do useful things for my tribe."

< Kiya of Chief Irakka's Tribe >

Six-year-old Kiya always kept sharp eyes on her mother and took in her every word. She learned every plant and its use. Kiya once harvested an undesirable weed. "That is not a useful plant, Kiya," her mother had told her.

"It *is* useful, Mother. I just haven't found out what for yet."

Vanam, Kiya, Pumi, Valki, Putt, Putt-pay, Breathson, Littlerock.

5. The Birth of Valki

Three years later; ages 13, 9, 3, 0.

The woman was panicked. She was birthing her baby, and the chief did not even stop the tribe for her. He did not allow a gatherer to stay with her. She squatted on the ground in the glaring sun; no water; no herbs; no ointments. *I don't deserve this. I know there is little food, but still—I don't deserve this. My chief expects me to die—wants me to die. Die with my baby. Anger will sap my strength. I need all my strength—all my will. I will have my baby. I will live. My baby will live.*

She successfully gave birth to a daughter and followed the direction the tribe had gone. Late that night, she saw the remains of the campfire. She had nursed her newborn baby. She had found edible vegetation along the trail. She would not starve and would produce enough milk for her baby. *My baby is alive. I will name her Valki. I will teach her to raise all who have fallen. The chief will not be pleased to see us. He wanted us to die. He might banish us from the camp. I need the camp for protection and scraps of food. If I stay out of his sight until they leave for the hunt, maybe they will be successful and make our chief happy. The elder woman is terrified of him and won't help me. A new mother should be given a season to nurse and care for her newborn. Perhaps the elder woman will not notice one of her gatherers has given birth and carries her child with her to gather.*

< Vanam and Pumi of Chief Saparu's Tribe >

Vanam had grown into a fine young hunter; everything Chief Saparu had hoped for. He was on the verge of manhood and would undoubtedly become a worthy chief when his time came. His little brother, Pumi, had survived but with slow growth due to a lack of proper nutrition as an infant. Pumi loved his big brother and never missed a chance to interact with him.

Vanam enjoyed his little brother. It was fun to have someone look up to him, was always thrilled to see him—and knew his place. Vanam felt grown-up as he taught his toddler brother the things a toddler brother should know.

< Kiya of Chief Irakka's Tribe >

Kiya grew into a mature, sophisticated, knowledgeable young girl. She was aware she had advantages—her father was the chief, and her mother was the elder woman—but she did not flout her high status. She was "just one of the girls" and giggled with the best of them. Sometimes, in the back of her mind but never expressed, *We can be silly sometimes.*

But always, she listened, learned the art and science of gathering, and sometimes discovered the use of a thing by herself.

Saparu, Palai, Moonman. Nanatan, Vivekamulla, Vaniyal, Littlestar. Irakka, Mari, Irul.

6. Pumi, Apprentice Stonecutter

Three years later; ages 16, 12, 6, 3.

As he often did, Pumi watched the old stonecutter chip away at his rocks. Now and then, Kattar stopped to admire a well-crafted spear point he had fashioned. The boy picked up a large, discarded chip and said, "In here."

Kattar looked at the six-year-old and asked, "What's in there, Pumi?"

Pumi replied, "One of those things—a spear point."

The stonecutter took the discarded chip from Pumi and examined it. "Maybe, with a little work, I could turn this piece into a spear point."

"No," Pumi said. "The spear point is in there. Just remove the rock from around it. The spear point will be free."

Kattar laughed. "Here," he said as he handed his cutting tools to Pumi, "set the spear point free."

With inexperienced hands, Pumi took the crafting tools and the rock. He set the rock on the anvil stone and tentatively made a first strike with the hammerstone. The boy frowned at the result. He repositioned the burin and struck the rock again. This time, a little more to his liking. Kattar was impressed. He had never told the boy how to hold the tools nor had given any other stone-cutting instructions. The boy's amateur strikes were learned by nothing but observation. Pumi struck the rock a third time and excess material flew away. What remained was one side of a spear point; the other side and the edges remained encased in stone, but a spear point was being set free.

Pumi looked at Kattar for approval.

Kattar grinned as he shook his head, "Yes."

With pride and excitement, Pumi repositioned the stone and struck it again and again. *This hammerstone is not good. It doesn't fit my hand. The balance is bad.*

The old stonecutter watched a reasonable spear point emerge from what had been a discarded chip. He asked Pumi, "Would you like to learn everything there is to know about cutting stones?"

Pumi looked at Kattar with wide-eyed excitement and said, "Yes, I want to learn how to set the things in the rocks free!" *And make a better hammerstone and a sharper burin that's easier to control!*

Vanam, Kiya, Pumi, Valki, Putt, Putt-pay, Breathson, Littlerock.

Kattar said, "The hunters will return soon. I shall ask Chief Saparu if you can become my apprentice at the next council meeting."

Pumi looked at the surrounding rocks. He saw a better hammerstone waiting to be set free. *I want to make EVERYTHING better!*

< Kiya of Chief Irakka's Tribe >

Aman held a private ceremony for her twelve-year-old daughter.

She said, "You are no longer a child, Kiya. You are now a woman. I have so much to share with you. You can now join the women in the gathering fields. I must tell you about men and their weaknesses. You must now take on the joys and burdens of being a woman. There is much to be thankful for and much to bear, but your body can now bring forth life, although, perhaps, unfortunately, you will need a male to do that. But time enough for these things. Right now, let us rejoice."

< Valki of an Unknown Tribe >

Valki no longer toddled.

The environment and conditions had forced the three-year-old to walk in straight, purposeful motions. To toddle was a sign of weakness. There could be no sign of weakness in Valki or her mother. Each day could bring their banishment. The mother made a show of taking little food. What she took, she shared with Valki. They were both gaunt, more so than the other women in the tribe.

The hunters took more than their share of food because "they had to maintain their strength" for the hunt. The chief, of course, needed to remain the strongest.

Her mother had taught Valki which plants were edible. Valki could explore the periphery of the camp and find a few edible plants; enough to ward off starvation, at least. Her mother held Valki tightly each night, softly singing songs, laughing with her, talking to her, stroking her hair, and being the best mother she knew how to be.

Valki grew to be a happy, caring child.

She knew no better.

Book One. The Beginning of Civilization: Mythologies Told True

< Vanam of Chief Saparu's Tribe >

Vanam sat between his two fathers at the council campfire.

The hunt had again been good, and Vanam was becoming a dominant hunter. He already commanded respect and deference from most of the other hunters. Only Saparu, Ramum, and maybe his friend, Valuvana, the strongest hunter in the tribe, remained his obvious betters. But Vanam was working on that problem.

As the council meeting ended, Saparu asked Palai and Kattar if they had more issues requiring his attention.

Kattar cleared his throat and said, tentatively, "Yes, Great Chief, there is one more issue I wish to bring to your attention."

Saparu hated hearing the words "Great Chief." That meant something was coming he did not want to hear. "Very well, what is it?"

"It concerns your younger son, Great Chief. And my pressing need for an apprentice stonecutter. I ask you to consider—if it might be possible—if it might be good for the tribe—if perhaps …"

Vanam snapped, "You wish my little brother to become your apprentice?

Kattar answered, "Just consider it. You can change your mind as he gets older. He's still a boy and may grow to be a full-sized hunter—but for now—he would be extremely useful to me—and he has a great talent for it—maybe a great hunter who also knows how to create spear points would someday be helpful—I was just asking for your thoughts on the matter—I told the boy I would ask." Kattar became silent.

Saparu asked, "What do you think, Vanam? Your brother, a stonecutter."

Vanam replied, "Better a good stonecutter than a poor hunter. Pumi isn't old enough for training hunts and he is too skinny to ever be a good hunter, anyway. Even if Pumi is a poor student and never becomes accomplished, there is no harm in it, and it will help Kattar. I would allow it."

Saparu roared, "I have decided! Kattar, you will take Pumi to be your apprentice stonecutter. Let us know when he makes his first spearhead so we can assess his progress. You are all dismissed."

Kattar was dismissed before he could present any of the spear points Pumi had already produced. Upon further reflection, Kattar decided, although he did not know why, this had been for the best.

Vanam, Kiya, Pumi, Valki, Putt, Putt-pay, Breathson, Littlerock.

17

7. Encounter with Chief Irakka

Two years later; ages 18, 14, 8, 5.

Moonman saw the reflections of the distant campfire in the night sky. He told Saparu and concluded with, "They will have seen our fire and will now be deciding what to do. How shall I proceed, Chief?"

Saparu replied, "An encounter, I suppose. We have a little food to offer, several young women to trade, extra spear points—pretty good spear points, at that. We need linen and rope. Take Ramum with you—and Vanam, take Vanam, too. Ask if they wish to encounter us. If you meet their delegation on the way to us, then whatever you decide will be my command."

"As you command, my chief," Moonman said as he hurried off to enlist Ramum and Vanam as emissaries to the unknown tribe.

Saparu sought Palai to advise her of the probable upcoming encounter. *These things are more women's work than men's. Too much planning, feasting, bartering, and visiting to be a man's work. I'll have to entertain the other chief. Who is wealthier? Us or them? Who is more powerful? Are they dangerous? Will they have anything of value to us? Can Palai trade off some of our young women? I had rather be out hunting!"*

Moonman and company were two thousand paces from their camp when they saw the torch of the other tribesmen approaching. They shifted their direction to meet them. Upon meeting, Moonman announced, "Two thousand paces."

"Three thousand paces," the opposing moonwatcher announced. "I am Irul, moonwatcher from the tribe of Chief Irakka. We have made an overnight camp on our way to the west. We seek to encounter your tribe."

Presumably, Irul and his company had begun their march toward Saparu's camp first and were, therefore, the presumptive moderator.

"I am Moonman, moonwatcher from the tribe of Chief Saparu. We have made our season camp and will remain here for the remainder of the hunting season. We, too, seek to encounter. My chief will accept whatever terms you and I might agree upon."

"Let us counsel," Irul suggested.

The six men placed their torches into the ground and sat down to work out the delicate details of an encounter between two tribes. Chief Saparu would eventually become the host of this encounter since his camp was long-term rather than temporary.

Saparu, Palai, Moonman. Nanatan, Vivekamulla, Vaniyal, Littlestar. Irakka, Mari, Irul.

Book One. The Beginning of Civilization: Mythologies Told True

The negotiators returned late that night and called a council meeting.

Saparu complained, "Oh, no. I'm the host? Must I provide the food?"

Moonman answered, "All we can spare. And they, unfortunately, are a large tribe. If they are honorable, then they will bring their share, but be prepared for the worst."

Sapuru asked, "Can you prepare the festivities, Palai? When do they get here?"

Moonman said, "Late tomorrow. That will give us time to prepare and leave time for our tribes to mingle. The feast will be held after the mingling. We will host trade negotiations the day after."

Palai said, "I will have the women prepare for many guests. They will be excited. The young women, especially. You must be both forceful and magnanimous tomorrow, Chief Saparu. This will be an exhibition of your greatness. You must make a good impression not only on their chief but on their hunters and gatherers. This is how your reputation will grow."

Saparu said, "My responsibilities are never-ending. But I shall be wonderful!"

Palai was excited. "I will call the young women together at sunrise and discuss our goals. I will get the older women to start preparing the feast. And our traders must review what we have to trade and the things needed."

She stopped and looked at Vanam. "Vanam, you are my best young hunter. I can command a great premium on one such as you—son of the chief—the heir apparent—the best young hunter in our tribe—and so tall—so handsome. Be prepared to accept a desirable young woman into your protection. And I have Valuvana and Maiyana, too. Oh, I have so many desirable young hunters. They are a large tribe, you said? I hope they have desirable young gatherers to exchange. How exciting!"

The young hunters groaned, "Tied to a woman?"

But they would, they all knew, do as their chief commanded.

Saparu was excited. "Don't forget. I have my tradition when we accept new gatherers into my tribe."

< Next Day After Highsun >

The tribes mingled to assess each other.

The eligible males gathered near the great fire pit, talking about hunting.

Vanam, Kiya, Pumi, Valki, Putt, Putt-pay, Breathson, Littlerock.

The eligible young women paraded around the fire pit; ostensibly visiting with the young women from the other tribe; comparing notes on gathering techniques and that sort of thing. They took no apparent notice of the young hunters nervously glancing in their direction.

Not that their preferences made any difference in this matter. Selecting a proper protector was far too important to be left to the young. The elder women would decide. The chiefs would approve. Those matched were expected to acquiesce. The right of refusal was sometimes offered, but not always.

Female candidates from Irakka's tribe were all aware of the tall hunter who was the chief's son and would probably one day be chief himself—and an excellent hunter—and provider—and so handsome.

Although most hunters thought a running antelope far prettier than a gatherer, several hunters from Saparu's tribe, including Saparu himself, were struck by the tall, dark-eyed, self-possessed beauty from Irakka's tribe. "The chief's daughter," it was said. Extra consideration might well be needed to acquire this one into a tribe. Saparu would be open to extra consideration—tradition, and all.

There would be a great feast that night—Irakka's tribe had contributed much. The fire was built. The feast was wonderful.

Tomorrow, trade negotiations would begin.

< Next Day >

Trade negotiations began:
"Your spear points are superb."
"This rope is not as strong as I would like."
"Your linen is nice but do you have finer?"
"Yes, I believe these pelts will do nicely."
"The spear shafts are straight but a little thin."
"You say this ointment will help heal open wounds?"
"This potion ensures the woman will not become with child."

And then, it was time. Matches would be made. Lives decided.

The two elder women secluded themselves with the two moonwatchers. The moonwatchers would speak only if spoken to. The chiefs stayed nearby amicably sharing hunting information, both pleased with the day's transactions.

The encounter had been beneficial for both tribes. All that remained was the negotiation of finding suitable protectors for the young women. The

Saparu, Palai, Moonman. Nanatan, Vivekamulla, Vaniyal, Littlestar. Irakka, Mari, Irul.

Book One. The Beginning of Civilization: Mythologies Told True

women and girls gathered around the fire pit, guessing which women would soon be joining their tribe—and leaving.

Moonman and Irul walked to the fire pit. Moonman called out, "Valvuna, come with me!"

Irul then called out, "Pen-Pu, come with me!"

Through much giggling, the two young adults dutifully marched into the area where the elder women were holding Court. Later, they returned. Valvuna was holding Pen-Pu's hand. She was smiling and blushing. After the night's final feast, Valvuna would stand before both tribes and vow to protect Pen-Pu from the dangers of the world and to care for whatever child she might bear.

The two moonwatchers again returned to those gathered at the fire pit. "Maiyana, come with me," Moonman commanded.

Irul commanded, "Pen-Alai, come with me!" The two walked through the giggles. Soon enough, they emerged to the cheers of the women and the catcalls of the men.

The process was repeated two more times with young hunters from Irakka's tribe and two young women from Saparu's tribe.

After that, the moonwatchers did not appear at the time expected—nor any time soon, thereafter. Negotiations must have been intense and difficult. It was obvious, to all who kept track of such things, that the two prime candidates for matchmaking had not been called—the most eligible, desirable hunter and the most eligible, desirable gatherer. Both were fathered by a chief. Both were superior to their peers. Vanam and Kiya.

Among those keeping track was Pumi. Although only eight, Pumi could size up people. Not yet physically mature, he could still see and appreciate Kiya's great beauty. Not only her physical beauty but, too, her inner beauty. Her self-confidence—the poise—her easy way with both women and men—young and old—her presence—she was the most impressive gatherer Pumi had ever seen. It was obvious what was under discussion was whether his older brother would agree to become her protector. And, maybe, too, if she would accept him. Pumi had never before considered his older brother taking a gatherer. Where would this leave Pumi in his relationship with his older brother? What would be his relationship with Kiya? Life was getting too complicated. Pumi needed his rocks.

Vanam, Kiya, Pumi, Valki, Putt, Putt-pay, Breathson, Littlerock.

In the negotiations, Sophia said to Palai, "It is not my decision to make. Kiya is adamant. Since she became a woman, she has always been adamant. I realize what a magnificent protector Vanam would be. He is undoubtedly man enough to protect several women. But he must agree to Kiya's condition. She will not negotiate. Chief Irakka will honor his daughter's desire. She will agree to always mate with her chosen protector whenever called upon and support him in all things. But whichever protector she accepts must agree to her demand that she need not mate with any man not of her choosing. I realize this puts you in an untenable position. You told me of Chief Saparu's tradition to be the first to mate with each new woman to join his tribe. I am sorry. To refuse a chief is unthinkable. Perhaps Kiya will agree to mate with your chief, but you must be prepared for her refusal to do so. It will be better for both us and our tribes if we do not make the match rather than having Kiya refuse the match—and know Chief Irakka will not command her to accept—and even if he did—she would still refuse—and she is well trained in the art of self-defense. If your chief came for her after she refused him—there would be an incident so horrible neither of us may even think of it. Let us put this match behind us, Elder Woman Palai. We have made four wonderful matches. That is sufficient."

"Let us rest, Elder Woman Sophia. I will counsel with my chief and ask him to counsel with his son. Let me find out if they have any interest in this matter. We must meet again later."

The two women walked to the fire, negotiations apparently over. There was an audible collective sigh. There would be no match between Vanam and Kiya.

Pumi was mildly upset. He walked to Kiya, who was standing alone. He said, "Hello, my name is Pumi. I am an apprentice stonecutter. My brother is Vanam. I thought maybe he would agree to become your protector. I guess that would make us related in some way. I'm sorry that didn't happen. You are so mature. You would have made our tribe much better."

She knelt on her knee so she could look up rather than down at him. "My name is Kiya, Pumi. It is so nice to meet you. This is my third encounter as a woman and Sophia has yet to match me to a protector. I may never find one. But if I do, I hope he will be the man that you will become."

She smiled, rose to her feet, and said, "And I would have loved to be related to you." She then left to join her mother, lost somewhere in the crowd.

Elsewhere, Saparu was beside himself. He said to Palai, "Refuse to mate with a chief? Is that even possible? I mean every woman should be thrilled

Saparu, Palai, Moonman. Nanatan, Vivekamulla, Vaniyal, Littlestar. Irakka, Mari, Irul.

to mate with a chief. Did you explain my tradition? Surely, she wouldn't reject such a fine tradition. I understand not wanting to mate with some of my hunters—but the chief? Palai, this is highly irregular."

Palai answered, "I understand, Great Chief Saparu. But she will probably reject Vanam if he does not agree to this. That would put him in an impossible position. If he agrees to her condition and if you came for her, she might aggressively reject you—then you would have to banish her—but your son would be her protector—so he would have to abandon his vow to protect her—which would make him unqualified to be chief. I see no way to make this negotiation work."

"This is what happens when you let a female have a say in who she mates with. Respect is going downhill. Wait! Do you think this is a negotiation ploy? Maybe they want me, the chief, to agree to be her protector. I may be able to do that. Would they agree to that?"

"Kiya is a young woman, Great Chief. A young woman can sometimes be quite vexing to a mature leader, such as yourself. Especially, for a leader who has chosen to never accept the responsibility of a woman and any children she might bear."

"I suppose you're right, Palai. Do you think Vanam would have any interest in this matter?"

"That would be for a father and a son to discuss and come to an understanding."

"Send Vanam to me. I will then decide what to do."

Vanam arrived. He and Saparu discussed the awkward situation.

Saparu said, "She might refuse me, her chief. That is not certain, but it would be her choice. A woman's choice over a chief's choice. Could that even be allowed?"

Vanam replied, "It could not be allowed, Father. The only solution is for the issue to never arise. You would simply never ask her to mate. The only condition appears to be I give the woman a choice. She might accept you but then she might not. That would create the impossible situation—for her—for me—for you."

Saparu asked, "Do you think she would refuse me? A chief?"

Vanam laughed. "Probably not, but she might. It would be easy enough for you and me to agree in private that you will never ask her. The situation will

Vanam, Kiya, Pumi, Valki, Putt, Putt-pay, Breathson, Littlerock.

never arise. I could then agree to her condition. Maybe I could get her to agree to tell everyone she wanted to mate with you, but you didn't ask. Understanding, of course, you will never ask because your son is her protector."

Saparu roared, "Yes! I have decided! Do that!"

Vanam then did the unthinkable. He requested a private meeting with Kiya so "they could get to know each other" before another formal meeting between the two Elder Women.

The campfire burned down. The feast had been wonderful and was now complete. The ceremonies began. The women and children were allowed to mingle with the hunters for this particular ceremony. The men and women sat and stood together without regard to rank.

Elder Woman Palai stepped to stand behind Chief Saparu, who was sitting beside Chief Irakka.

On her right was Valvuna. On her left was Pen-Pu. She let the adoring crowd adore the scene for a while and then stepped back. In a loud voice, she asked, "Valvuna of the tribe of Saparu, do you agree to protect this woman, Pen-Pu of the tribe of Irakka? Do you agree to protect her from harm, to provide food for her nourishment, to help her raise any child she might bear, and any child she might adopt? Do you promise to do these things upon your honor and upon your manhood?"

Valvuna took Pen-Pu's hand in his, raised them into the air, and, with an adoring look from Pen-Pu, loudly proclaimed, "I promise to do these things!"

Palai returned to the fire with Maiyana and Pen-Alai by her side. To the delight of the crowd, the process was repeated.

It was then Sophia's turn. There had been two additional matches made. Twice, she brought a hunter from her tribe and a young woman from Saparu's tribe. The two young women would leave everyone they knew to join their protector in a tribe they had never before seen. The women were strangely unafraid.

The ceremonies were apparently over. Those sitting began to rise.

"Wait!" Palai commanded. "There is one more ceremony to perform!"

The crowd hushed in anticipation.

Sophia walked to stand behind the two chiefs, where she was joined by Palai. From out of the darkness stepped Vanam and Kiya. There was a collective gasp from the witnesses. Palai began, "Vanam of the tribe ..."

Saparu, Palai, Moonman. Nanatan, Vivekamulla, Vaniyal, Littlestar. Irakka, Mari, Irul.

Kiya held up her hand for silence and said, "Elder Woman Palai, before I ask the Great Hunter Vanam to consider being my protector, I wish to confess a weakness directly to your Great Chief Saparu so his son can make a wise decision. Can this be permitted?"

Palai feigned confusion even though the act had already been agreed upon by all participants. Palai said, "Well, if my chief agrees to this request, then I am sure he wishes to hear your confession."

Kiya went and knelt between the two chiefs but addressed Saparu so all could hear. "Great and wise chief of this great tribe I desperately wish to join, I feel you must know this about me. I have never before mated. It is my understanding it is your tradition that a maiden is introduced into your tribe by your being the first to mate with her. I am inexperienced in these matters, and I know I would bring dishonor to my tribe by not being satisfactory in my first mating. I do not wish to dishonor my tribe, but I leave it to the wisdom of my protector and his chief to decide such matters. I did not want the greatest hunter in the land to agree to protect a woman without being aware of the problems she would present."

Saparu laughed. "Ah! I shall command my son to welcome you into our tribe instead of me. Who you mate with will be left to you and your protector!"

Chief Irakka stood and said, "Great wisdom leads this tribe. I am well pleased my daughter will be accepted into your tribe!"

Pumi was impressed. *Nicely done. Who came up with that?*

Kiya rose. With wide eyes and a soft smile, she looked into the eyes of her soon-to-be protector as she walked to stand to face him. The tall, full-bodied, dark-haired, dark-eyed beauty accepted the hand of the muscular, imposing, self-confident Vanam. The two beautiful people turned to face the enthusiastic approval of the two tribes.

And their turbulent future.

< Valki of an Unknown Tribe >

Valki's mother had lived too long on too little food.

She knew she could not survive tomorrow's run to the next camp. "Please, Elder Woman, find a mother for my little Valki. She is a wonderful, resourceful, loving child. She deserves to live. Please—find her a mother."

There was no one listening to their conversation. An elder woman should never lie, but—what harm could it do this once? Besides, no one else was

Vanam, Kiya, Pumi, Valki, Putt, Putt-pay, Breathson, Littlerock.

listening. The elder woman replied, "If the child survives the run to the next camp, I will find her a mother. Valki will grow into a fine, strong woman."

The starving woman tried to embrace the elder woman, but the elder woman pushed her away.

The woman said, "Thank you, elder woman. You are kind and merciful!"

The woman returned to her pallet and her sleeping child. She held the child tightly through the night.

< The Run >

Her mother woke Valki before the sun rose. She said, "Today is our great test to see if we live. I will stay at this camp, and you will run with our tribe to the next camp. You must run by yourself all the way. When you arrive, find our elder woman and ask her who your new mother will be. She will find you a new mother to love and take care of you."

Valki was confused. "But I don't want a new mother. I want my real mother. I don't want to leave you."

"You must do what you must do, Valki. Always remember I have loved you with all my love. You have brought me great joy, but it is your duty to live. And to live, you must leave me and run by yourself to the next camp. No one will help you. But once you prove you can do it, the elder woman promises to find you a new mother. Elder women do not lie."

In the distance, the tribe was beginning its run to the next camp.

Her mother embraced her and said, "Hug me, Valki. Then run with your tribe. Do not stumble."

Valki hugged her mother and then ran after her tribe.

Her mother's request to the elder woman was reasonable. When a child could perform a migration run without assistance or other consideration, the child was no longer considered a burden on the tribe. Valki was young but her mother had trained her daughter well. Valki was as developed and much better trained than other children her age. Although all women and children in this particular tribe were undernourished, Valki's mother had provided Valki with sufficient food for her to develop normally but her short legs could not command the stride to stay up with her tribe even though it was not a fast run. She would fall behind but then catch up when the tribe stopped to rest. At long last, nightfall came, and the tribe stopped to make camp.

Saparu, Palai, Moonman. Nanatan, Vivekamulla, Vaniyal, Littlestar. Irakka, Mari, Irul.

Valki saw her tribe stop in the distance. Valki ran. The tribe was eating their meager rations when Valki arrived. All the food had been distributed. There was none for Valki. Valki presented herself to the elder woman. "My name is Valki. Mother told me you would find me another mother when we made camp. Which woman will be my mother, please?"

The elder woman was in disbelief that the child had made the run. She said, "We run again tomorrow. Find me when we make camp and we will discuss finding you a mother."

Valki said, "Thank you, Elder Woman. You are kind and merciful." She went to the edge of the camp to find an edible plant or root.

Valki would live another day.

Vanam, Kiya, Pumi, Valki, Putt, Putt-pay, Breathson, Littlerock.

8. The Liberation of Valki

Valki had risen early to find food to carry on her day's run.

She had been successful in her search the night before; edible roots, three grubs, and an earthworm. Not an abundance but enough to get her through another day of running. One more day and she would have a new mother. She mourned for her real mother, but it was Valki's duty to live. If she did not survive then all her mother had sacrificed for her would have been to no avail. *I am ready, Mother. I will run and I will not stumble.*

Valki was stronger on the second day's run because she had been successful the day prior and her confidence had increased.

This time she knew there would be no food for her, so she scavenged outside the camp before presenting herself once more to the elder woman with her request for a new mother.

The elder woman was resigned to facing the issue. She said, "I will counsel with the chief at tomorrow's council. The chief will advise me on how to proceed. In the meantime, find a place to sleep and stay out of the way during tomorrow's gathering."

Valki was happy. She wasn't too hungry, and she was going to get a new mother.

< >

The council met the next night. The chief was not happy to hear of another potential mouth to feed. He answered, "What woman would want another child? We have too many children. They don't do anything useful!"

The elder woman was fearful, but replied, "Great Chief, our tribe doesn't have *enough* children. We die faster than we are replaced. Many of our children have already died and many women, too. That this one still lives attests to her great strength and worthiness. Your tribe is barely large enough to function. I don't have enough gatherers. I believe that I can send Valki into the fields and she would find more food than she would eat."

The chief roared, "Silence! If you find a woman who will take her, let her stay. But let it be understood that the child's rations will come from the mother's rations. If a mother cannot be found, send the child away. Anything else?"

"No, Great Chief. I understand." The elder woman made a cursory attempt to find a woman willing to adopt Valki, but the sharing of already barely sustainable rations was simply not feasible.

Saparu, Palai, Moonman. Nanatan, Vivekamulla, Vaniyal, Littlestar. Irakka, Mari, Irul.

Out of pity, Valki was given a child's ration from the community dinner that night. Valki was excited to have a real meal for the first time in many days and excited, too, that she would soon have another mother.

The chief came to inspect the women as they ate. He saw Valki sitting by herself in a corner—eating.

The chief demanded, "Who is this girl's mother?"

All the women looked down in silence at their food. The elder woman hurried over. "I am still looking for a mother for the child, Great Chief. While I look, I gave her just enough food to sustain her."

"That food is MINE!" the chief shouted as he hurried over and took Valki's food. Let the mother of this girl stand—NOW!"

He looked around and seeing no one stand, demanded, "Send the girl away. Tell her not to return to my tribe!" The chief stormed out with Valki's food.

The woman sitting nearest Valki shoved her ration to Valki. "Take this. I'm full," the woman said as she rose and left.

Valki was sad because the woman had obviously not eaten enough. Valki took the offering and gave it to, other than herself, the youngest girl in the tribe. The girl had earlier rejected Valki's efforts at friendship. Valki said, "Here, I wish you to have this." She then surveyed the room and asked, "Will anyone be my mother?"

The women stared at their food. No one spoke.

Valki left the women's fire and walked to the edge of the camp to search for roots and grubs.

< >

In the night, Valki sat beside a trail leading to the campsite. She would have to remain near the camp for safety. She could slip into camp late each night and leave before sunrise. For the first time in her life, she was lonely. She wanted to cry but crying would not help. She stared across the trail and imagined her mother sitting across from her. *I am still alive, Mother. But the elder woman did not do what she promised—you are still my only mother—I like that—I didn't want another mother, anyway.*

The mother in her imagination seemed so real. Almost like Valki could cross the path and embrace her. *What will I do, Mother? No woman will have me. The chief will beat me if he sees me in his camp. If I leave, an animal will eat me.*

Vanam, Kiya, Pumi, Valki, Putt, Putt-pay, Breathson, Littlerock.

The image of her mother segued into the image of a nice young man; one who would be nice to her. She jumped up and ran to embrace him. "Bubba, Big Bubba," she said.

He seemed so real, just like he was really there. She thought she could feel him returning her embrace. Her mind heard him say, "Little sister, you are so sad. Why are you sad?"

She kept her eyes clenched closed, savoring the embrace of her imagined "Big Brother."

She said, "I am alone, Big Bubba. I have no place to go. No one wants me. If I stay here, I will be beaten. If I leave, I will be eaten. I don't know what to do. I don't know how to stay alive for another day. Mother will be sad."

"Well," said the image in her mind, "will this tribe take care of you?"

"No, the elder woman will not do what she promised, and the chief will beat me."

"Then should you stay or leave?"

"I should leave but then I will be eaten by a wild animal."

"How could you not be eaten by a wild animal?"

"I don't know."

"Who would know?"

"I guess a hunter would know."

"I see. If you weren't eaten by a wild animal, what would you do?"

"I would walk until I found another tribe somewhere."

"I see. If you found another tribe, what would happen?"

"Maybe, I could find another mother."

"Yes, that's possible. You will need a traveling bag with a knife. Where would you get that?"

"The chief has one and it has apples in it, too. I have seen it."

"I see. The chief took your food away from you, didn't he? For no good reason other than he could."

"Yes, the chief took my food."

Saparu, Palai, Moonman. Nanatan, Vivekamulla, Vaniyal, Littlestar. Irakka, Mari, Irul.

"I must go now, little sister. You seem to have learned that to solve an unsolvable problem, simply break it into many smaller problems. But I have stayed too long and talked too much. My associates will be angry with me. I must go. I hope you can stay alive another day."

With that, she felt her embrace returned—firmly—like her mother when Valki left her. She savored the feeling, then opened her eyes. No one was there. *Ask a hunter how not to get eaten. Get a bag with a knife. Walk in a direction the tribe will not go. Find another tribe. Stay alive another day.*

Valki was thrilled. She had a plan. She sneaked into the edge of the camp and slept well.

< Staying Alive >

The next morning, Valki surveyed the campsite. The women had left to gather. The chief had kept one of the younger women from the fields to keep him company for the day.

Two young hunters sat on the ground pitching stones into a circle. She approached them as innocently as she could. For a child, especially a girl, bothering a hunter was always a risk. She asked, "Are you afraid something will eat you at night when you're out hunting?"

A hunter looked up at her. "Nah," he said. "We just keep the fire going. Animals are afraid of fire."

She asked, "What would you do if the fire went out?"

He replied, "Keep my trusty spear ready."

His friend laughed. "Trusty spear? You would go climb the nearest tree. High up the tree, so a leopard wouldn't get you."

"Nahhh. We don't have that many leopards around here."

The two young males then forgot about the girl standing there as she soaked up their every word about staying alive on the hunt.

Valki hung around the outskirts of the camp until the night before the camp would pack. All would retire early in preparation for the difficult coming day. The tribe would move to the east for the next hunting season.

After the camp had been silent for a long time, Valki quietly walked to where the chief slept, picked up his traveling bag and spear, and quickly walked southward into the night. If she were fortunate enough to not be eaten during her first night, she would be far enough away to build a fire or sleep in a tree.

Vanam, Kiya, Pumi, Valki, Putt, Putt-pay, Breathson, Littlerock.

On this night, she could only rely on the beating of the spear against her traveling bag so the noise would hopefully ward off any tentative predator. She would stand little chance against a determined predator, anyway. But the young hunter had demonstrated how he would use his spear to try to fight off a lion or a bear. "Good luck with that," his friend laughed.

She had prepared the best she knew how. She simply knew she had to be far away from the camp when the chief woke up and could not find his equipment. *He isn't smart, though. It was a fair trade. He may never figure out what happened to his bag and spear, anyway.*

She walked well past sunrise and then found a suitable tree in which to sleep.

Valki was an expert gatherer. Her mother had trained her incessantly. She found protein crawling in trees and protein in the ground. She wondered why her mother had not simply left the tribe and lived off the land. Things could hardly have been worse. But she remained thankful for each day she stayed alive. There was surely something out there waiting to eat her.

But, in the meantime, she was alive.

She traveled south for a full season; walking, trotting, resting, foraging, building fires, climbing trees, and staying alive for one more day. *I hope Mother knows.*

The sun was high in the sky when she, at last, saw motion on the distant horizon. She walked toward it. Motion became a gatherer. She saw more gatherers. She walked toward them. A gatherer looked up and saw Valki approaching. She stared at the girl. Another gatherer saw her, stood, stared, and loudly called out, "Elder Woman Vivekamulla—come quickly!"

Valki continued to walk through their midst. Gatherers continued to stand and stare. A woman came running up, fell to her knees, and faced Valki. She asked, "Child, where did you come from? What has happened to you?"

Women gathered around the two.

"My name is Valki, Great Elder Woman. My mother died. My elder woman would not find me a new mother like she promised. The chief commanded me to leave his camp and not come back. I took his hunting bag and spear because he took my food. I'm searching for a new tribe and a new mother. Will you be my mother?"

Vivekamulla stared into the eyes of the filthy, emaciated young girl and said, "We will find you a mother, Valki. And all the food you can eat."

Valki returned the embrace with unimagined strength.

Saparu, Palai, Moonman. Nanatan, Vivekamulla, Vaniyal, Littlestar. Irakka, Mari, Irul.

Book One. The Beginning of Civilization: Mythologies Told True

9. Pumi

Seven years later; ages 25, 21, 15, 12.

< Rockplace >

Pumi once more returned to Rockplace. He stared at the large outcrop of stone. He walked to it, closed his eyes, and ran his fingers absent-mindedly across the smooth, hard surface, thrilling to its touch. His fingers crossed a deep crevice formed in the outcrop. The sudden change in texture and feel excited his senses. He let his mind imagine what secrets lay hidden inside the crevice—how he might take advantage of this knowledge. *I love my rocks. There can be no greater thrill than to look at a rock and to understand it—to make it part of your mind—part of yourself. Not animals—not plants—not sky—not water. Only stones. Stones—a gift from the earth, herself.*

He let his fingers trace the outline of the crevice and then slipped his fingers into it to explore the wonders that lay within. *The texture of the stone is different inside and it becomes more moist the deeper I go. This knowledge will be useful. I love my rocks. I love life!*

He placed his forehead on the outcrop and reached in to brush his lips against it. *It is the taste of earth and stone. It is wonderful!*

Pumi broke from his reverie, opened his eyes, and looked around.

He walked to his favorite rock—his flat table of stone—and climbed onto it. He stood tall upon his table but saw nothing on the eastern horizon except the endless low, scraggly bushes. His constant surveillance pleased the women and children under his protection. He was accomplished with a spear and did well enough in training hunts. His wards were safe under his watchful eye.

Not yet being allowed to participate in a major hunt with his father, uncles, brother, and cousins did not discourage him. His greatest talent—his greatest love—was here—with his rocks.

Among his tribe, among all other tribes he had met, he was the most accomplished creator of spearheads, blades, and cutting knives. Pumi could look into the rock and see the wonderful shapes hiding there. He knew where to tap, and how hard. He could work the stones into smooth, efficient, deadly instruments. His spearheads and cutting blades were desired by all who saw them.

The rock upon which he stood had been his favorite source of material. He had begun his learning here, still a young child. His grizzled teacher had been delighted when Pumi took to his craft so eagerly and so skillfully.

Vanam, Kiya, Pumi, Valki, Putt, Putt-pay, Breathson, Littlerock.

Pumi's teacher was no longer part of the tribe. Eventually, he had been unable to keep up with the children and old women. He had been given his ration of food and water and left at a camp. There were neither old man nor any remains when they returned the following year.

The boy missed his teacher.

His rock had become flat by accident. Pumi had simply kept cutting away the rounded top of the rock because he visualized the beautiful spearheads inside. He would cut down to a certain depth and then start again at the top. He eventually began sitting in the spot from where he'd cut the stone away. The area became larger. The women began sorting their herbs and seeds on the flattened portion of the rock. He saw seeds get lost in the roughness of the flattened stone, so he made it flatter, without rough spots.

After five camps at the rock bed, he had created a perfectly flat rock upon which to shape his stones, upon which the women could organize their plants, and, eventually, upon which the hunters would butcher their prey. After studying the butchering, he made larger sharpened rocks, ones shaped to a man's hand. These rocks increased the efficiency with which the hunters could strip the flesh from their game.

The boy considered this to be his personal rock.

The previous time they had hunted from this camp, the men had returned without game and the tribe had been left without food. They'd survived on the herbs and fruits the women had collected during the previous season. There had been hunger.

Pumi thought, *This hunt will be different.*

He visualized what the hunters would surely see.

He sat down on his rock, and, with his punch, carved the figure of an antelope into its smooth surface. He had never thought of such a thing before, but the shape of the creature flowed from his hand through the punch and onto the rock table. The antelope looked alive. He carved two more. Then he saw his older brother, arm in throwing position, ready to deliver his spear to the heart of the antelope. The vision flowed into the stone table.

The boy looked at the figures and became concerned that his father would punish him for wasting time.

Nonetheless, for good measure, he carved the figure of a fallen antelope.

Saparu, Palai, Moonman. Nanatan, Vivekamulla, Vaniyal, Littlestar. Irakka, Mari, Irul.

Book One. The Beginning of Civilization: Mythologies Told True

< Valki, Now of Chief Nanatan's Tribe >

Valki was the only child allowed to join the women in the gathering fields. In part, because it had been Elder Woman Vivekamulla who accepted Valki as her own daughter and, in part, because Valki was the most accomplished gatherer in the tribe. She was faster, more accurate, and more discerning. She was the first one to the fields, and the last one out. Valki was still thin but proper nourishment had allowed her to grow a healthy body.

After receiving training on proper grooming, Valki kept herself the most presentable and well-groomed woman—girl—in the tribe. Every suggestion, every criticism, and all training was listened to, incorporated, and acted on with twice the effort and determination of any of her peers. It was unfortunate that her peers, both the girls and the women, considered her to be too tall—too thin—her blue eyes too different from their brown eyes—her hair not the dark black color it should be, but rather the color of washed-out straw. And, sometimes, she was just too clever. They soon found, however, that no matter how many times she may have been snubbed or walked away from, Valki always met them with friendliness. She became tolerated as a member of the tribe.

Valki continued to stay alive for one more day.

Vanam, Kiya, Pumi, Valki, Putt, Putt-pay, Breathson, Littlerock.

10. Scouts Pumi and Kiya

One disadvantage of Rockplace Camp was the lack of shade for the children and the old women. The gathering women were scattered around the area trying to find useful herbs and grasses, but the oldest women spent their time tending and nurturing the babes and small children.

Shade would have been a great blessing.

The only shade at all was behind the two twin outcrops of rocks tilted at a great slant, located on the slope of the hill. They were less than the height of a man and during the middle of the day, they no longer provided any protection from the sun. Pumi could not make the rocks taller, but he could lower the ground below them and extend the protection of their shadow. He ordered the four largest boys to remove as much of the dirt as they could and pile it between the two rocks. It was a manly and meaningful task. Each boy tried to outdo the others.

The other great disadvantage of this site was the lack of meaningful vegetation in the area.

The women were diligent in their work, but there were simply few plants to harvest. As the sun climbed higher into the sky, he wondered if there might be more plant life farther to the south.

He went to his digging boys and gave them each a spear. He charged them with the protection of the children and women until he returned. The four boys were ecstatic, eager to take on the task. "Yes! We will protect the camp. We will move the dirt. Yes!"

The hunters always set off due east from this camp. Pumi wondered, *Maybe there's better foraging in the southwest.*

He took three spears and set out toward the southwest in search of better fields. A half-mile from the camp, he came upon Kiya and several other women—gathering.

Pumi acknowledged his older brother's mate as he walked past. Of all the women in the tribe, Kiya was recognized as the most accomplished in finding, identifying, and utilizing plants. She was to plants as he was to stone. She was older than him, a full-grown woman while he was still considered to be only a boy. Who better than Kiya to evaluate new areas for useful plants? She was tall and could easily keep his pace.

Saparu, Palai, Moonman. Nanatan, Vivekamulla, Vaniyal, Littlestar. Irakka, Mari, Irul.

He hesitated and then returned to face her as she continued her futile search for useful plants. It was unheard of, but he said, "Pen-Kiya, I am going to run to the southwest to look for more abundant vegetation. I will be back before the sun sets. If you and I search together, we might have better fortune finding such an area. Will you travel with me?"

Kiya was in an awkward position. Pumi had not yet been acknowledged to be a man and she should ignore him. She was on duty—gathering. To interrupt her in her work was unacceptable. To leave her duties would be grounds for punishment. *But he is my protector's brother and son of my chief. He is well thought of and will be a man soon enough.*

She said, "Pumi, I cannot leave. I have to stay here and work. We don't have much food and I must gather my share. But thank you for asking."

She returned to her gathering.

Pumi thanked her and turned to continue on but then stopped, turned again, and said, "I shall ask Elder Woman Palai for her wisdom in this matter."

She replied, "As you will," and continued her work. *You are an aggressive young male. Everyone thinks you're cute but, somehow, they always do your bidding. They aren't even aware of it. Of course, you are a stonecutter in good standing—equal in rank to a good hunter. In my father's tribe, you would sit on my father's council, along with his moonwatcher, elder woman, and second-in-command. Chief Saparu and Vanam don't pay you any notice. They see you as Vanam's little brother—a plaything. And yet, you always get your way. You are a very persuasive boy—man—whatever.*

A while later, Palai found Kiya and said, "Let's rest a while, Kiya. Pumi told me of your conversation and your proper dismissal of him."

Kiya laughed. "Yes, but …"

Palai returned the laugh. "Yes, but … what is your view of his suggestion? Do you believe it has merit?"

"Great Elder Woman, we both know everything Pumi suggests has merit. Whether we can act on it carries the risk of displeasure from our chief. That is something I do not wish to face."

"You are wise, Kiya. Nor do I want to face it. That's why I will not command you to accompany Pumi on his scouting mission. I told him not to expect you to join him but to continue with his plan. You have been working too hard, Kiya. I dismiss you from your gathering for the remainder of the day. Do whatever may amuse you. Enjoy yourself."

Vanam, Kiya, Pumi, Valki, Putt, Putt-pay, Breathson, Littlerock.

Palai nodded and returned to continue monitoring the other gatherers.

Kiya muttered, "Yes, but…" and considered the many possible complications. She then, as she knew she would, began her brisk trot due southwest.

She soon overtook Pumi and joined his trot. He quickened his pace slightly but made no mention of any past conversation. He merely greeted her with, "This may be promising. Look—far in the distance toward our right. That could be a band of trees—that would indicate a stream nearby—that would suggest lusher vegetation. I am hopeful."

The farther they traveled, the more fertile the land became. Kiya asked to stop and survey the vegetation around them, but Pumi pressed on until he found what he was looking for—a hillock rising gently but significantly over the surrounding plains.

He ran to the crest, looked down at her on the plains below, and said, "Here!"

Kiya was thrilled. She hurried across the landscape, stopping to harvest this plant, and then that one, and then another. The land was fertile and rich in diversity. This was a wonderful place for gatherers to find healing herbs and grains. Her gathering bag was already overflowing.

For a gatherer, this was paradise.

Pumi said, "I shall name this place 'Pumi's Hill.'"

He walked to the top of the hill and drove his longest spear into the ground. "We will camp here next year. The choice will be Father's to make; not mine. But I will help him decide. Our world will be a better place if this is where we camp."

Suddenly, Kiya realized the sun had set, and they were far from camp. She panicked. No matter how important their discovery was, neither she nor Pumi had been given permission to make this scouting expedition. She shouted, "Pumi, the hunters will be back! We are in trouble!"

Pumi laughed. "You're correct. We *are* in trouble. But we would be in trouble even if we had gotten back before dark. Oh, well, it's me Father will notice. Stay far behind; he will not even see you in the dark. Facing Father's displeasure is easy enough for me. You slip in and make things right with my brother. That's my only concern."

They both ran full speed, back to their camp.

They arrived well into the night, a travesty on its own.

Saparu, Palai, Moonman. Nanatan, Vivekamulla, Vaniyal, Littlestar. Irakka, Mari, Irul.

< >

The hunters had returned from their hunt much earlier. Chief Saparu met Pumi with full fury. Pumi stood beside the campfire in front of his father. The chief shouted the litany of sins his young son had committed during the hunters' absence.

Vanam had directed the dressing of the antelopes. He now sat on the table next to the four butchered antelope gazing at the engravings of four antelope carved into it. Last season's hunt had brought back no game. This season's hunt was rich. He ran his fingers across the etchings. The flickering flames made the figures look alive and real. *How did you know this, Pumi? Was it us or you who delivered four antelopes to this table? Or the flattened rock itself?*

Kiya slipped in and joined Vanam sitting cross-legged on the flat rock listening to his father's tirade against his younger brother. She tried to look into his eyes for some indication of her likely fate, but her gaze was not immediately returned.

His fingers continued tracing an etching of an antelope. *And you, my mate—returned from an adventure with my little brother. How nice! What did you do?*

When Vanam finally met Kiya's waiting eyes, he smiled a tight, strained smile.

< >

This hunt had been an embarrassment of riches. The catastrophe of last season had been replaced with an overabundance of game. Four antelope carcasses had been butchered on the flat rock table.

When he and his hunters had returned to camp, Saparu had looked in vain for his youngest son, who should have been protecting the camp. He had found instead four boys proudly proclaiming they had successfully protected everyone and inviting him to come look at the shade tree they had dug.

Disobedience was not to be tolerated. His young son must face his wrath; to learn the inviolate rules of the tribe, to learn his place in the tribe. Ignoring the great supply of spearheads his young son had left proudly piled upon the flat rock, ignoring the new place of shade the four male children wanted to show off, ignoring the happiness of the old women and the contentment of the small children, the chief angrily ordered the antelopes to be laid upon the great flat rock his youngest son had single-handedly carved. In fury, he had waited for Pumi's return.

At last, Chief Saparu lay down to sleep. It had been a difficult day, a difficult hunt. The wear on his body was taking its toll. *Vanam is capable of leading my*

Vanam, Kiya, Pumi, Valki, Putt, Putt-pay, Breathson, Littlerock.

tribe. He is a good hunter and would command the tribe with great authority. Pumi is such a disappointment, but he does make great spearheads and tools. He may be tall, but he is too lean with not enough muscles like Vanam. And Pumi has no great lust for the hunt. He has an unhealthy interest in the words and deeds of women and the old. These were not qualities that gladdened my heart. The boy might still become an honored member of my tribe, but he will certainly never be chief. Only a stonecutter. But Vanam, my son. You are ready to become chief. The greatest chief to ever live.*

< >

The next day, Pumi requested a meeting with Moonman, Palai, and Kiya. He presented his scouting report on his expedition to the southwest. He told of the high hillock with the spear driven into the ground, of the wealth of vegetation nearby, that it was but a half day's run further southwest.

He said to Moonman, "Such decisions are the ones you and Chief Saparu must make but I know how much he relies on you to make wise decisions. I wanted you to know of this wonderful site since the chief would not know anything about it. When we return to Rockplace again, you could show your knowledge and wisdom by suggesting this new site instead of Rockplace. There is no need to mention my name. I just wanted you, Palai, and Kiya to be aware of this place in case it comes up in other, private discussions."

Moonman was unaware Kiya had already been there, been thrilled by the location, and had told Palai about it. Kiya had told Palai, "It would be so wonderful if our chief decides to camp there next year."

The night finally came when the moon did not appear overhead. Moonman proclaimed this hunting season ended. The tribe should leave this camp and begin trekking back toward the northern lands where they would find and make a suitable camp, usually at a location used in the past.

Moonman helped Chief Saparu decide these things.

< And so ... >

With each new moon, a new hunting season began, and everyone became a season older. Pumi remained excluded from the hunts. Although he had participated in several, his lack of skill and enthusiasm was obvious to Chief Saparu and Ramum. It seemed as if his father expected Pumi to be a poor hunter—an expectation Vanam encouraged.

Saparu often said to Vanam, "I'm so happy I have you as a son. You will lead our tribe to great heights. Your little brother will always be nothing but a stonecutter. You will always be the better man."

Saparu, Palai, Moonman. Nanatan, Vivekamulla, Vaniyal, Littlestar. Irakka, Mari, Irul.

Book One. The Beginning of Civilization: Mythologies Told True

Vanam was aware his little brother usually attacked his projects obliquely; not head-on as a man would. Pumi did not speak of the wonderful gathering fields that lay a half day's run southwest of Rockplace Camp—but his desire to move the camp there was obvious. Vanam heard Pumi's words in Kiya's voice as they talked in the night's darkness. He heard Palai's inquiries to Saparu, "Can you take us further southwest past Rockplace Campsite next time we are there?" At least once each season, Pumi asked Moonman if he had yet considered suggesting camping farther southwest of Rockplace. *You are annoying, devious, thorough, and persistent, little brother. Whatever shall I do with you?*

Vanam, Kiya, Pumi, Valki, Putt, Putt-pay, Breathson, Littlerock.

11. Return to Pumi's Place

The next year in Year 26; ages 26, 22, 16, 13.

Eleven hunting seasons passed.

The tribe eventually returned to Rockplace. Pumi was excited to return to this camp and to his personal flattened rock table. His father had allowed him to take an apprentice rock cutter, Littlerock. Pumi and Littlerock arrived at the rock site several days before the remainder of the tribe.

During those days, Pumi selected and prepared rocks for shaping into spearheads. He had his apprentice begin fashioning spearheads, watching and guiding him through each strike of the burin. To their delight, Littlerock eventually fashioned each spearhead to their satisfaction. Their quota was met before the tribe arrived. Chief Saparu entered Rockplace first, followed by Vanam and his most able hunters. The chief surveyed the area and made note of the spearheads laid out upon the rock table. *This is excellent. My hunter's spears needed replenishing and reworking. We will make camp here and set out on the hunt at sunrise.*

"Great Chief Saparu," Moonman said, "we already have our new spearheads. Have you considered setting the camp further southwest? The vegetation might be more plentiful."

Saparu did not like change, but Palai's words echoed in his mind, so he asked, "What do you think, Son?"

Vanam felt like he was being used by his younger brother, but Kiya had been adamant. "Vanam, the vegetation in the southwest is unbelievably plentiful. Pumi drove a spear into the ground on a hill. You could easily find it. Every gatherer would praise your name if you led us there."

Vanam replied to his father, "I hear there is a spear in the ground on a hill a half-day run southwest and there is a great deal of vegetation for our gatherers nearby. I don't know about the game."

Vanam glanced in the direction of Pumi. The boy sat with his back toward the decision-making, busying himself at his rock table.

Saparu roared, "My wish is to camp further to the southwest."

Before the tribe continued their journey, and with some resentment, Vanam required each hunter to pass by the great flat rock table and brush their hand across the graven antelopes captured there. The tribe then moved southwest, toward a spear in the ground on a hill.

Saparu, Palai, Moonman. Nanatan, Vivekamulla, Vaniyal, Littlestar. Irakka, Mari, Irul.

< >

Pumi already missed his flat rock. It had been a large part of his life. It was there he had learned the craft that had captured his heart, the place where he refined his skills, a place of joy and accomplishment. But moving the campsite to where the women could gather plants until their hearts were content was more important. It was easy enough to make the stone tools quickly and in great quantity. Pumi's skill was immense, and he was passing it along to his apprentice. Good stones were more plentiful than good vegetation.

The medicines the females could make from the plants were unbelievable to Pumi. Hunters did not appreciate the healing powers administered so expertly by the women. He knew these powers required the correct plants. The women could rub a plant on a hunter's wound and the wound would heal quickly. They could cause the fires to give off a pleasing smell by burning certain plants. They could turn certain plants into food to supplement their meat. They could add meat and plants into a container of water and turn the water into delicious, thick, liquid food.

With happiness, sadness, and Littlerock beside him, Pumi trotted southwestward with his tribe.

Littlerock asked, "Can we take it with us?"

Pumi asked, "What?"

"The flat rock table, can we take it with us to the new camp?"

Pumi asked again, "What?"

"Your great rock. The women harvest plants, the hunters harvest animals, we harvest rocks."

Pumi dumbly asked, "Harvest rocks?"

"Leave it if you like, but I would like to take your flat rock with us."

Pumi stopped. "Take it with us? How can we? How can we take it with us?"

Littlerock replied, "I don't know. You are the master. I am the apprentice. But I know you could take it with us if you wanted to."

Pumi considered Littlerock's words and then said with finality. "Yes. Yes, we will take the flat rock with us."

< >

Saparu led the way, but Vanam saw the spear first. "There—on top of that hill. Is not that a spear driven into the ground?"

The chief trotted to the top of the hill and studied the spear. It appeared to be one of his tribe's spears, one of Pumi's. He asked, "Strange. Have we been to this place before?"

Vanam said, "No, Father. But it appears to be a good site we can easily find again—a good camp for the children and women. What do you think?"

Saparu roared, "We will make camp here. Our hunt will begin at sunrise tomorrow."

As the tribe set up the campsite, Pumi gave no recognition of the hill, the spear, or the surrounding fields. Vanam looked for a smug look on his face. There was none.

< >

Pumi slept fitfully that night. *Move the rock? How do I pull a great stone from the earth that grew it? How do I harvest a rock table?*

In the night, as the waxing crescent of the moon reached its greatest height, as the others slept, as the wind moved silently through nearby trees, as the sky bathed the ground in silver light, as overwhelming silence spread through the camp, Pumi sat up. *I see the spearhead waiting in each stone. I see the cutting blades waiting to be set free from each rock. I have only to apply my burin to set these things free. I shall set my rock table free.*

Saparu, Palai, Moonman. Nanatan, Vivekamulla, Vaniyal, Littlestar. Irakka, Mari, Irul.

12. The Rock Table and the Tall Stone

Pumi was ready and waiting as the tribe awoke and prepared for their day. He held his spear awkwardly and waited dutifully for his father to call him to the hunting party. Without apology, his father informed Pumi he must stay behind to protect the camp. As always, Pumi was stoic and resigned.

The hunters set off. The gatherers left to find plants.

Pumi stared toward the northeast. Today he needed to survey the area to ensure the camp was completely safe. But tomorrow was tomorrow. He called the four oldest boys to him and gave them each a spear. He told them, "Come with me. I will teach you how to keep the camp safe."

The next day, he left two of the excited boys in charge of the camp, then set off with the other two and Littlerock to Rockplace. He had only to conceive of the concept of the flat rock's imprisonment to see each stroke needed to set it free. He had the boys start to clear away dirt so he could reach the striking places. This would take many days to accomplish, and he needed to check on the camp each day.

That night he placed Littlerock in charge of the two boys. They would remove dirt from around the rock as late as they could and resume early the next morning. Pumi returned the next day bringing several older girls with him.

By day's end, the girls and two boys had removed dirt from around the rock to a great depth. He sent the two boys to escort the girls back to Pumi's Place. He stayed with Littlerock, working long into the night chipping away at the base of the table. At morning's first light, he sent Littlerock back to the camp, to ensure all was running safely and smoothly. Meanwhile, he continued to chip away at the base of the rock without stopping, through the day and into the night.

The next day brought bittersweet triumph. He pushed the great stone table onto the ground. But moving it from its fallen position, even with Littlerock's help, was impossible. The amount of stone remaining made the table too heavy. He began removing excess stone, but a fundamental problem remained. *How can I convince hunters to move this table to Pumi's Place?*

< Suggestions >

Pumi was at Pumi's Place when the hunters returned.

Again, the hunt had been good. Saparu ordered the butchering tables to be erected, and the butchering began. Pumi noticed a single wolf sitting in the

Vanam, Kiya, Pumi, Valki, Putt, Putt-pay, Breathson, Littlerock.

far distance watching the tribe. He retrieved a portion of entrails, and as inconspicuously as he could, headed toward the wolf. The wolf had a white circle around her left eye. She watched Pumi approach for a while and then rose to run away. He stopped immediately. Keeping his eyes downcast, he knelt and placed the entrails in a pile. Rising slowly, he turned and started retracing his steps. After twelve paces, he looked back in the wolf's direction. She was still watching him. Pumi left her to consider his gift.

That night the tribe feasted around the campfire and filled their bellies. After everyone else had retired for the night, only Vanam remained at the fire, lost in thought. Pumi sat down beside him.

Vanam said, "Ah, little brother, the butchering would have gone faster if we'd had your great table here, rather than at Rockplace."

Pumi merely said, "Yes, it would have. I could move it from Rockplace to here, but I don't have the strength to do it. But I wonder …" His voice trailed off.

Vanam asked, with resignation, "What do you wonder?"

Pumi answered, "Well, who is the strongest hunter in our tribe? You are the best. Everyone knows that. But you are not the strongest. I wonder who is."

"Maybe Maiyana, or perhaps Valuvana. They are both interested in impressing the women with their muscles."

"Tomorrow is a day of rest. Instead of resting, maybe the hunters could perform a trial of strength to determine the strongest. The admiration of the women might be better for them than actual rest. The women could give the strongest a garland of flowers to wear for a day. It would be an inspiration for the young ones."

"And what would this great test of strength be?"

"Dragging a heavy rock a great distance. Women could watch and cheer them on. The hunter who could drag it the greatest distance would surely be the strongest."

"Perhaps a stone table from Rockplace to this camp."

"What a wonderful suggestion. We can talk more tomorrow after you consider it." Pumi asked as he rose to leave, "Oh, do wolves interfere with the hunts?"

Vanam answered, "No. Wolves are helpful. They're fast, and when they grab the neck of the prey, it makes it easier to bring the animal down."

Saparu, Palai, Moonman. Nanatan, Vivekamulla, Vaniyal, Littlestar. Irakka, Mari, Irul.

"When I was watching the butchering today, it occurred to me gutting a carcass in the field would make for a lighter trip home. Plus, the wolves would have a reason to join in more hunts." Pumi turned and strode toward his sleeping pallet, then stopped, looked back toward his brother, and said, "Think about dragging that heavy rock idea. Remember, I happen to have one that needs dragging."

< Garlands >

Valuvana turned out to be the strongest, with Maiyana next. Both wore their garlands proudly, but Valuvana's massive garland ensured everyone knew who was strongest. The boys ran to feel Valuvana's flexed biceps. The women watched with interest.

Chief Saparu, at first totally against the competition, grudgingly admitted the tribe's spirits had never before been this high. The contest seemed to have renewed the spirit, strength, and happiness of his tribe. Had anyone other than his oldest son suggested it, he would have dismissed it outright. The chief sought out his oldest son, clasped him by the shoulders, gave him a once-in-a-lifetime bear hug, and said, "What a wonderful idea you had. Much good has come of it—including getting that butchering table to a campsite we will come back to many times. Well done, my son!"

Vanam said nothing but instead forced a smile to his face. *You are challenging me for domination, aren't you, Pumi?*

< The Tall Stone >

Meanwhile, Pumi and Littlerock sat on their stone table. They had placed it due south at the base of the hill.

Pumi stared up at the spear on the hill and said, "An experienced eye can see our hill from a great distance but ..."

"But?" asked Littlerock.

"The site could be seen from a greater distance, more easily, with even greater excitement if a much taller spear—maybe one made completely of stone—four times the height of a man—sat on the hill. There would be no mistaking that this was Pumi's Place. The tall stone would be unmistakable. We could carve a pointed top—like a spear. It would be lighter than the table. It would be much taller but not nearly so wide. Valuvana, Maiyana, and two others would be able to drag it from Rockplace in a day. We would have two days to fashion it and one day to transport it. It doesn't have to be perfect, only standing erect within three days. Get ready to go to Rockplace. I will ask my brother for permission."

<>

By the third night, the Moon had completely disappeared. Elderly Moonman advised Saparu that this hunting season had ended and the tribe should head back northward for the next season's hunting.

At dawn the next day, the tribe broke camp. Pumi and Littlerock had little sleep in the last four nights, but the tall stone stood on the hill; not as finished as it would someday be, but, for now, it would do.

Pumi left the camp with a deep feeling of accomplishment. Pumi's Place was the tribe's best camp, ever. It had a great abundance of plants, plentiful game nearby, and a large flat rock table upon which the gatherers could sort plants and hunters could butcher game.

Plus, it had a great tall stone standing on a hill to proclaim its glory—Pumi's Place.

Book One. The Beginning of Civilization: Mythologies Told True

13. Encounter with Chief Nanatan

Encounters were always random. They were almost always good. Usually, there would be a feast, food permitting. The hunters would discuss the game in the area. Gossip and stories of great hunts would be told, some of it true. Goods would be bartered. Pumi's spearheads and cutting tools were always of great interest. They commanded exchanges of straight and strong shafts of wood, animal hides, and long lengths of strong weaving material. The women would discuss the use of plants and share women's stories. Which young women, if any, would be exchanged? Which male would be her protector? Herbs and plants would be exchanged, as well as information regarding their best use. The elders of both tribes would gather to make important decisions.

On their way north, Chief Saparu's tribe encountered a large tribe traveling south—the great tribe of Chief Nanatan. Chief Saparu's tribe was overloaded with game and plants; Nanatan's tribe was completely without food. Their last two hunting seasons had been disasters. Their supply of spearheads had been depleted too early and the spearheads they had were crafted from poor stone.

With Saparu's disgruntled permission, Vanam ordered a large feast. The hungry tribe would reciprocate if they ever crossed paths again, an agreement that salved the pride of the southbound tribe. The show of respect and mercy without condition was noted by the hunters of the hungry tribe—and its chief.

Pumi suggested to Palai that the women make the soft bread they had recently learned to bake. Kiya had discovered they could add wild bee honey to create bread that was both delicious and nourishing.

After protocol was performed and overnight camps made, the chiefs met and then allowed their tribe's people to mingle. The young women casually strolled around the campfire where the eligible young males had gathered, each group studiously ignoring the other.

After the evening feast, Pumi wandered through the camp, listening to the stories. He listened to his father, Chief Saparu, counsel Chief Nanatan. "There is a large herd of antelopes to the southwest. Travel until you find a hill where a tall thin rock four times the height of a hunter stands."

Vanam interrupted. "We call this place Tallstone Camp and it's a good location. From Tallstone, travel a half-day due east and you will find plentiful game."

Vanam, Kiya, Pumi, Valki, Putt, Putt-pay, Breathson, Littlerock.

Pumi was hurt. He had named the camp Pumi's Place, but his brother had just renamed it Tallstone Camp. *Nothing to be upset about, I suppose. It's still a camp I founded, and it's named after the tall stone I placed there.*

Pumi went about his business and found one of the other tribe's senior hunters. He told the hunter, "A pack of wolves live in the area in which you will be hunting. They are quite useful in assisting in your hunt. Just leave some innards of your prey for them. They will be happy to hunt with you."

During his wandering, Pumi came upon Vaniyal, the skywatcher of the southbound tribe, engaged in conversation with Moonman. Vaniyal had an apprentice younger than Pumi, named Littlestar.

Both Vaniyal and Littlestar were intensely interested in how often and during which seasons Pumi's tribe hunted in the land to the south. Was game always plentiful? What about the weather? Was it ever too hot? Too cold? What were the markings in the heaven when they traveled to this place? Was there water nearby? What of predators? How much protection was needed at the camp?

These men referred to themselves as "skywatchers" rather than "moonwatchers," a distinction Pumi immediately noticed. He felt a pang of sympathy for his tribesman. These skywatchers seemed immersed in the knowledge of the heaven and the lands in which their hunters hunted. Moonman did little more than track the moon and make rote decisions.

Pumi was aware there were many more points of light in the heaven than just the great moon, but he had never wondered whether these lights provided useful information, or whether decisions could be devised from the ever-changing sky. *Do the lights contain meaning? Is it possible to read these lights like hunters read markings on the land?*

Pumi overstepped his bounds when he blurted, "What are the markings in the sky right now? What do they look like? What do they mean?"

Vaniyal arrogantly rebuked Pumi for not keeping his place. Pumi was penitent. Littlestar, wisely, did not speak.

The evening feast ended.

The fires burned low as Littlestar found Pumi. They sat together around the embers of the fire as Littlestar shared his knowledge of the night sky. "Overhead is a ceiling of lights. The lights are constant and run in a complete circle around the ceiling. It takes twelve seasons for the cycle to begin again. My master calls this amount of time a 'year' and says the shortest night is the end of a year. The next daybreak begins another year."

Saparu, Palai, Moonman. Nanatan, Vivekamulla, Vaniyal, Littlestar. Irakka, Mari, Irul.

Littlestar removed two leather pouches containing small, polished pebbles from his belt and spilled their contents to the ground, careful not to mix their contents. He said, "This bag is for the nightfalls since the beginning of this year. This bag is for the nightfalls remaining until the end of this year. Each nightfall, I move a pebble from the second bag to the first. This way we know exactly where we are in the year. The hunters consider this information to be of great mystery, but it is a simple matter of looking at stones—and knowing the next year has as many nightfalls as the last. Knowing the number of nights in a hunting season alternates between twenty-nine and thirty allows us to know how many seasons remain in the year. This is useful in predicting where the best hunting sites are likely to be. Vaniyal can also see which hunting season we are in, and where we should hunt next, by looking at the orientation of the five bright lights in the night sky he calls 'Stillhunter.' Stillhunter will soon appear to be standing with his leg pointed due north. This marks the hunting season when night and day are of equal length. After this time, the nights grow shorter, and the days grow longer. In this way, we know the growing seasons."

Pumi was overwhelmed. That such knowledge even existed was exciting. To be in the presence of someone who understood these things was a privilege of unimaginable proportions. Pumi asked to be shown the five bright lights and committed their positions to memory. He bowed his head to Littlestar to show thanks and subservience. After leaving the apprentice, he retired with his stone working tools and favorite small rocks. By the time he had finished his project, he was exhausted. He slept fitfully.

Vaniyal and Littlestar rose the next morning to the humming activity of the tribes breaking camp to continue their treks. To the puzzlement of the old man—and the delight of his apprentice—next to each of them lay a round rock flat on both sides. On one side was etched a perfect depiction of a hunter. On the other, the five points of "Stillhunter."

< Sunrise >

Pumi watched the southbound tribe depart. Later in the day, his tribe would continue northward. *So much knowledge in the world. So much to know. What if our new friends do not find the tall stone? Of course, it makes little difference whether they find it or not. Still ...*

He sought his older brother. His thoughts and words were half-incoherent as he said, "I could lead them to the tall stone. I could make sure they find it. They are a large tribe, a rich tribe. Even without food, they had many items to trade and many women—and much knowledge. It would be our

Vanam, Kiya, Pumi, Valki, Putt, Putt-pay, Breathson, Littlerock.

good fortune to encounter them again. I could guide them to Tallstone Camp and return to our tribe long before the end of this hunting season. I could stop at Rockplace and replenish the spearheads we traded. Do you think there is more they could teach me? Should I ask our father if I can leave the tribe for this season? I don't know what to do."

Vanam listened patiently. *Even if nothing comes of it, having Pumi as a liaison to such a large tribe would be a good thing. Having too many friends is not possible. That, plus Pumi would be away from my tribe— and Kiya!*

"Yes," Vanam said as Pumi paused to draw breath. "I will consult with Father so he can decide you should guide our new friends to Tallstone Camp." *Your power grows, little brother. Too much!*

< Next Day >

Pumi caught Chief Nanatan's tribe the next day. He remained away from their camp until sunrise, at which time he presented himself to Nanatan and said, "My father commands that I offer my poor services to you. I can guide you to a field rich in rock where your stonecutters can gather many fine stones. From there it is but a half day's run to Tallstone Camp of which my father spoke. I shall leave or provide my poor service, as you wish."

The chief studied Pumi. His tribe treated him as a boy, but he was a rock cutter of the highest order and the son of a chief who had shown courtesy and hospitality. It was true Vaniyal had complained that the boy was disrespectful, but that was a common complaint from the old man. "Yes," replied Nanatan, "a guide would be helpful. You may accompany us."

Pumi was overcome with excitement.

< >

On the second day, the tribe arrived at Rockplace. Their stonecutters were elated. "The key to making good tools is having good stone to work with," they told him.

Pumi said nothing but watched carefully as they selected rocks and made exploratory cuts. *This is true. But knowledge in selecting the stone, having good tools, and skill in cutting are also useful.*

Pumi had made a point not to approach either Vaniyal or Littlestar. The old man did not accept familiarity and would have been infuriated had he known his apprentice had shown interest in Pumi.

Saparu, Palai, Moonman. Nanatan, Vivekamulla, Vaniyal, Littlestar. Irakka, Mari, Irul.

Book One. The Beginning of Civilization: Mythologies Told True

The old skywatcher had questioned where the flat, engraved rocks had come from, and how the engraver knew about Stillhunter. "Your fame is widespread," the apprentice had answered. "Their stonecutter wanted to honor your knowledge with a small token of admiration. I assume their skywatcher had heard of Stillhunter, and adequately described it to their rock cutter. What a wonderful gift celebrating your great knowledge. Are you pleased?"

"Humph," replied the old man. "I suppose that's acceptable."

Now, Vaniyal saw Pumi standing nearby with the tribe's two stonecutters. He and Littlestar walked over to join them. Vaniyal sat down on a small boulder as his apprentice sat on the ground.

Littlestar risked angering his master by saying to Pumi, "Your skywatcher did a good job of describing Stillhunter. Your reproduction is almost adequate."

"Yes," snorted Vaniyal, pleased with his apprentice's words. "I will have my apprentice give you a better description so you can improve upon the likeness."

Pumi said, "It would be my honor to make many reproductions for you. If they are to your liking, you could give them to skywatchers you encounter on your journeys. Your fame would spread."

"That's a fine idea," said the old skywatcher. He looked toward Littlestar. "Take this boy around with you; teach him as much as he can learn. Especially all that is known concerning Stillhunter. But remember, he is only a stonecutter. Don't drive him mad with too much knowledge."

Vaniyal rose stiffly from his rock. "That rock is pointed and uncomfortable," he grumbled. "A comfortable seat is difficult to find."

As the old man walked off, Pumi studied his butt.

At the next daybreak, Pumi found Littlestar and took him to the stone boulder Vaniyal had sat upon the previous day. The boulder had been rolled onto a net of vines Pumi had begged from the women. The netting was attached to two heavy spears he had solicited from a hunter. Pumi said to Littlestar, "Using these poles, four hunters can carry this rock to Tallstone Camp for your master. I have carved the rock's surface to fit him. He should find it comfortable to sit on. Stillhunter is etched on the top. He can claim the rock as his own. Find four hunters to carry it to Tallstone Camp and set it due east of the tall stone on the hill."

Pumi left Littlestar and placed himself near Nanatan as they continued their journey to Tallstone Camp.

Vanam, Kiya, Pumi, Valki, Putt, Putt-pay, Breathson, Littlerock.

14. The Tall Stone and Nanatan

The chief and his skywatcher always led the tribe to the next campsite. They chose the direction and pace of the trek. They would select the campsite.

Pumi maintained a respectful distance as they trotted. Only rarely did he suggest to Nanatan that perhaps he should veer more toward the west. Finally, with much relief, Pumi saw the top of the tall stone reflecting brilliant sunlight. He said nothing. Eventually, Vaniyal triumphantly announced the site visible in the distance.

The tribe arrived, made camp, and prepared for the hunters to begin their hunt at the next sunrise.

Littlestar and his four helpers arrived later with the sitting rock. They placed the rock beneath the hill directly east of the tall stone; a fine place to study the night sky. Littlestar hurried off to find Vaniyal.

Pumi watched and wondered, *Will Skywatcher Vaniyal receive the rock seat with delight or with disgust?*

Pumi's flat rock table had been placed below the hill due south of the tall stone, a convenient location to bring and butcher the hunter's game. He retired and sat upon his rock table, pleased with the successful completion of his projects. *Are there any other things I can try? Brother thinks it helpful for the hunters to touch the images of the antelopes as they leave for the hunt. He said it helps focus their minds and quicken their step. Would the hunter I told about the wolves be interested in this? He had seemed interested enough.*

Pumi bid his time until the senior hunter passed close enough that Pumi could attract his attention. *Oh, well, at worst I will only be humiliated, reprimanded, and driven away.*

"Master! It is I, Pumi. The son of the chief from the last tribe you encountered."

The hunter looked at Pumi with amusement. He approached Pumi, who had risen and stood at the end of his flat table.

The hunter asked, "Of what service may I provide you, boy-man?"

Pumi replied, "I wanted to tell you of the great success you will have with tomorrow's hunt, and to remind you to gut one in the field."

The hunter laughed. "Oh, yes. For the enjoyment of wolves."

Saparu, Palai, Moonman. Nanatan, Vivekamulla, Vaniyal, Littlestar. Irakka, Mari, Irul.

Pumi bowed his head slightly. "Yes, sir, if they have helped in the hunt. By the way, my older brother is one of my tribe's senior hunters. He commands each of his hunters to brush his fingers across the images of the antelope carved into this table when they leave for the hunt. Something about focusing everyone's mind."

"Interesting," the hunter said.

< Graven Images >

The next morning, the hunters rose. There was tremendous pressure on them for a successful hunt. Upon leaving, each man ran his fingers over the antelope images carved into the rock table.

< Valki >

The young girl was infatuated with Pumi. She maintained a respectful distance, but her eyes were always on him.

He was still considered to be a child as was she, but he had a great deal of respect from the elders. She had little respect from anyone, only tolerance. Few of the girls in the tribe wished to associate with Valki because she was different. The women did not want to admit that Valki was simply more talented than them as they gathered in the fields.

Pumi noticed Valki and smiled. She was thrilled, but she dared not approach a boy, especially one who could be considered a man.

The morning of the departing hunt gave way to evening. Pumi's work there was surely done. He could begin his trek to catch up with his tribe. But on the other hand, Vaniyal might warm toward Pumi and share some of his immense knowledge. He decided to seek the skywatcher and try to speak to him. *What is the worst that could happen?*

Pumi had brought a small amount of food with him and did not burden the tribe by partaking in their meager evening meal. After the meal, when most of the tribe had retired, Pumi found Vaniyal sitting on his customized rock, holding court with Littlestar. Pumi discreetly approached the two.

Seeing Pumi, Vaniyal exclaimed, "There is the builder of this fine rock! Come here, boy. I wish to speak to you."

Pumi approached respectfully and deferentially listened to Vaniyal expound upon rocks, the sky, and the heaven. The skywatcher found he had an interested, respectful student. That evening, he was inspired.

Unseen in the distance, watched Valki.

Vanam, Kiya, Pumi, Valki, Putt, Putt-pay, Breathson, Littlerock.

< Sunrise >

Pumi woke, his mind agitated. *I will never see Vaniyal or Littlestar again! I wish to see them both in future days. How can I make this happen?*

With a new problem to solve, Pumi became excited. *I need a plan. It will be days before the hunters return. What shall I do? I will go explore. I have not seen the lands in the southwest. I will walk there. A plan will come to me.*

As he entered the fields to begin his journey, Pumi felt someone looking at him. He turned and saw two piercing blue eyes staring at him. Valki quickly averted her gaze lest she be reprimanded. Pumi smiled and turned to resume his walk. Long ago, he had broken all protocol and invited Kiya to travel with him. Trouble had ensued, but so had great success. *That girl is ignored by all the women except their elder woman. She would probably not even be missed if she went with me. She's only a child but I heard that she is an accomplished gatherer. She might prove useful.*

He turned toward Valki and motioned to her. She came to him.

He said, "I'm going on an overnight hike to explore the land and find what types of vegetation grow southwest of here. I understand you are knowledgeable about such things. Will you travel with me?"

Joy—pure, unadulterated joy—is not something often experienced. Valki showed no emotion, no hint of joy, and no hint of excitement. She calmly replied, "Yes, I know all the plants and their uses. I will keep up with you and not slow your pace. I would be pleased to journey with you. Let me inform Mother and get my things."

"Yes, of course," said Pumi. "I'll wait here for you."

Valki returned shortly with Vivekamulla's permission. Pumi and Valki began their journey.

The land grew even more fertile as they traveled farther southwest. Grains and plants grew more varied. They discovered a large flowing stream with trees and underbrush growing along the banks. The two travelers stopped to drink their fill from the stream. They returned to the open fields to continue their journey, but Pumi kept the stream in his sight.

Valki slowly lost her stoic composure and excitedly began collecting grains of einkorn to make bread for her hungry tribesmen. Her gathering bag was overflowing as evening approached. They made a basic camp and Pumi shared the remainder of his food with Valki. They settled onto their bed with what little coverings they had.

Saparu, Palai, Moonman. Nanatan, Vivekamulla, Vaniyal, Littlestar. Irakka, Mari, Irul.

The rain came. Torrential rain. The fury of an angry sky unleashed. He protected Valki as best he could, but the torrent became even more oppressive. He rose and gathered brush and grass, attempting to create protection for them. It was not much. He could not stop the cascading water from running under their bedding and over them. Valki did not complain. She did not whimper.

He placed his arms around her to shelter her from the onslaught of the downpour. He felt her body form itself into his.

Valki's mind flooded with memories; her mother holding her close; singing soft songs; her mother's love. She unconsciously grasped Pumi's arms with her hands, holding on tightly. Valki was not aware of the rain. Only that a human was holding her, protecting her. *Do not feel happiness. It will disappear. It is only passing. Do not try to hold onto this. The rain will stop, and I will be a little child again—different. Do not feel anything. No one will ever touch me again.*

She could not help it. She trembled and cried silent tears of happiness.

Pumi did not sleep. He felt the intensity of the girl. He felt her tremble. He thought that she was miserable from being pelted by the endless rain. The indignity of the situation ran through his mind. Worse yet, someone under his protection was experiencing the same thing. *What could I have done to prevent this? The temporary tents we raise when it rains hard would not be able to withstand this deluge. A cave is the only full protection, but there's no cave nearby. How does one build a cave? Is that even possible? If I come to this place again—to bring Kiya to see the abundance of grains—how could I make sure this indignity is never repeated? What will I do, and when will I do it?*

< Sunrise >

Daybreak brought the sun.

Valki rose and faced the day without complaint, even though her carefully harvested einkorn had been washed away, streaming across the field. All lost.

Pumi joined her, and they explored the surrounding area. She made careful mental records of the vegetation, again gathering as much einkorn as she could. At dusk, they made camp once more, this time feeling pangs of hunger. Valki found edible roots and plants for them.

< Sunrise >

They broke camp and returned to Tallstone Camp.

Upon arrival, they discovered the camp in a state of excitement. The hunters had returned the previous evening, and there was food for everyone. No one seemed to have missed the visiting stonecutter or the girl Valki. But now there was food for the two of them and laughing praise for the effects of touching antelope engravings when leaving for a hunt. And, yes, a wolf pack had chased the antelopes with the hunters, slowing the prey for easy kills. And, yes, the hunters had left entrails for the enjoyment of the wolves.

The women took note of Valki's association with Pumi.

It was a good day.

< >

That evening, after another feast, Pumi found Vaniyal on his sitting rock, watching the sky. "Ah, stonecutter, the night is fast approaching. This will be the longest night of the year, Winter Solstice, a night of great joy. We will all make merry and there will be much rejoicing. Each day grows longer after this night, and each night shorter. It is difficult to observe exactly, but the day the sun rises lowest in the sky will mark the day and the solstice always occurs in the season of the Stillhunter. I have been watching the shadow cast by your tall stone. I believe that I might be able to identify the exact moment of Highsun each day by simply reading the shadow. Even more importantly, it may be that I can tell the exact moment of the Winter Solstice by observing the shadow. I have commanded my apprentice to lay small stones where the shadow falls from sunrise to sundown. We shall soon see if there is a story to be told."

Pumi was tired but excited by this new knowledge. He had already observed that some days were shorter than others but had never stopped to consider that the change was consistent and knowable. His tall stone might yield such knowledge. *Wonderful! What other information might be revealed?*

Before retiring for the evening, he sought Valki to thank her for her valuable assistance and to tell her good night. The girls and women took note. Inside, Valki was thrilled. Outside, Valki was stoic.

Pumi retired and slept happily but fitfully. *What of the shadows cast by the tall stone? How does one build a cave?*

< Next Day >

Vaniyal watched the sky. Was Highsun lower than yesterday's Highsun? Would it be even lower tomorrow? It was difficult to say with certainty, but he was the tribe's skywatcher. His endless years of experience counted a great deal. Who, better than he, to declare the coming night the shortest of the year? The days would grow longer. Warmer weather would soon arrive.

Saparu, Palai, Moonman. Nanatan, Vivekamulla, Vaniyal, Littlestar. Irakka, Mari, Irul.

Book One. The Beginning of Civilization: Mythologies Told True

The earth would give forth its full bounty. Life would be good.

Vaniyal so declared, and the preparations began. Tomorrow night would be the Winter Solstice!

Pumi and Littlestar spent the day refining their new art of marking the track of a shadow from sunrise to sunset. In the late afternoon, Vaniyal ambled by to criticize their efforts. After eagerly accepting the criticisms, Pumi blurted, "How would one build a cave?"

"Build a cave? What kind of cave? Why would you want to build a cave, anyway?" Vaniyal asked.

"For when I am in an open plain," Pumi answered, "and torrential rains come, and there is no protection and there are weaker people to protect. We could go into a cave for protection against the terrible rain. Or animal attacks."

"Oh. I suppose it would depend on what materials are available." the skywatcher replied. He had only a passing interest in the matter, but interest, nonetheless. This was an opportunity to demonstrate his vast knowledge, even if only to his apprentice and the strange stonecutter. "There are structures, especially much farther north, called huts. I suppose they are a form of a cave. Some are built of stone, some of wooden timbers, and some are no more than mud mixed with straw. They are flimsy, but mud is readily available near rivers. But then so are trees that could be cut. In the far north, axes are common—clubs with heavy pieces of sharp stone that a strong man can swing to fell and trim trees. None of our tribesmen have this tool or skill or knowledge. It is not something we need."

"Your wisdom exceeds the glory of the night sky," Pumi said.

Littlestar thought this excessive. Vaniyal, however, seemed pleased.

Pumi thought, *Strong men and axes. I'm not especially strong, but I believe that I can make a club with a sharp-edged heavy stone.*

Pumi and Littlerock had stashed an emergency rock supply nearby in case spears or arrowheads came to be in short supply at Tallstone Camp. Pumi disappeared to visit his cache of materials. The site also hid a collection of wooden shafts with which spears could be fashioned. *Heavy pieces of sharp stone, swung by a strong man.*

He visualized a strong man hitting a tree with a sharp stone attached to a club. Hefting through the various rocks in his collection, he at last found a heavy stone that could be fashioned to have a sharp edge. He quickly shaped the ax head, and then bound three spear shafts together and attached them to his ax head. Pumi tested the weight. He would need a strong man.

By the time Pumi returned to camp with his improvised ax, the festival was well underway. Drumbeating, singing, dancing, feasting, storytelling, and laughter were everywhere.

Pumi casually asked various hunters, "Who is your strongest hunter?"

< Sunrise >

The tribe rose early to prepare for their largest feast of the year.

As the tribe prepared for the upcoming festivities, Chief Nanatan and his counselors met to discuss the tribes' triumphs, problems, and concerns of the previous year and make plans for the coming year.

That evening, the chief sat at the head of the low-burning fire, facing his entire tribe. Beside him sat Vaniyal and Vivekamulla. The hunters, according to their rank, sat facing the trio. The women milled around in the background, separating the children from the men. Pumi remained with the children.

Everyone feasted, laughed, and talked.

Then, with great deference, the chief commanded his two councilors to speak to the tribe.

The skywatcher spoke first. Vaniyal spoke of the signs in the sky, how the signs had influenced his decisions, and what great things he had accomplished this year.

Elder Woman Vivekamulla then spoke of births, and of young women who had been traded into and out of their tribe. To nervous laughter, she identified the hunters who would soon be accepting women from other tribes to take in and to protect, and the young women now old enough to be joining other tribes.

Chief Nanatan then spoke. He reviewed the events since the last festival—deaths, old members left behind, the bad seasons of hunting, and how successful this season had been. He praised the excellence of the hunters, singling out the best of them, and he praised Vaniyal and Vivekamulla for their wisdom and guidance. He praised the gatherers for their medicines, healing herbs, fruits, and berries. He thanked the young stonecutter, Pumi, for his contributions to the tribe, and as he did so, Nanatan searched for the face of the young man. He did not find him. "Have we chased our guest away?" the chief asked. "Where is he?"

Saparu, Palai, Moonman. Nanatan, Vivekamulla, Vaniyal, Littlestar. Irakka, Mari, Irul.

Book One. *The Beginning of Civilization: Mythologies Told True*

All were silent until a girl far in the back shouted, "Pumi is here—with us."

Pumi, flustered, raised his hand, and said, "I am here, Chief Nanatan."

"Well, come here, stonecutter. Why would you not be with the men?"

Awkwardly picking his way through the densely gathered tribe, Pumi arrived before the chief. "I have not been inducted into the brotherhood of men, Chief Nanatan. I am not worthy to sit with great hunters."

"Nonsense," said Nanatan. "You have accomplished much, even during the short time you have traveled with me. You may be a boy in your tribe, but in this tribe, you are an honored man. Act so."

"Yes, my chief," Pumi replied. "I shall not fail you or this tribe." He saluted the chief, pumping his fist over his heart, and then turned toward the assembled tribe and repeated the salute. He then strode to the back of the gathered hunters and sat. *I no longer need to be circumspect. I can implement my projects with direct words and actions. Will this be easier or more difficult?*

< Next Day >

Pumi sought Vaniyal and found him alone on his sitting rock and said, "Your plan to trace the shadow of the tall stone could well reveal new knowledge about the sun. Already, the traces give useful information. Your apprentice is accomplished and could be the Master Skywatcher in any other tribe. If you command him to stay here and trace every day until his tribe returns in twelve seasons, you and he could then consider what has been uncovered. Training another apprentice would be difficult for most Master Skywatchers, but you are wise and an excellent teacher, and you have many years to train a replacement. You could apprentice more than a single skywatcher. No one knows what new knowledge Littlestar may discover from the tall stone. It is a task that requires someone with great knowledge to understand what is being revealed. This would be of great risk, of course. Littlestar would have to be trained in the art of gathering so that he could feed himself. He is not a hunter so he might be eaten. But tell me, how many more nights before you command the tribe to break camp?"

"Three," Vaniyal replied, his mind now elsewhere.

"Thank you," Pumi said as strode off to find the chief.

Vaniyal was vaguely aware that something had just happened, but unsure of precisely what. The old man thought, however, that he should start training new apprentices.

Vanam, Kiya, Pumi, Valki, Putt, Putt-pay, Breathson, Littlerock.

Pumi waited for an opportune moment to speak to the chief. When one arrived, he approached respectfully and requested an audience.

"Speak," the chief said.

Pumi said, "Vaniyal told me it would be three days before you break camp. May I ask some of your tribesmen to accompany me on a three-day excursion that may prove beneficial in the future?"

Nanatan was a patient man, but Pumi was pushing the chief's limits. "You may ask, but I will not command them to obey. Do as you can. That is all."

Pumi thanked Chief Nanatan and left to recruit at least two hunters to become something other than hunters. *This being a man thing—so far, so good.*

Pumi sought out women and hunters alike. "Who are the strongest and smartest hunters in your tribe?" he asked. His questions generated curiosity, and soon the hunters were asking themselves the same questions.

That night after the evening meal, he rose and, holding his great ax, addressed the hunters lounging before their fire. "At sunrise tomorrow, I will run a half-day toward the southwest. I will build a hut there made of timber and mud. The hut will be large enough to accommodate the women and children in your great tribe. If the women decided to gather in that place while the men were away, the hut could protect them from predators and rainstorms. I will need men of great strength to cut and fashion the trees. I will need clever men to design the hut. I leave at sunrise. If you are strong or clever, I invite you to accompany me for this great task."

Pumi saluted the hunters and left them to talk amongst themselves. He found Valki. He said, "It was you that called out during the council when I stood with the children. Why did you call out?"

"To repay your kindness for letting me travel with you, that time."

"Will you travel there again? I hope several hunters will volunteer to return there with me. Your knowledge of the vegetation would be a great help, and perhaps decide where exactly this hut should be built. Plus, the hut is for children and women, and although you are a child, you are especially insightful. Your observations would be beneficial."

Valki was breathless. "Yes," she said, as she studied the ax he held. "May I bring extra rope? Just in case your cutting thing comes apart."

"Yes, much rope." He had made a good decision.

Saparu, Palai, Moonman. Nanatan, Vivekamulla, Vaniyal, Littlestar. Irakka, Mari, Irul.

< Sunrise >

The camp came alive. Most of the tribe's hunters gathered before Pumi. Nanatan and Vaniyal came to observe.

Pumi had already risen and prepared for the trek. Valki had joined him with her gathering sack and rope she had begged from Vivekamulla.

Pumi was overwhelmed. *What have I done? I cannot lead this many men. I don't know what I'm doing.*

He looked over the gathered hunters, raised his fist high into the air, then turned toward the chief and skywatcher and smartly saluted. He looked back to the hunters and said simply, "This way."

Under his breath, Nanatan muttered, "He's taking all my hunters."

"And my apprentices," Vaniyal groaned.

Pumi set a fast pace. At mid-morning he called for a brief rest, and afterward commanded, "Those of you who are strong, travel on my right. Those of you who are clever, travel on my left."

He soon saw the river for which he had been searching. As Highsun approached, they came upon the remains of the disastrous camp Pumi and Valki had set the previous week.

"We will stop here and scout this location," he commanded. "Each member will comment on the advisability of where to build a hut. The strongest will report on building resources; the cleverest on where and how it should be built." Pumi was pleased when he realized that all unplanned, he had shifted decisions from himself to his followers.

The clever ones reported back first. "There is a small hill to the west. It's near enough to water and some trees. It will provide good visibility, and rain will not flood it. It would be easy for hunters to find."

Pumi called for the strong ones and the expedition headed toward the hill.

"What do you think of this place?" he asked Valki when they arrived.

"The women would have rich fields from which to gather all manner of grains and herbs," she said. "This place is good."

"And the building materials?" Pumi asked the strong ones.

"Whatever you wish, we can do," they assured him.

Vanam, Kiya, Pumi, Valki, Putt, Putt-pay, Breathson, Littlerock.

Pumi directed four spears to be placed marking the corners of the hut. After discussion, the spears were moved around until the corners were agreed upon.

Pumi looked at the strong one in charge of the ax and said, "Very well, now build us a hut."

The strong ones looked at one another and complained, "We haven't ever built a hut and don't even know what one looks like!"

A clever male, still only a boy and the smallest in the tribe, broke in and said, "Let's look at the trees we have to work with, then decide how to start. We will make a plan and begin building at sunrise."

< Next Day >

Valki helped Pumi reassemble the ax several times, and, too, their other tools were not well designed for the tasks at hand. Pumi noted what didn't work well and envisioned a better design. He encouraged, praised, and offered suggestions to his teams.

As work progressed, the small, clever boy began making subtle changes and offering design suggestions. "There should be openings on the front and back sides so that air can flow through. The roof should be pitched so that rain will run off. Mix mud and twigs to put on it for more protection."

Pumi named the small, clever boy "Putt."

By trial and error, a hut was built. It was not a fortress, but it would stand for several years. More importantly, Pumi and Putt had gained experience in building. Pumi could envision how to fashion and combine stone with wooden handles to make the work easier.

That night, Pumi, Valki, and Putt slept in the newly constructed hut. The hunters slept under the open sky.

Pumi named their camp "Urfa."

< Sunrise >

The troupe set off to return to Tallstone Camp. Pumi set the fastest pace the group could sustain. He was afraid of raising Nanatan's ire for keeping most of the hunters away on the probable day of breaking camp.

The group arrived back in mid-morning. The chief was not irate but was not especially interested in the result of the venture. Vaniyal had decided they should break camp and migrate to the next hunting site the next morning at sunrise. The chief so commanded.

Saparu, Palai, Moonman. Nanatan, Vivekamulla, Vaniyal, Littlestar. Irakka, Mari, Irul.

Book One. The Beginning of Civilization: Mythologies Told True

< >

A flash of fear went through Valki's mind. *I will never see Pumi again. He is so nice to me. I want to see him again. What can I do?*

She was lost in thought as she sought Vivekamulla to present her with a sack overflowing with medicinal herbs. The old woman was taken aback, thrilled with the great treasure. Valki graciously accepted Vivekamulla's praise but still, in the back of her mind, *What can I do to see him again?*

< >

Pumi found Vaniyal sitting on his rock, watching his apprentice lay a small stone on the tip of the shadow cast by the tall stone. The skywatcher did not shift his gaze when he spoke to Pumi. "This is interesting, stonecutter. The meaning cannot yet be divined, but the traces of the rocks appear to be slightly different each day. And—Nanatan will allow Littlestar to leave the tribe and remain here, laying the stones. Perhaps with a year of traces, we can understand what the sun and the tall stone are revealing. There may be great knowledge to be discovered here."

"To remain in one place without company is a great hardship."

"Oh, he won't be alone. Nanatan also released one of the older boys to remain, the one who calls himself 'Putt.' When he heard of Littlestar being allowed to remain here, the boy petitioned me to ask the chief if he, too, could remain. He knows a little about hunting and using a spear. He said he could learn the art of gathering quickly enough. The boy appears to be interested in improving the hut he helped build. This Putt wasn't going to become much of a hunter anyway. The two of them can assist each other and, who knows, maybe bring in smaller game. They won't starve. Maybe another tribe will see the tall stone and decide to camp here. It doesn't matter. Gaining new knowledge is worth my risk."

Pumi nodded in agreement.

This was the last night before the tribe broke camp.

Late that evening Littlestar found Pumi and gave him a parting gift; two pouches, one of which contained 365 pebbles. Pumi was humbled by the gift. They both expressed hope that they would someday meet again. Pumi spontaneously embraced Littlestar and said, "Stay well, my friend!"

Littlestar turned and walked away.

Vanam, Kiya, Pumi, Valki, Putt, Putt-pay, Breathson, Littlerock.

< >

After the sun had set, Valki summoned all her courage and found Pumi. She rambled on about how much he had accomplished but ended with "Mother Vivekamulla told me our chief intends to return to this camp to celebrate the next Winter's Solstice. Besides, Vaniyal needs to return to measure the progress of Littlestar and his markings given by the tall stone. Wouldn't it be wonderful if *your* chief decided to camp here at the same time? Our tribes could have another encounter."

Pumi was clever. He knew he was clever, but it was as if this girl had revealed another world to him! *So obvious! This was so obvious. I simply did not consider what I already knew! I did not know how to think!*

Her wisdom flowed over and through Pumi like a great river. He embraced Valki in a bear hug, released her, and gushed words of praise about her wisdom and cleverness.

Valki accepted Pumi's praise but did not allow herself to feel anything.

Pumi began formulating a plan to ensure the first-ever planned encounter between two tribes.

< Sunrise >

Pumi found Chief Nanatan organizing his tribe for their run north. Pumi spoke briskly, hoping the chief would take time to listen. "Chief Nanatan, I seek your counsel. It is important to my tribe, and I will be brief."

Nanatan snapped, "Be brief!"

Pumi began, "Your yearly festival is of great impact and accomplishes much for your tribe. My tribe has no such festival, not even a yearly council. You are wise. I would like to invite my chief to bring our tribe to Tallstone during the season of Stillhunter. This would be a planned encounter, with all that an encounter brings. My tribe could observe and maybe join you in your festival. Perhaps my older brother could observe your yearly council. He will someday be our chief. He could learn much from you."

Chief Nanatan was surprised that such wisdom came from someone so young. He briefly considered the suggestion and said, "Yes. I will be happy if both tribes camp here during the next season of the Stillhunter. An encounter would be beneficial to both tribes."

"Thank you," Pumi replied and dismissed himself.

The once-boy would now set off to find his tribe as a man.

Saparu, Palai, Moonman. Nanatan, Vivekamulla, Vaniyal, Littlestar. Irakka, Mari, Irul.

Book One. The Beginning of Civilization: *Mythologies Told True*

15. Pumi Returns to His Tribe

After leaving Tallstone, Pumi spent three days at Rockplace gathering rocks from which to fashion spearheads. He also experimented with fashioning building tools, especially axes. He stashed the tools away and set out for camps he knew the tribe used in previous years. He found no sign of his tribe, but he encountered a small tribe traveling east with whom he traded spearheads for food and information.

"Yes, there had been signs of a recent camp," their chief said, "but it was farther west. We have seen no sign of a tribe traveling north. And beware, game to the west is in short supply."

Unsure, Pumi turned west, and after some days found signs of a recent camp. He followed the traces. If it was not his tribe he followed, then perhaps it would be a tribe that might have information.

He camped for the night but woke under a full moon. He had been dreaming uneasy dreams. He knew that it was past time for him to couple with a woman. He had often considered his options—mate with a woman from his tribe—but they might be related, which he did not find appealing. He could go to one of the hunters and ask to mate with the woman under his protection. Protocol dictated that he obtain the hunter's permission since the hunter would be responsible for raising a child that might result from the union. The woman still had the right of refusal, but, with her protector's approval, a mating privilege was usually granted.

He considered all such women in his tribe. He had long ago decided that it should be a woman he was attracted to in some way.

Only one attracted him—Kiya.

Therein lay the problem. Pumi was not at all sure how Vanam would react to such a request. Well, yes, he was sure. Vanam would grant the request but would then be bitter when Kiya accepted Pumi; assuming she did; which she wouldn't. At her ceremony, she had made it clear that she would not accept Chief Saparu. And he was the chief. The match almost didn't happen because of this. Pumi believed that Vanam was the only hunter Kiya had ever mated with. Plus, Kiya was noticeably standoffish whenever Pumi came too close to her. Pumi did not know which to fear more—that he would be rejected or that he would be accepted. He knew he was attracted to her. He also knew it was in everyone's best interest that he remained sexually frustrated for the foreseeable future.

Vanam, Kiya, Pumi, Valki, Putt, Putt-pay, Breathson, Littlerock.

< One Summer Morning >

Pumi finally found his tribe. He was euphoric to find their campsite, even though the hunters were away hunting.

As was appropriate, Pumi walked through the women and children to find the tribe's ranking member when the hunters were away—Palai. He found her and stood before her, asking, "Are you well, Mother?"

She gasped in surprise. "My little stonecutter, you have returned! Welcome back, child. Sit. Join me. Tell me about your adventures."

He sat and recounted his tales, making the woman gasp and laugh with joy. "And what of you, Mother?" he asked when he was done.

There was a long silence. "The hunts have not gone well. We live on what little we can scavenge. There is much hunger."

Pumi asked, "What of the grains the women collect?"

"There is little in this land. That which we harvest is almost inedible. The times are hard, extremely hard."

"All will become better, Mother," Pumi said. "Now rest. Let me inspect the camp before the hunters return with fresh game."

She smiled and again bid him welcome back.

< >

Kiya had seen Pumi arrive and had moved away, resolving to tactfully avoid him. *When he looks at me, his gaze is too intense, more interested in me than even Vanam when he returns from a hunt. It was amusing but it grows worse. I will just stay away from him.*

But Pumi saw her and now walked toward her.

Kiya smiled, but not too greatly. *The look in his eyes is still there! It's best not to encourage him. He has grown so tall.*

"So, sister, how does our tribe fare? How do *you* fare?"

Kiya's expression softened into sadness. "Vanam is worried," she confided. "He fears Moonman can no longer read the sky to choose where the hunting is good. He is concerned that Saparu blindly takes Moonman's advice and leads us to poor camps. I should not say these horrible things, but the tribe is hungry and Palai grows weaker. It becomes harder for her and Moonman to maintain a good pace as we travel. It's still many days before the hunters will return and I'm afraid what little food we have will be gone."

Saparu, Palai, Moonman. Nanatan, Vivekamulla, Vaniyal, Littlestar. Irakka, Mari, Irul.

She paused, then said, "Welcome back to your people, Pumi."

"Yes. It's good to be back and to see you again, Kiya. We will talk later."

< >

He left Kiya and sought his apprentice. Pumi found Littlerock watching over lethargic children, who were lying and drawing pictures in the dirt.

Pumi asked, "We have spear points?"

Littlerock answered, "Yes, master, and welcome back."

Pumi laughed. "It's good to see you, Littlerock. I have much to tell you. The knowledge we must learn, the things we must build, and the things we must do are great and unending. I will be excited to start these tasks, but first ..."

"But first," said the apprentice, "we are starving. What shall we do?"

"Give a spear and a cutting blade to each boy. Give a gathering sack to each girl. We have half the day remaining. The land in which I just traveled is barren. We will scout toward the south. If we find nothing, we are none the worse off, and we will have gained information. I will obtain Palai's permission and we will leave when you have gathered the children."

The makeshift troupe gathered—giggling girls, so grown up, strutting males excited to be carrying a spear like the hunters.

Pumi said to them, "You boys follow Littlerock. If it moves, flies, slithers, or jumps, it is food. Kill it. The girls will follow me. Consider any growth to be food unless you know it's not. Everyone spread out but remain within each other's viewing distance. If you cannot keep up, or if you get lost, place the sun on your left and start walking. Our search will be good. Let us begin."

They began.

After an hour of running, the vegetation became slightly denser. The girls were beginning to find plants that might be edible. A boy found and decapitated a small snake. Pumi picked up a faint wind, slightly cooler, and turned the troupe slightly westward. In the far distance, he saw a tree line. *Yes. Yes!*

They pillaged the spoils of the creek, not filling their bags, but finding some edible vegetation, spiders, frogs, and insects. The sun began to set, but there was a partial moon.

"We will return to camp now," Pumi commanded. "Follow Littlerock. Stay close together. Boys, keep your spears ready. Do not be afraid. I will be behind you. You will be safe. Let's return to camp."

Vanam, Kiya, Pumi, Valki, Putt, Putt-pay, Breathson, Littlerock.

In the camp, the women were frantic for their children. Upon seeing them return in the moonlight, they rushed, arms outstretched, toward them.

Pumi held up his hand and commanded them to halt and stand straight. These were hunters and gatherers returning from a successful outing and they would be greeted with the respect they were due. The women stood back and watched their children's triumphant return to camp.

The children presented their sacks of food to Palai, who ordered them to be sorted for use. Pumi commanded all the edibles prepared for consumption that night. The children would eat their fill, and the women would have whatever remained. One woman blurted out that the food should be saved for the returning hunters. Pumi harshly silenced her, and said again, "Tonight the children will eat their fill."

With apprehension, the women prepared the collection of grains, roots, bugs, frogs, and a headless snake. As they worked, Pumi sought Palai and said, "Tomorrow, the children and all of the women will travel to the creek we have discovered. The hands of the women are quicker and surer than the children's, but all will participate. I will show the boys how to better harvest the creatures living in the water and along the banks. A day of gathering will provide as much food as the camp will need, at least for a few meals. We can return for more if the hunt goes badly."

Palai shared the news of the upcoming adventure, readying the tribe.

< Sunrise >

The women and children rose, excited and ready to begin their hunt to the newly discovered fields near the creek. The boys were ready to learn the art of hunting. They set off. Littlerock and Pumi led the way.

At the creek, Kiya led the girls into the fields, showing them how to identify what was edible and what was not. Pumi had attached a gathering sack to three spears and showed the boys how to capture small fish and other aquatic creatures in a sack.

The morning and afternoon were fruitful. The hunter-gatherers returned to the camp and prepared a small meal for themselves. There would also be food for the returning hunters.

After the meal, Pumi and Littlerock sat discussing plans for the days until the hunters returned. Eventually, Littlerock retired for the night, leaving Pumi alone by the dying fire with his thoughts.

Saparu, Palai, Moonman. Nanatan, Vivekamulla, Vaniyal, Littlestar. Irakka, Mari, Irul.

Against her resolve, Kiya came to him, foolishly putting the two of them alone. Pumi watched her approach. She saw intensity burning in his eyes, but he did not smile nor offer frivolous compliments. He merely commanded, "Sit. We will talk."

She sat. There was silence for many minutes.

Eventually, Pumi said, "Your words are troubling. Littlerock and Palai have said much the same thing. It is not my place to command the tribe. It is my chief's place. And yet Moonman leads our people into a foodless land, and my chief does nothing. Moonman does not have an apprentice. How did this happen? Why did he not train his replacement? How did our chief allow this to happen? Our people are starving, and yet our chief does nothing. Not only can my brother lead, but he would lead much better than our chief. My father does not have the wisdom to name Vanam as chief. Our tribe will perish."

Kiya's cheeks glowed red at such criticisms of her elders. She had never heard such words spoken about a chief. With a downturned face and closed eyes, she murmured, "What shall we do?"

Pumi answered, "A girl in Chief Nanatan's tribe once told me that to solve a large problem, break it into smaller problems and solve the small ones. This, then, is what we shall do: Saparu will retire and name Vanam the new chief. Moonman will retire immediately and no longer offer counsel. Vanam will lead the tribe toward the northeast, where we have found game in the past. When the time comes, he will turn south and lead us to a planned encounter at Tallstone with the great tribe I traveled with. We will barter with them for a new skywatcher. Probably, both Palai and Moonman will be ready to make their last camp at Tallstone Camp. It is simple enough."

Kiya exclaimed, "Simple? And what will bring these things to pass?"

"Perhaps the stars will whisper that which must be done to those who must do it. Or, perhaps, we shall whisper these things ourselves. I am sorry to leave your company, but I must speak to Palai. I will join you later if you are still here when I finish. We can—visit."

Pumi rose and reluctantly left Kiya sitting pensively by the glowing embers. He found Palai still awake. "Palai," he asked, "when shall it come to pass that Saparu will pass the robe of leadership to Vanam?"

The question agitated the woman. "We do not discuss these things. The robe will be passed when Saparu decides. He is not yet old. He can lead for many more seasons."

Vanam, Kiya, Pumi, Valki, Putt, Putt-pay, Breathson, Littlerock.

"And when, Mother, will you make your Last Camp?"

"You may be the chief's son, stonecutter, but you shall not be impertinent!"

Pumi feigned contrition. "Yes," he said. "You are right, of course. And yet you are the only person who can save our tribe. I may not be as wise as you, but I do know that Saparu must pass the robe. As do you."

He rose abruptly and bid her good night, leaving the woman angry, confused, and distraught.

Pumi returned to the dying fire to hopefully visit Kiya. He knew she would not be there.

< >

For the next three days, Pumi led his child hunters and gatherers to the creek. They were successful.

On the third day, the adult hunters returned. They were *not* successful.

The women rejoiced to see them, even though the hunters had no food. The women surprised the hunters with a meal from the food they had gathered. There was enough for the hunters to regain their strength and survive for many nights.

Pumi stayed away from the camp that evening.

< >

The next morning, Pumi sought Saparu to present himself back into the tribe. The chief was not pleased to see Pumi, another mouth to feed. Pumi revealed little of what had transpired in his own life, changing the subject instead to ask about the bad times that had befallen the tribe. There were many reasons, none of which involved bad decisions by the chief or the skywatcher. Pumi listened politely and sympathetically. After a while, he excused himself to seek his older brother.

Vanam had been observing Pumi and Saparu from a respectful distance and coolly welcomed his brother. "Little brother, where did you find the bountiful harvest?"

Pumi answered, "The children found it and the women gathered it."

"Yes, I'm sure. I hunt and *you* feed the tribe. How interesting."

"Brother," Pumi said, "the tribe appears to be much farther to the west than it has been in my lifetime. What signs lead you in this direction?"

Saparu, Palai, Moonman. Nanatan, Vivekamulla, Vaniyal, Littlestar. Irakka, Mari, Irul.

Vanam snorted in annoyance. "Moonman has been adamant that our hunts move to the west. He offers no justification. Father needs none. He accepts the advice of Moonman. We travel where our moonwatcher suggests."

"I see," said Pumi. "As I searched for our tribe, the land looked fertile toward the north where the tribe usually hunts, but not so much in this direction. A moonwatcher has powers of observation beyond my understanding. Perhaps he will share this knowledge with me. He knows that I have always had an interest in his knowledge of the sky. I'm happy to see you again, Brother. I have much to tell you about Tallstone Camp and my time there. I am pleased with the things I have learned and done. But now, let me pay my respects to Moonman."

"Yes, little brother. We will talk at the campfire. I suspect you have much to tell."

Pumi left his brother and found Moonman napping. He sat down beside the sleeping moonwatcher. Moonman had been old for many years and appeared even older after these last few seasons. Saparu had been regularly commanding rests when no one but Moonman needed it. Even Palai had been maintaining the chief's pace.

Pumi studied the moonwatcher as he slept. *And so ... and so ...*

The moonwatcher woke.

"Ah, good master," said Pumi, "you return from your reflections on the sky. It is good to see you again."

Moonman, mildly confused, finally remembered Pumi as the tribe's stonecutter. "Welcome back, stonecutter. I did not expect to see you again."

"You cannot dispose of me so easily, Moonwatcher. You know that I have always been impressed with your unending knowledge of the sky. If only you had taken me as your apprentice back when I was a child. I would have a much higher status in this world. But, no, you did not choose me."

"You were not clever enough to learn everything about the sky," Moonman said. "Your talent lay in your hands. That is what Saparu decided, and, I will say, he appears to have made the correct decision."

"Yes," said Pumi. "You see wondrous things that are beyond my knowledge. Such as the things that lay in the western sky. Few moonwatchers would be so bold as to trek directly west away from proven hunting grounds. What great thing is it you see in the sky?"

Vanam, Kiya, Pumi, Valki, Putt, Putt-pay, Breathson, Littlerock.

Moonman did not hesitate. "There is a great sea in the west. Water as far as anyone can see. It is a wondrous place. I saw it when I was a child and yearn to return to it again before my Last Camp. I might make my Last Camp there, beside the great sea."

"Ah, yes," replied Pumi and then lied as he said, "A tribe I encountered not too long ago was traveling from the west. They spoke of this great sea, although not as happily as you. Barren and without life, they said. It is twelve seasons to the west."

"Twelve seasons!?" repeated the moonwatcher.

"At least twelve," Pumi said, "maybe more. Hard traveling, too. Many of our weak will die before they reach this forsaken place. You are strong, of course, although Palai would probably make her Last Camp during one of these hunts. But so be it."

Moonman was silent, thinking.

"Allow me to tell you of my recent adventures," continued Pumi. "I made another camp southwest of Tallstone, in an even richer land. I named it 'Urfa Camp.' I had hoped that Palai might make her last camp there. We have built a sort of cave there that would protect her from the elements and predators. Grains and herbs are plentiful, as is water. The water is not as great as the sea of which you speak, but it is a vast expanse of water, nonetheless. Without the hardship of keeping up with the tribe, she might live for many more seasons, gathering grains, making bread, perhaps napping during the day, and reflecting on the great bounty of the land and sky. It is a pity that there is no one else to stay at this place with her. She would enjoy the company and the conversation. Although I imagine that there would be regular encounters with other tribes. Plus, it is only a half-day run back to Tallstone. So much has happened at Tallstone since you were last there. There is an apprentice skywatcher who is assigned to stay there, studying the shadows cast by the tall stone for at least twelve seasons. I worry that he needs another master skywatcher to continue this learning and to improve his work around the stone."

"This apprentice does not travel with his tribe but stays twelve seasons at Tallstone?" asked Moonman. "His chief will allow this?"

"His chief not only allows it; he commands it. The work is so important that it will give the apprentice great value to his tribe—a giant among skywatchers, I imagine. Ah, but you have paid me much respect by listening so long to my prattle. Let me seek my apprentice. I have much to share with him. But if you wish to consider Tallstone and Urfa further, I would be pleased to share what I know of these wonderful places." Pumi rose, smiled, and nodded to the old man, and then quietly crept away, leaving the old man lost in thought.

When he found Littlerock, Pumi told his apprentice, "When my brother becomes chief, I shall ask him to make me skywatcher. This would make you the tribe's master stonecutter. Are you prepared?"

"No," said Littlerock swiftly. "I am not. There is much I cannot do well. My skill in finding the best rocks is small. Seeing the spearhead within the rock is hard. I ruin more stone than I make spearheads. I will say, however, that the land we are now in provides an abundance of stone. Not much game or plants, but plenty of rock."

Pumi laughed. "Yes, there is at least plenty of rock. Let's take advantage and hone your skills in selecting rock and releasing the tool that resides inside. There are new types of tools that I require. I will show you what must be done, and we shall design tools that will aid in the doing. There is much left to learn. We shall be old men before we understand everything there is to understand."

The two talked and worked for the remainder of the day. The moon would disappear in the coming nights. As soon as it did, Moonman would advise Saparu to break camp and move to the next hunting site.

Pumi considered the moment with apprehension.

< Sunrise >

Pumi and Littlerock continued with their work. Palai came to them in the early morning and asked, "Why did you not tell me of this Urfa?" she demanded.

"Oh, Palai, I should have told you of that wonderful place," Pumi replied. "There are fields of grain and herbs as far as the eye can see. We have built a large hut on a hill. It provides safety and shelter. The breeze is always cool and refreshing. A great river flows nearby, providing more water than anyone could ever need. How did you hear of it?"

"Never mind," she snapped as she stormed off.

Pumi said to Littlerock, "Find Moonman. Mention how exciting the work being done at Tallstone and Urfa is. Mention how much I have always wanted to be a skywatcher if only a great teacher would agree to instruct

Vanam, Kiya, Pumi, Valki, Putt, Putt-pay, Breathson, Littlerock.

me. Most importantly, tell him that if he is unsure where the tribe should travel for the next season, say that the skies have not been clear and to ask Vanam for a suggestion."

The apprentice understood and rose to find Moonman. Before leaving, he looked at Pumi and asked, "Are we smarter than hunters, or do they simply not think?"

Pumi laughed and said, "We are stonecutters. It is our nature to release that which is hidden."

< >

The night came when no moon rose.

At the campfire, Moonman intoned that camp would be broken at sunrise and the next hunting grounds would be sought. Unexpectedly he said, "The skies have not been clear. Several directions might yield plentiful game, but I am not ready to recommend which."

Saparu was confused. How could a chief command if he had not been told what to command?

"Perhaps Vanam could provide guidance," Moonman suggested.

Saparu was unsure how to proceed. He merely stated, "We must break camp tomorrow. How shall we decide on the direction?" He turned to Vanam. "What do you think, Son?"

Vanam suggested, "The northern regions have been good for us in the past. We could travel northward. Do you agree with that, Moonman?"

"Pumi has recently traveled from the east," Moonman observed. "I have been instructing him on how to read the sky, not as an apprentice, of course, but he listens and observes. He might one day become an apprentice moonwatcher if he is not too old to learn. What do you say, Pumi?"

Pumi replied, "Several tribes that I encountered suggested that there was good hunting to the north and the east. I don't know if they spoke the truth, but they had plenty of meat."

"I have decided," Saparu bellowed. "We travel toward the northeast at sunrise."

< Elders >

Being old brings with it much respect. Knowledge and experience are of great value to a tribe. It is the old who has these things.

Saparu, Palai, Moonman. Nanatan, Vivekamulla, Vaniyal, Littlestar. Irakka, Mari, Irul.

The loss of stamina is not good. Without it, one cannot keep up with the tribe as they move between campsites. The tribe can sometimes assist the person—slow down the pace or make an early camp—but each of these actions has a cost. They are not long-term solutions.

When a chief observes a member slowing his tribe, when one must stop too often to regain their breath, the chief will begin intimate conversations with the member. "Which is your favorite campsite? When is your favorite season? What do you enjoy most about life?"

The subject is never openly discussed, but everyone knows that at some future camp, sooner rather than later, the overly tired member will be invited to remain at the campsite rather than move on with the tribe. They will be given shelter, food, and water for a season. They will be given a spear. They will be left behind. Remains will not be found.

Generally, it was being very old that stole one's stamina.

Moonman and Palai were very old.

< Change >

Change did not all happen at once.

But in the coming seasons, Pumi was appointed apprentice skywatcher. Palai told the chief of her desire to make her last camp at a place called Urfa, southwest of Tallstone. Moonman told Saparu that he, too, might like to make his last camp in that area. The chief saw his support group melting away. It made him uneasy. *Vanam might be better to make life-and-death decisions for my tribe.*

Faithfully, each night, Pumi moved a stone from one pouch to another.

< >

At last, the time came for Pumi to consult his brother. The hunters had returned from a successful hunt and would rest until the coming new moon a few nights away. Vanam and his father had counseled together, and the chief had retired for the evening, leaving his eldest sitting contemplatively in front of the dying fire.

Pumi approached his brother with trepidation. "May I speak with you?"

"Yes, sit," his brother replied. "Of what shall we talk?"

Pumi was silent.

Vanam, Kiya, Pumi, Valki, Putt, Putt-pay, Breathson, Littlerock.

"Oh, yes," Vanam said. "We should discuss my becoming chief and leading the tribe to Tallstone during this season of a 'Stillhunter.' Discuss having a pre-arranged encounter where we will barter for a new skywatcher. Discuss leaving Palai and Moonman at this place called 'Urfa.' What other plans do you have, little stonecutter? Will you become the chief of all chiefs, so that they come to you for every decision to be made? Will any of us survive without your continual meddling and scheming and teaching the stars to do your bidding? Are these the things we should discuss, little brother?"

Pumi remained silent, then quietly replied, "No harsh words my father has ever hurled upon me have inflicted the pain your words inflict. I do not and have never wished to be a chief of any tribe or any people. That which I do, I do because it is the right thing to do. The right thing for *you* to do is to talk with our father. Tell him you know of the stress he constantly feels from the burden of continuously making life-and-death decisions. Tell him that when this burden is passed, he will once more experience the thrill of the hunt and the happy rejoicing that comes from the absence of responsibilities. Tell him he could have many more seasons as a hunter, but only a few more as a chief. Tell him that when the robe of power is passed, he will always be known as Great Chief Saparu. Tell him that if you are anointed his successor, you will be known only as Chief Vanam. Tell him that he has trained you well and that you would be honored if he named you as his successor. Tell him of the great excitement and pageantry if the robe of power were transferred at Tallstone, the camp that he alone has made, and which shall be his legacy. Tell him these things, and if it pleases you, tell him that the stars have told you this."

Pumi paused—his expression cold. "May I go now, Brother?"

Vanam sat silently staring at the fire. Finally, he whispered, "So it is Pumi that shall make me chief."

"No," replied Pumi. "The stars shall make you chief."

Pumi rose and left without permission.

Saparu, Palai, Moonman. Nanatan, Vivekamulla, Vaniyal, Littlestar. Irakka, Mari, Irul.

Book One. The Beginning of Civilization: Mythologies Told True

16. Tallstone and Chief Saparu

The next year in Year 27; ages 27, 23, 17, 14.

Chief Saparu led his tribe into Tallstone Camp.

Nanatan's tribe was already there. Their hunters had left for the hunt and their women were gathering in the fields. The children ran toward the new arrivals but kept a respectful distance.

"Hmm," said Saparu. "Moonman, there is already a camp here, full of children. Where shall we make our camp?"

Moonman replied with contempt, "We should chase the interlopers away. This is *our* camp, not theirs."

Saparu asked Pumi, "Hmm. Where does the apprentice skywatcher suggest we camp?"

Without pause, Pumi said, "We should camp on the southern side. It is a superior location to their camp on the east. We will even have the great flat rock table. They are the larger tribe, but we shall have the better location."

Chief Saparu commanded, "We will camp below the great stone table that I have placed here!" He reflected, *Perhaps this will be the last camp I command. Perhaps I will relinquish this robe of power. After all, my oldest son is a respected, powerful hunter—and he is my son. All would obey him, but he would continually consult me. I would be called "Great Chief Saparu." The transfer of power would be impressive with an appreciative audience. Moonman and Palai wish to make this their last camp— not that I require their advice, of course, but still, it was sometimes useful and would no longer be available. Making decisions is tiring. Commanding is difficult. I have commanded for so long. I am tired. Perhaps. Perhaps.*

Pumi could barely keep his attention on the proceedings. On the top of the hill by the tall stone stood Vaniyal, Littlestar, Putt, and several young males watching the proceedings. But Pumi made no move to dismiss himself. He had to be careful. His chief was distracted and would not be patient. Vanam was cold and any misstep could undo everything. A loose, inappropriate word from Moonman could bring down the wrath of his father and his brother. Best not to be seen and not to be heard. Pumi was patient until he could disappear. He then motioned Littlerock to go with him to the top of the hill, where their peers waited.

At the tall stone, the reunion was joyful. These were men burning with a thirst for knowledge and with information that needed to be shared,

Vanam, Kiya, Pumi, Valki, Putt, Putt-pay, Breathson, Littlerock.

understood, and applied. There was talk of building huts. Words flowed. Words of shadows traced upon the ground, of possible meaning, of suggestions for improvement. Gathered for the first time were hunters who had similar interests that were neither hunting nor gathering. The things they hunted were ideas, concepts, and learning. They were something new—scholars.

Pumi had found his council. For the first time, he was home.

< >

Afternoon moved toward evening.

Women began returning from their gathering. Children from both tribes ran to the periphery of the camp to greet them. The women of Pumi's tribe waited respectfully at the edge of their camp, waiting for the elder women of the two tribes to properly meet and invite the other women to mingle.

Pumi noticed the returning women and excused himself from the deep discussions in which he had been involved. He walked beyond the tall stone to the edge of the hill, midway between the returning women's camp on the east side of the hill and his own tribe's camp in the south. He scanned the horizon watching the returning women.

In the distance, he saw her. She was unmistakable. Her long, straw-colored hair blew in the gentle wind. Her stride was long. In the last year, she had matured from a child into a woman. An imperceptible warmth swept through Pumi, one that he associated only with Kiya. Yet it was Valki who approached. His stoic little adventuress. The little girl who looked upon Pumi with such large eyes. Who followed him wherever he asked. Valki.

The women came closer to their camp. Pumi could see Valki scanning the two camps. She saw him and raised her hand to wave. A gross impropriety. Her pace seemed to quicken. She seemed to smile broadly at him. Pumi carefully made no sign of recognition. His expression did not change. He watched her return to her camp.

< >

After the women met with their elder women, after the fruits of their labors had been identified and separated into the appropriate piles and safely stored, only then did Pumi approach the elder woman.

"Do you remember me, Elder Woman Vivekamulla?" Pumi asked.

Vivekamulla replied, "Of course, I remember you. You are the little stonecutter. The one who erected the tall stone. My, you have grown very tall. I cannot call you 'little' anymore. You must be ready to accept a young woman into your protection. I have many candidates in my tribe. I shall go immediately to your elder. We will discuss many things, including proper matchmaking."

Pumi laughed. "No woman yet, Elder Woman Vivekamulla. I have much growing to do, and many quests to make."

"Nonetheless, I will consult your elder woman." She waved him away.

He turned to go, then suddenly turned. "Although, with your permission, I would like to say hello to Valki. Does she learn her gathering arts well enough?"

Vivekamulla laughed. "She has been my best gatherer since she was a child. Yes, you have my permission."

Pumi found Valki. She was sitting on the ground in a circle with five other young women. Seeing him approach, she rose to her feet and, with forward impropriety, spoke to him. "The boy has become the man without the baby fat of a child."

Pumi accepted the familiarity without rancor. "And the girl has become the woman. Sleek and comely."

Neither noticed the giggles coming from the circle as the other young women quickly and quietly excused themselves and left the two standing figures to themselves.

Valki smiled. "The women's gossip said that our two tribes had planned an encounter for Winter Solstice. I have been hoping that it would come to pass so that I could see you again. You were kind to me. The other girls changed their attitude because of your kindness toward me. They accepted me as one of their own."

Pumi, seldom at a loss for words, found himself stammering. "Y-you were a wonderful companion. I enjoyed your company. You were more mature and clever than all of the other children, and most of the women, that I have known. It's good to see you again. Have you been well?"

Valki blushed and replied, "Yes, extremely well. Thank you. I was admitted into the company of women a season after we parted. No one seems to notice my differences anymore, not the women anyway. Maybe the men do. You have grown so tall—so muscular. Will I be permitted to go with you when you return to Urfa? I am sure you will want to return there, as I do. Vivekamulla will surely grant me permission."

Vanam, Kiya, Pumi, Valki, Putt, Putt-pay, Breathson, Littlerock.

That caught Pumi by surprise. He had long wondered how he could manipulate the situation so he could show Kiya what had been built at Urfa. He wanted to do so, not only to impress her but also to gain her insights into the viability of the surrounding land—but mainly to impress her. Unexpectedly, Pumi was overcome with confusion and embarrassment. He realized that both Kiya and Valki warmed him. Urfa existed because of Valki, but it had been inspired by his wanting to protect Kiya.

"Of course, I will go to Urfa," he said. "And you shall go, too. We will wait until the hunters leave. I'll tell you when the time comes."

Valki smiled, replied, "Thank you, Pumi," and left him to his confusion.

< >

Several nights passed.

After the hunters from Pumi's tribe left for their hunt, Pumi put together an expeditionary force to return to Urfa.

Moonman was the senior man in the party. His interest was in seeing the hut where he might make his last camp, and to see the nearby mighty river. Accompanying Moonman was Palai, who was resigned that she would remain there, never again to join her tribe as they moved from camp to camp.

Accompanying Palai was Kiya, a candidate for the position of the tribe's elder woman. She was too young, but her knowledge of plants was greater than any woman in the tribe, and, besides, she would be the new chief's woman. No one would complain too vigorously if she were selected. Littlerock and two interested boys also traveled with them.

Members of Nanatan's tribe included Vaniyal and Littlestar, who both had a general interest in new things. Putt was there, of course, plus several boy apprentices of Putt's choosing. Vivekamulla, who had been influenced by Palai's decision, requested inclusion.

And Valki.

The expedition set forth.

Pumi set a slow trot for Moonman's benefit.

Early afternoon brought them to the hut.

Putt was anxious to show Pumi the improvements he had made. Littlerock unpacked the new tools that he and Pumi had fashioned to be used in constructing such things as this hut. Everyone admired Putt's "house." It

Saparu, Palai, Moonman. Nanatan, Vivekamulla, Vaniyal, Littlestar. Irakka, Mari, Irul.

was larger than just a "hut" and had much more room than Palai and Moonman would ever need. It could house many people.

Palai was ecstatic. She said, "This is a wonderful Last Camp. There is so much vegetation here that I can gather on the last day of my life."

Vaniyal was impressed. "A cave, boy. You said you wanted a cave. This place could protect a tribe from an attack by lions."

Vivekamulla announced, "When my time comes, I will choose this place as my Last Camp."

Moonman thought it grand but wanted to see the vast river he had been told was nearby. He set out to look for it.

Palai, Kiya, and Vivekamulla inspected the surrounding fields. They were pleased. The fields were richer with growth than even Tallstone.

Valki searched for last year's rain-drenched camp.

From the distance came a cry. "Is *this* the great river I was told of?"

"Excuse me," Pumi said. "I have to attend to something." He scurried toward the cry, already arranging comforting words of reassurance.

Valki found the remains of the camp. She was struck dumb by what she saw. She stared at it for a long time.

Excitedly, she returned to the women. "Come. Come and see what the earth has given us. It is thick and beautiful. It is more einkorn in one place than I have ever seen. More than I have ever imagined."

Palai and Kiya, unfamiliar with Valki's knowledge, were amused at the young woman's excitement, but nevertheless, they followed.

Vivekamulla knew well of Valki's expertise. Her blood quickened with excitement as she ran with Valki.

There, before them, lay a field of einkorn, so thick that it crowded out all other growth. A field where a gatherer could gather a week's worth of einkorn in a single morning. It was rich beyond belief. The four women stared at the treasure.

Finally, Valki stammered, "This is where Pumi and I made camp when that torrential rain came. That is where my einkorn was carried away by the deluge. See, this is where we made our bed. This field is where the einkorn would have been returned to the earth. How can such a place be, Vivekamulla? What kind of place is this?"

The four women stared in silent disbelief at the great field of einkorn.

< >

In the late evening, the troupe set out to return to Tallstone.

Valki ran with Vivekamulla. "Can I stay in this place, Mother Vivekamulla, with Palai and Moonman? Putt would think it wonderful to live here, too. He could build more things and improve his buildings. Surely everyone would want to make their Last Camp at Urfa. They could die in peace and dignity. We could have little ceremonies when they die. They would all die happily. It would mean a great deal if I could help all of those people. And there is the einkorn field. How did that happen? I need to learn its secrets. Do you think my chief might release me from his tribe to live here? And release Putt, too? How would I request these things? What do I have to offer? You are his elder woman. How can I make these things happen?"

She replied, "There is much happening this season. Negotiating a release from a tribe is difficult unless the chief views you as a liability, which in your case, he doesn't. But I will think about it."

Saparu, Palai, Moonman. Nanatan, Vivekamulla, Vaniyal, Littlestar. Irakka, Mari, Irul.

17. Winter Solstice Festival I

Chief Nanatan's hunters returned from their hunt. It had been a great success. Entrails had been left for the wolves.

Nanatan was pleased to find that Pumi's tribe had returned to Tallstone Camp for the Winter Solstice. The chief decided that this would be the greatest celebration ever. Not only for his tribe but for the tribe that had shown such generous hospitality in his time of need, the tribe that had produced the little stonecutter boy who had erected the tall stone, which his skywatcher's senior apprentice had been studying for an entire year. Yes, this would be a momentous celebration—a festival—the first-ever Winter Solstice Festival.

The two tribal chiefs found one another. They warmly exchanged greetings and retired to discuss the responsibilities of chiefdom and make plans for the remainder of the season. Before retiring, the chiefs signaled that the two tribes could mingle. The two elder women, Vivekamulla and Palai, also retired with one another. There was the matter of young, unattached men and women to be addressed, plus other pressing matters.

The two chiefs agreed that Nanatan would host the encounter feast on the night of the Winter Solstice. The feast would have been held even without an encountered tribe. Vanam and his father would be invited to attend the tribe's council meeting the following evening.

A few days later, on the eve of the new moon, Chief Saparu would conduct the ceremony for transferring the robe of power to his son, who would, therefore, be anointed the new chief of his tribe. Vanam would be known as Chief Vanam, and his father would be known as Great Chief Saparu. Both tribes would observe the transfer ceremony.

Meanwhile, the scholars had retreated to the tall stone. It was obvious that they had to recruit neophytes. There were far too many questions and unknowns for themselves alone to resolve. They debated on how to proceed, how to acquire apprentices, and how to survive here year-round, without hunters and gatherers. Who, if any of them, could stay year-round studying the building of structures and the shadows of the sun?

During the discussions, Pumi, without a clear vision, commanded Littlerock to take whichever of their party wished to go with him to Rockplace, and harvest two sitting stones like the one Pumi had carved out for Vaniyal. Littlerock delayed the task until the next morning. Pumi's high

Vanam, Kiya, Pumi, Valki, Putt, Putt-pay, Breathson, Littlerock.

status as a stonecutter had raised the interest of young boys in the art. Two boys interested in learning begged to be allowed to go with Littlerock.

< >

The day before the Winter Solstice came.

The anticipation of the celebration was great. Pumi added more excitement by organizing a challenge to see which tribe had the strongest hunters. The challenge was to move a large rock from Rockplace to Tallstone. Hunters from each tribe would select two of their strongest to run to Rockplace, select one of the waiting sitting rocks, and return it to Tallstone. There would be garlands for the first team to transport their rock back.

Girls were thrilled to be tasked with collecting vines and plants and then constructing the garlands.

Toward sunset, the first of the exhausted hunters returned, placed their rock at the designated location, and claimed their garland. The winning team was Valuvana and Maiyana from Saparu's tribe. Within minutes, two hunters from Nanatan's tribe arrived with their rock. They, too, received garlands, but less impressive.

Pumi announced to the crowds that each of the two tribal chiefs would be awarded their own personal sitting rock, just like Vaniyal had his own personal sitting rock. These sitting rocks were larger of course, as befitted chiefs. The two chiefs, already glowing from the excitement of the contest and the imminent Winter Solstice Festival, were delighted.

Pumi said Saparu should select first from the two rocks because his hunters had won the competition. Saparu was grateful but deferred to Vanam as the tribe's soon-to-be chief. Vanam bowed to his father and thanked him profusely for the unnecessary but appreciated kindness, then made a great show of inspecting the two sitting rocks closely before pointing to one and declaring it to be perfect.

"That's the one I wanted," shouted Nanatan, with feigned frustration.

"Well," announced Pumi, joining in with animated theatrics, "since Vanam selected the first stone, Chief Nanatan, you will be first to select the sign that you wish carved into your rock. This will inform all people that this is your sitting rock and yours alone."

"Ahhh," said Nanatan. "What manner of a sign shall I select?"

Saparu, Palai, Moonman. Nanatan, Vivekamulla, Vaniyal, Littlestar. Irakka, Mari, Irul.

Pumi replied, "Vaniyal has an engraving of 'Stillhunter' on his sitting rock because it is special to him. Select an image that everyone will associate with you when they see your sitting rock."

Nanatan roared, "Aahhh! Cut the figure of a great lion, the greatest hunter there is. He fears nothing, and all do his bidding. Yes, a lion will tell everyone that this is Nanatan's sitting rock."

Pumi said, "It will be done before the night is out. You will sit on it tonight. I will see to it myself. Now soon-to-be Chief Vanam, what sign do you wish carved into your sitting rock?"

Vanam said, "The mighty lion is already taken. The lion fears nothing—except—maybe the serpent. Yes. Carve me a mighty serpent."

"Well played," exclaimed Nanatan loudly, laughing. "Well played." The two chiefs and the chief-soon-to-be walked arm-in-arm toward the hunter's fire to finalize the next day's wonderful event—the greatest celebration ever—the first-ever Winter Solstice Festival.

Valki found Pumi watching Littlerock engrave the chief's sitting rocks with their icons. She requested an audience to present him with an idea she had. She told him, "The more tribes that come to the festival, the greater the riches to be bartered. There would be more choices for matchmaking. There would be more information to be exchanged and learned. This area has abundant game and vegetation and would support many tribes gathering at one time. Maybe the two chiefs could encourage every tribe they encounter to meet at Tallstone at the next Winter Solstice. You could make stone coins for the chiefs with an image of Stillhunter on one side and Tallstone on the other. The chiefs could give the coins as gifts to encountered tribes. Their chiefs and skywatchers might have the desire and expertise to find their way to the event."

Pumi was awestruck. "Many tribes at one camp at the same time?"

Without thought he embraced her. She melted. He put his hands on her shoulders, pushed her back to arm's length, and, with excitement, stared at her as he said, "Why didn't I think of that? I can make the coins tonight. We will need to prepare a sitting rock for each chief so it will be here at the next festival. We will start with four more. Each chief will have to select a symbol for his tribe. We will need some long-term plans to accommodate growth for the festival. That is the best idea ever—at least since the last best idea you had last year. Valki! You are so clever! Of course, the chiefs will

Vanam, Kiya, Pumi, Valki, Putt, Putt-pay, Breathson, Littlerock.

agree with this. I will meet with Vaniyal and Littlestar tonight. They will both be excited and will have suggestions on how to proceed. You are the smartest, greatest gatherer that's ever been."

He smiled broadly at her and then left to find Vaniyal.

Valki stood there—trembling. *Mother, I am still alive.*

< Sunrise >

On the day of the great Winter Solstice Festival, the skywatchers and stonecutters held an impromptu meeting while everyone else gathered in the fields for the planned gaming events. Pumi reviewed Valki's great plan with the scholars, which he would propose to the two chiefs at tonight's campfire meeting. They planned on two additional tribes next year and four more the year after that. The festival might eventually grow to accommodate up to twelve tribes. Their immediate problem was to decide where the chief's sitting stones should be placed. Placing two stones was one thing. Planning for twelve chiefs at a single encounter was something else entirely. Much to Vaniyal's delight, it was decided the two new sitting stones for the chiefs would be placed immediately due east of his sitting stone with five more undesignated stones on either side of the two new ones. This would be a good, central location for Chief Nanatan to proclaim the beginning of the festival. All were in agreement—how could any chief not be delighted with their proposal?

Littlerock missed the day's festivities. He took three apprentices to Rockplace to begin harvesting ten more sitting stones.

< Nightfall >

The first day ended with Chief Nanatan's yearly council meeting around the great campfire. Chief Saparu and his son were honored guests. Spectators from both tribes stood a respectful distance away while Nanatan conducted the yearly review of the trials and victories of his beloved tribe.

As the meeting started, Pumi saw Valki standing across the crowd with the other women. She was staring at him.

He returned the stare, but Valki did not look away. *Where have I seen that look before? Oh, I remember. That is the look I have gazed upon Kiya with. She always looked away. Now I understand why. I wanted more from her, and she knew it. More than talking—more than even coupling—I wanted HER. I didn't realize I found her to be the most interesting, confident, commanding person I had ever known—and—*

Saparu, Palai, Moonman. Nanatan, Vivekamulla, Vaniyal, Littlestar. Irakka, Mari, Irul.

sexually desirable. I seldom admitted even to myself that I had a fantasy of Kiya standing naked before me—inviting me. But that was not right—she was my brother's mate. I understand now that she was the only female that I ever wished to couple with. But now—Valki—my friend—my explorer—my always-there-when-I-have-a-problem-companion—Valki. More interesting than even Kiya. Valki—your hair, the color of a golden sunset—your voice, music—your touch, gentle—you love all, even those that spurn you—you are the morning and the evening—you are life itself—Valki.

He began walking toward her.

She saw him walk toward her and moved through the women to meet him at the edge of the gathering.

He did not speak, nor did he smile. He held out his hand. She took it.

She walked with him up the hill to behind the tall stone. Everyone else was at the chief's campfire. They looked down upon the great congregation. She started to tell him what a wonderful thing that he had brought to pass but he held his finger to her lips to silence her.

He untied the string around her neck that held her tunic. Her tunic slid to the ground.

She had been counseled in these things by Vivekamulla. "If you choose to accept him, raise your tunic to your waist, fall to your hands and knees, and present your rear to him. He will enter you, thrust several times, make a strange sound, stand, and leave. If he is courteous, he will help you rise and thank you. There is no more to it than that."

But still, she listened to the gossip of the mated women.

One gatherer had said, "It excites me when a male removes my tunic for me. I think he's interested in more than just entering my body. Maybe he wants intimacy or something. Who knows what they want?"

But all agreed—he wanted *you*. Not some random woman. He wanted *you*.

And Pumi had removed her tunic. *Mother, I have never been afraid before.*

Pumi stared at her naked body. *You trembled in my arms when I was trying to protect you from the rain. It was not the rain that made you tremble, was it?*

He remembered the times he had caught her staring at him. The look of pleasure in her eyes when they met after a long absence. The joy and laughter in her voice when she talked to him. *You are trembling now.*

He pulled the strings to his tunic. It fell to the ground. He stepped toward her.

Vanam, Kiya, Pumi, Valki, Putt, Putt-pay, Breathson, Littlerock.

Valki immediately turned, fell to her hands and knees, presented her rear to him, clenched her hands, and waited. *Mother Vivekamulla told me I would do everything correctly. Please, let me please him. Please!*

Pumi knelt and stared, mesmerized, at the vision before him. He placed a hand on each of her cheeks—still hypnotized by the sight of her waiting, willing body. His need grew with each passing moment. *I am going to mate with Valki!*

She waited with clenched fists. *What is he waiting for? Am I not desirable? Am I deformed? Am I not presenting myself correctly? What is wrong?*

Finally, she felt his hands on her shoulders.

He rolled her onto her back, dropped down, pulled her legs upward, and worked himself into her. He lowered himself to his elbows and began thrusting. As he did, he whispered, "I want to see your face while we do this thing—to see if I please you—to see if you take any pleasure in the doing—to see if you care."

She released a low, guttural moan as she wrapped her arms around his shoulders and whispered with disbelief, "Please me? Do *you* please *me*?!"

She began thrusting in time with him. She threw her head back and sank her fingernails into his shoulders.

Pumi, through the fog of his actions, saw her exposed neck. The sign of completely vulnerable prey surrendering to an overpowering predator—or of complete trust. Without thought he reached down and wrapped his open mouth around her throat.

A continuous, low moan began flowing from her. Her embrace became unbreakable. She slowed the rate of their thrusts from fast to slow. She looked up at him with half-closed eyes and parted lips.

He forced his lips onto hers, opening her mouth wider and sending his tongue deep into her mouth.

She responded in kind; their mouths became one; their hips, one. Her hands began exploring his body; his hands, hers.

His fingers found her nipples; her body trembled. *She likes that.*

To delay the release he knew would be soon coming, he stopped his thrusts and began grinding his groin into hers.

Her eyes rolled back, her body shook, and a moan came from deep within her body. She tensed and her entire body shuddered. She loosened her grip and became totally limp.

Saparu, Palai, Moonman. Nanatan, Vivekamulla, Vaniyal, Littlestar. Irakka, Mari, Irul.

Pumi the hunter then released himself into Valki the gatherer.

He lay on top of her, embracing her. He was tired but pleased. *I'm not at all sure I did that correctly, but it went well enough, I suppose. She seemed to like her nipples being rubbed—and my lips on hers—and something happened to her when I began rubbing against the outside of her body. I'll need to explore those things some more. I'll ask her after she wakes up if I did what I was supposed to. But for now—I think I'll rest.*

< >

He awoke several hours later, lying beside her. He was strangely refreshed. Pumi remembered what they had done and found the remembrance arousing. *I need to find out the things I did wrong, but I also need to know what I am working with. A stonecutter must always know his rocks. I suppose her body is at least as complicated as a rock. I should understand these things.*

He raised himself to his elbows and hovered his body over hers. He pulled her legs up and apart as he lowered himself down her body.

Half-asleep, she placed her hands on his head and gently messaged it.

He lowered himself until he could see her body in detail. The moon lit every crevice and mound. The blond hair reflected like wild grain in the moonlight. *Do you mind if I study you, Valki?*

His hands explored her. She did not discourage his touch as he caressed, prodded, and probed. He noted subtle changes in the pressure of her caresses as he explored. *This is more complicated than even Rockplace!*

He remembered his explorations of the outcrop at Rockplace. Changes in the crevices the deeper he explored; the taste of stone; the different textures. He explored Valki. He discovered a great deal.

He remembered how sweet her open mouth had tasted. *What about your other parts, Valki?*

His lips and tongue explored. He ventured from the crevice to the little stone-shaped mound above it. Her gentle touch became a tight grip.

"Oh, yes," she moaned. "Right there, Pumi. Touch me right there."

He explored a while longer until she suddenly sat upright, rolled him onto his back, and mounted him as she guided his erection into her body. She fell to her elbows and began slow thrusts.

Vanam, Kiya, Pumi, Valki, Putt, Putt-pay, Breathson, Littlerock.

Pumi accepted her commands and wound up looking at her breasts gently swaying above him. In a mist, he thought, *A good time to explore the landscape, I suppose. Find out what works and what doesn't.*

He raised his head to suck one of her breasts into his mouth. His tongue found her nipple. *She likes that!*

He stopped his testing long enough to mutter, "Valki, I don't think we're doing this right."

Her reply came from deep within her throat, "Aahh oonntt aaaree."

Pumi replied, "You're right, Valki. I don't care, either!"

They continued their research until they reached a mutually satisfactory stopping point; then they rested.

< >

A few hours later, Pumi awakened with a strange sensation. He silently savored the feeling for a moment and then looked down to see the top of Valki's bobbing head. He asked, "What are you doing, Valki?!"

Valki stopped what she was doing, looked up, and said, "It's only fair!"

She then resumed her experiment. After her self-imposed task was climatically completed, she lay her head on his contented chest and murmured, "No one told me about any of these things, Pumi. We must experiment until we try every possible combination and position. Would you like to try something different now?"

< >

They awoke at sunrise. Valki insisted they welcome the sun. She commanded, "You must be tired. Here—I will get on top and do all the work. You just lay there and inspire me!"

They eventually finished, rested, rose, and dressed. Pumi took her hand as they walked to the campsites and found Vivekamulla and Palai. He declared to both that he would protect Valki and any children she might have.

Both elder women approved of this excellent match.

Valki displayed happiness.

< Sunset >

On the eve of the new moon, the Clan of the Serpent gathered around a great campfire. The Clan of the Lion watched at a respectful distance.

Saparu, Palai, Moonman. Nanatan, Vivekamulla, Vaniyal, Littlestar. Irakka, Mari, Irul.

Book One. *The Beginning of Civilization: Mythologies Told True*

Chief Saparu, in his robe of power, conducted the business of the tribe. He announced that his close advisors, Elder Woman Palai, and the tribe's longtime moonwatcher, Moonman, would make their Last Camp at nearby Urfa. He then said, "I shall not appoint those who will replace my loyal council. That will be for the one who replaces me to do. I hereby declare my oldest son, Vanam, to be Chief of the Clan of the Serpent. He will lead this clan to greater wealth and power than I have even dreamed."

He talked on for a while, then called for his son to stand before him. Saparu and Vanam stood. Chief Saparu removed his bear-skin robe and placed it on Vanam's shoulders. Chief Saparu announced loudly, "You are now Chief Vanam of the Clan of the Serpent."

Vanam bowed to his father and said, "No chief will ever be as great as you, Great Chief Saparu. But I will lead your tribe to the best of my ability, and I have been taught by the best."

The tribe began to chant, "Va-nam … Va-nam … Va-nam …"

Finally, Vanam held up his arm and commanded silence. He said, "Does any tribesman have an issue that should now be addressed?"

Pumi stood with Valki by his side and said, "Chief Vanam, I have a request for you to consider. I wish to protect the woman Valki from all harm that might otherwise fall upon her or her children. Both elder women will allow it. I beg that you permit it."

Without emotion, Vanam commanded, "Palai, your last act as an elder woman will be to administer this ceremony for Pumi and Valki. Elder Woman Vivekamulla may assist."

Vivekamulla joined Palai. They motioned the man and woman to come to them. There were silent tears of joy in Vivekamulla's eyes.

And Valki's.

< What Pumi Wants >

Sunrise.

Valki lay cuddled in Pumi's arms. She dared not move lest Pumi wake and roll away. *Mother, your suffering was not in vain. I live. My life is bountiful beyond all hope you had for me. How did you do it? Even now I remember your suffering, your hunger, the evil of our chief. Mother, I do not deserve this happiness—happiness beyond bearing. But I shall always try to do what is right—to help those less fortunate than me—to make you and Pumi proud of me.*

Vanam, Kiya, Pumi, Valki, Putt, Putt-pay, Breathson, Littlerock.

She felt Pumi shift his position. She rolled over so that her nose almost touched his. She reached down between them and gently began stroking him. He opened his eyes to stare into hers, less than a pebble away. She said, "Good morning, Pumi. How shall we begin our day?"

He smirked and then, together, they began their day.

Afterward, Pumi lay with Valki in the crook of his arm looking up at the morning sky. Valki purred with contentment.

He told her, "I have too much to do today. I'm going to ask Vanam to release us both from his tribe. He is jealous of things I do and now it will get worse. He will have mixed feelings about it. He wants to be rid of me, but I am his best excuse for a moonwatcher and by far his best stonecutter. I did not dare ask for my release before he became chief. Now, I can ask—but I need a plan."

Valki sleepily replied, "Get Littlestar to be Vanam's skywatcher for a year. He can train some apprentices. You can trade Littlestar for our release. Tell Vanam that I will live with Moonman and Palai at Urfa. That will keep them both alive a little while longer. I will accept everybody's weak members so that their tribes will no longer be burdened by them. Both chiefs would like that. My newcomers can help me learn about einkorn. Now that that's solved, do you want to start our day again?"

After restarting their day, Pumi rose mid-morning and set out to find Chief Nanatan. He was talking with Chief Vanam. Pumi would wait until he could talk to Nanatan alone. Pumi looked for and found Littlestar near the tall stone. He went to him and said, "Littlestar, my dearest friend. I have come to ask a favor of you. It might be a large favor—an extremely large favor—and Vaniyal might not be in favor of it—or Nanatan—or you."

Littlestar stared at Pumi and asked, "So, only Pumi will be pleased?"

"Oh, yes, dear friend Littlestar. Pumi will be extremely pleased."

Littlestar laughed and said, "Well, let's hear it!"

Littlestar "heard it" and replied, "Even if I agreed to be your brother's skywatcher because—well, I have no idea why I would do that—but if I did agree, neither Vaniyal nor Nanatan would agree to such a thing. You need a different plan, Pumi."

Pumi countered, "Of course Vaniyal will agree. He will agree because his greatest protégé ever, second only to Vaniyal himself in the knowledge of

Saparu, Palai, Moonman. Nanatan, Vivekamulla, Vaniyal, Littlestar. Irakka, Mari, Irul.

the sky, is so excited to spend a year passing on Vaniyal's vast knowledge to at least two new eager apprentices in the Clan of the Serpent; a clan that will someday become second in greatness only to the Clan of the Lion. And I, of course, will be free to spend half my time throughout the year working with the current inhabitants of Tallstone; surely these are bargaining tools. And the chief? I will dedicate a full quarter moon each month at Rockplace, making countless exquisite cutting tools for the Clan of the Lion. And, if your chief has any older members considering making a Last Camp in the coming year, I will help Valki prepare a place for them."

Littlestar asked, "Now, tell me why I should agree to this?"

"Don't you see, Littlestar? For all of this to happen, your chief will have to convince Vaniyal to release you from the Clan of the Lion. You are allowed to stay at Tallstone only at the leisure of your chief. If Nanatan will release you, you will be free to stay at Tallstone forever. Your only cost is one year of service to Vanam, plus you will be fed well during your service. My bigger problem is that I need Vaniyal to also trade his newest and best apprentice skywatcher, Voutch, to Vanam to become your apprentice. With your training, Voutch will be a good skywatcher within a year. You can leave the Clan of the Serpent knowing you have made it stronger. You will be free to learn all the secrets of the tall stone and teach it to all who seek knowledge of the heaven. You will become Littlestar of Tallstone. Say yes, my dear friend. Our futures await our freedom from our tribes."

< Negotiations >

Pumi found Valki. He said, "Negotiating with Littlestar was difficult, Valki. My plan is complicated, but Littlestar sees more good than bad in it. I will go to Vaniyal this afternoon. If he will listen, then these things may come to pass."

Valki replied, "You poor man. You look exhausted. Come. I will renew you."

Later—tired, but otherwise renewed—Pumi found Vaniyal monitoring the activity at the tall stone and asked, "Great Wise Master Skywatcher Vaniyal, may I counsel with you?"

Vaniyal groaned. "What is it you wish of me, Master Pumi?"

Pumi answered, "You misjudge my motives, Great Master Vaniyal. I only wish to speak of that which makes a tribe great. The Clan of the Lion is the greatest tribe in all the lands. I have wondered, 'Why is that?' So, I ask Vaniyal, 'Why is that?'"

Vanam, Kiya, Pumi, Valki, Putt, Putt-pay, Breathson, Littlerock.

Vaniyal replied, "My tribe *is* great. And it is because our chief is great. He is strong, wise, and just. No skywatcher could ask for a greater chief than Chief Nanatan. That is why, Pumi."

"Well said, Vaniyal. And all so true. But I believe there to be a second reason." He paused. "A great chief must surround himself with great advisors. Vivekamulla may be the wisest elder woman who has ever lived. And Nanatan's skywatcher? What of him?"

They were both silent.

Finally, Pumi said, "You are the greatest skywatcher who has ever lived, Vaniyal. This is not flattery. This is truth. We both know it. You have walked side-by-side with Nanatan as he has created a tribe of great wealth, size, and power. He would have been great without you, Vaniyal. But with you—he is the greatest chief who has ever lived. You helped make him so. There you have it. And what is it I want? You know what I want. I want my Clan of the Serpent to be great. I want Vanam to become a great chief. I want, too, something more subtle. You know that I love knowledge; knowledge that is shared with all who seek it. What shall be your legacy, Vaniyal?—'The greatest skywatcher who ever lived'—when you someday make your Last Camp, what is it you leave behind? What shall be your glory then? Thank you for counseling me. I see Littlestar. I need to talk with him."

Pumi rose and walked toward Littlestar, leaving Vaniyal lost in thought.

After a while, Vaniyal rose and joined the two men. He asked, "What is it I am to do?"

Pumi told him.

< Interesting Thoughts >

Pumi found Vanam in the afternoon. "Chief Vanam, do you have time to meet with me?"

Vanam was still in the euphoria of being anointed chief. "Yes, skywatcher or stonecutter or scholar or whatever you are today. Let us meet. What is it that I wish you to do—for the good of my clan?"

Pumi laughed. "For the good of my older brother, get rid of me and Valki. I am a thorn—a sore in your side. Get rid of me and my mate and move without impediment into your great and wonderful future. I believe that I could then negotiate both skywatcher apprentice Voutch and maybe even Littlestar, himself, into your tribe. Even Voutch, as he is now, would serve you much better as a skywatcher than me. A year of training under Littlestar would give you a Master Skywatcher. Shall I continue with my thoughts?"

Vanam stared at Pumi in silence—considering. He said, "Continue. These are interesting thoughts."

< Renewal >

Valki was surprised to see Pumi return early. She asked, "Did your meeting go well?"

"Yes, both of them. The two clans will meet to negotiate at this evening's campfire. In the meantime, I am extremely tired."

Valki jumped up with excitement, squealed with delight, clapped her hands, and exclaimed, "Let me renew you, Pumi!"

< Evening >

The evening's meal was completed as was tribal business. The two chiefs retired to negotiate a matter of paramount importance—the trade of tribal members. Pumi, looking somewhat haggard, and Vaniyal were allowed to join them. Without Vaniyal's resistance, Voutch might be available for the Clan of the Serpent but, as Chief Nanatan understood the transaction, the Clan of the Lion would be losing Littlestar, Voutch, the boy Putt—not much of a hunter, but still—Nanatan would be losing many valuable resources and would only be receiving some spear points in return. "This is not an equitable trade," he complained.

Pumi offered, "Chief Nantan, I have seen a toddler in your tribe. I believe he is called 'Breathson.' He appears to be afflicted and a burden to your tribe. A tribe as large as yours probably has several members who are a burden and will always be so. A burden that Valki of Urfa could lighten. If Chief Vanam releases her and me from his tribe, then Valki will accept all those who burden your tribe. You can rid yourself of them with honor for you and dignity for them. All she desires is trading privileges at the next festival, a space south of the Clan of the Serpent campsite. She extends this offer if you two great chiefs come to a mutually satisfactory agreement in your negotiation and she becomes, in fact, Valki of Urfa."

Nanatan asked, "You say that she would accept the boy, Breathson?"

Pumi replied, "As her own son."

"I may have others. I would need to meet with Vivekamulla to finalize a list of such tribesmen."

Vanam, Kiya, Pumi, Valki, Putt, Putt-pay, Breathson, Littlerock.

Pumi said, "She needs no list. Tomorrow at Highsun, if Chief Vanam releases the two of us, Valki will sit in the field where she wishes her trading area. She will accept all who come to her. Have Vivekamulla lead them there. Valki will want to know their stories. And Chief Nanatan, if this comes to pass, I will spend the next month at Rockplace making you the finest cutting devices I can. Leave any rock cutter apprentices you wish with me. As I fashion your tools, I will train them to the best of my ability. Great Chiefs, I have offered all that I have to offer. I shall remain silent and await the wisdom of your decisions."

< Celebration >

Exhausted, Pumi returned to Valki late at night and said, "It is done. You are now Valki of Urfa—einkorn, Breathson, Putt, everything."

"Wonderful!" she exclaimed as she jumped up. "We must celebrate!"

< Pumi and Kiya >

Sunrise.

Pumi and Valki began their day the traditional way.

Then Pumi set off to the tall stone—perhaps to rest.

On his way there, Pumi passed Kiya sitting with the women bidding farewell to Palai and telling stories of her greatness. Pumi waved her an invitation to join him when she finished. Kiya nodded in recognition and later found him at his stone table to the south of the tall stone. He looked up at her and smiled.

Kiya took note that there was no longer intensity in his eyes. She happily returned his smile and teased, "The gossip is that once more Pumi has everything that Pumi desires."

He replied, "Everything that is right for me to have. What is right and what I desire are not always the same things. You know that, I suppose."

She laughed and said, "The gossip is that Pumi now has his hands full. And now, you are leaving the tribe of your father and your brother— and me. You are taking up residence with that young woman—Valki. Valki of Urfa?"

"We are mated, you know. You saw our Ceremony."

Kiya replied, "Mated many times my giggling gossip girls tell me."

She became serious and said, "Valki is a superior woman, Pumi. You did well. She will match your thirst for life, maybe surpass it. You and I were

Saparu, Palai, Moonman. Nanatan, Vivekamulla, Vaniyal, Littlestar. Irakka, Mari, Irul.

born into good fortune. Whatever good fortune Valki has, she clawed from the depths of despair. I have great hope for Pumi and Valki and for Vanam and Kiya. Time has been kind to us."

With concern in his voice, he asked, "Will Vanam wear the robe well?

Kiya laughed. "Last night, he took his robe off and threw me on it. We celebrated his becoming chief. He commanded me to conceive a male child before the night was out. And, yes, he will wear the robe well. He has hungered for it—planned for it. I am to take a female toddler from Nanatan's tribe as my own. Vanam feels that if I adopt a girl from each tribe we encounter, it will strengthen his relationship—and control—over that tribe. Their elder woman has a candidate for us to consider. A child whose mother already had three daughters when her protector was killed in a hunt. Four are too many for her to care for by herself. I will meet with the child, Themis, and her mother this afternoon. We will have a little adoption ceremony with her sisters. Leaving a tribe is difficult for a grown woman. For a child—I cannot imagine. Yes, Pumi, your brother is determined to have the largest, wealthiest, most powerful tribe in all the lands. His father told him every day of his life this was his destiny. Vanam is obsessed with making it so. And, for whatever reason, he has become jealous of your increasing power. I suppose you know *that*."

"Yes. That's one reason I wanted to leave the tribe. That, and to let Valki make Urfa a comfortable Last Camp for Palai and Moonman—*and* so I could stay near Tallstone. But Vanam needs me out of his life. I get credit for much that I don't do. Things just go well when I'm around. These things created jealousy in him. Maybe Vanam will not be so serious after I am gone from his life."

"He will be even more serious. I felt it when he rose from our bed this morning. He had no time to greet me. He simply rose and left. It might help me conceive his child if I felt his arms around me and heard warm words. But no matter, I am accomplished enough in mixing elixirs to bear him a male child from his celebratory contribution."

"And what a fine son he shall be. One any man would be proud of." He paused and asked, "Did Vanam tell you if he will appoint Panti as his elder woman? She is the natural heir to Palai. The women would be pleased."

"He shares nothing with me, Pumi. He will do whatever brings him the greatest power."

Vanam, Kiya, Pumi, Valki, Putt, Putt-pay, Breathson, Littlerock.

"I see," Pumi said. He took her hand and pulled himself to a standing position. He released her hand and offered, "Come, Kiya, you have never seen the glory of the tall stone. Let me show you."

They walked up the hill toward the tall stone.

In the distance, out of sight, without expression, Vanam watched Kiya accept Pumi's hand and then climb the hill to disappear.

Out of Vanam's sight.

< >

In the meantime, Valki found Palai. "Urfa is now to be my permanent camp, Elder Mother. You and Moonman will live there with me and my new son. Pumi told me others may join us. I am to wait in the field and at Highsun, Vivekamulla will bring those Chief Nanatan will release from his tribe. We will be considered a tribe with all trading and meeting rights. I wish you to be Urfa's elder woman. I ask you to go to Chief Vanam and invite him to send those who he wishes gone from the Clan of the Serpent to join us at Urfa. You probably already know who they are. We will need so much help—so many hands. Most will be too young or too old or too infirm to be of much help, but you and I will make this work. This is so exciting. We have seen how men command a tribe. Let's find out how well women do."

They laughed.

< Highsun >

The burdensome came to Valki in the southern fields. Pumi stayed away.

Valki surveyed the new citizens of Urfa. They were beautiful. She told them to sit in front of her and introduce themselves. She already knew the women and children from her old tribe, but she wanted all—women, men, and children— to know all others in their tribe—to create a sense of togetherness—of family.

Valki began with Moonman and then Palai. They introduced themselves and told their stories, about how they wished the festival to be their Last Camp and how they would now remain at Urfa awaiting their fate.

Valki then pointed to the oldest male. "You, Great Hunter, what is your name and what is your story?"

He answered, "I am Pavett. In my youth, I was the fastest hunter in my tribe, but the hunts have taken all my speed. My arm is strong and accurate but now the game must come to me to die. I can no longer run after it."

Saparu, Palai, Moonman. Nanatan, Vivekamulla, Vaniyal, Littlestar. Irakka, Mari, Irul.

Valki replied, "Welcome to your new home, Hunter Pavett. We will find you a place to sit and wait while our dinner comes to you."

She pointed to the young hunter missing a leg. He said, "I am Nonti. You can see that I run even slower than Hunter Pavett. I once fought a lion. My tribesmen made sure that the lion lost the battle, but my leg was the price to be paid. My chief—my once-chief—now wears the robe and the head of the lion. Chief Nanatan was kind and merciful to me. He allowed me to stay with his tribe even though I was a burden."

Valki replied, "A burden on a tribe that must move to a new camp each season, Hunter Nonti. But not so great for a camp that does not move. I have wondered how Urfa would obtain meat to supplement our bread. Between you and Pavett, I believe we will have sufficient game. And I see that we have some young boys that you might be able to train. Small boys but ones who will grow into fine young men, nonetheless. What is your name?" She pointed to the oldest of the boys.

He replied, "I have no name and will not hunt. I don't like killing things. The men don't want me around them."

Valki told him, "Then you will be a builder. You will build things. You will be Putt's apprentice. Your name is now Putt-pay."

She continued to point to each new citizen of Urfa and hear their story.

With each story, Valki's confidence increased.

Vanam, Kiya, Pumi, Valki, Putt, Putt-pay, Breathson, Littlerock.

18. Valki of Urfa

She and Pumi, with Breathson, led the soon-to-be citizens of Urfa southwest to their new home the next morning.

Pumi told her, "I don't want to miss your triumphant entry into Urfa, Valki. This is a major responsibility you have undertaken—taking care of old and young—just you and sometimes me."

"We will take care of each other," she said. "You did not talk with them. You don't see all the talents they have. We are going to do well. Palai already looks more vigorous than she did at the beginning of the festival. Urfa is nothing more than a rickety building, but it is grander than anything they have ever had before. Putt is an amazing builder and now he has an apprentice. They are both extremely proud."

The journey was normally less than a half-day trot but this time it took almost a full day.

Pumi separated himself from the troupe before they arrived late in the evening. He told Valki, "You and Palai lead them into your city. It's not fitting that I be part of your grand entry. I'll watch from far away and come to you after your day is done. You will be too tired to celebrate but I want to spend your first night here with you."

She smiled and called Palai to join her at the head of the procession. "I have brought enough food for all to have a small meal tonight. But you must begin gathering early. At sunrise, lead any of the women and children capable of gathering and find out how proficient they are. I will meet with the men to find out what needs to be done for them to scout for the possibility of nearby game. We have the woods. There will be small animals there. Assign everyone an area to sleep; either under the heaven or in the house as is their preference. I would like a space in the back, near the back door, large enough for me, Breathson, and Pumi. Pumi won't be here most of the time, but whenever he is, I want a space for him. Is all this too much to ask of an old cast-off elder woman?"

Palai laughed and said, "You know the kind of fields in which I have had to find food. I could be blind and still gather enough food from these fields by myself to make ample bread for this evening's meal. Do not concern yourself with the work of the gatherers. Concern yourself with determining how to keep your other castoffs busy throughout the days to come."

Saparu, Palai, Moonman. Nanatan, Vivekamulla, Vaniyal, Littlestar. Irakka, Mari, Irul.

"Thank you, Palai. After our people are fed, I will leave them under your expert care. I would like time to get to know Breathson. Vivekamulla told me much about him, but she does not know why he is the way he is."

< >

After everyone was fed, Valki sat with Breathson and tried to engage him. He was still too young to talk, and he showed no signs of understanding communication. After a while, Valki simply took Breathson in her arms and held him close. She sang him the song her mother had sung to her. Breathson did not object to being held. She laid him on his blanket for the night and walked out the back door to look at the heaven.

Pumi looked up at her from the rock he sat on and asked, "Long day?"

She walked to him, sat down at his feet, and put her head in his lap. "Yes. A long, long day."

"We have a lifetime to celebrate, Valki. Tonight, you are going to rest. I will spend the night with you but with our nightclothes on. I will be gone before sunrise. You must establish your authority in this place. It would confuse them if I were here, especially the men. I looked in and saw you with Breathson. Your life is full. And for now, I would be a burden on you. I will be back in a quarter moon. Reserve a time to celebrate with me."

"Come to bed. But I have misplaced my nightclothes."

< Sunrise >

He was gone.

She had felt his arms disengage from her body, but she did not challenge him. *Better to let him silently disappear. Today will be long and what happens today will establish our pattern of life.*

She rose, checked on sleeping Breathson, and walked out her back door into the early morning light. *What shall I do? How can I possibly take care of all these people? I know nothing of what I am supposed to do.*

She remembered a night long ago—a lost child sitting alone—no idea of how to survive—she had learned to reason. *Break the problem into small parts—solve the smaller problem—keep thinking—keep solving—keep going.*

She relaxed. *The men. What do men do when they rise? They need to train the women in self-defense. That will give them something manly to do. They need to scout the woods to find out what game might be there. That should entertain them. Nonti must use a crutch to move around. I wonder if Putt could construct a wooden leg so that Nomi could*

Vanam, Kiya, Pumi, Valki, Putt, Putt-pay, Breathson, Littlerock.

walk without the crutch. I will ask Putt about that. Oh, and Putt and Putt-pay must identify building projects to start. I wonder if they could build a separate house just for the gatherers to sort and store their plants—and make their elixirs—and bake their bread.

She watched as the residents of Urfa began rising. *Putt is so clever. These "chairs" he made are remarkable. Sitting places made of wood rather than rock. They are comfortable and portable. I can sit in one for hours. He told me he could make them to fit a specific person. I will ask him to teach Putt-pay how to do that—make one especially for Palai and Moonman—and a small one for Breathson. And he made a table of wood that we can all sit around on "benches" when we eat. Pumi will be so jealous that I now have my own table. His is made of stone and can't be moved. Mine is made of wood and can be moved wherever I want it to be.*

Valki greeted Palai as Palai began the task of organizing the gatherers. Palai said, "I will take the children with me. Some of them will be useful. The young girls can tend to Breathson. They will like that. If you approve, he may take to gathering."

Valki agreed and went to meet Putt and Putt-pay, who were just rising. "So, my builders finally wake. You grow lazy in your new home."

Putt said, "We talked late into the night, Mother Valki. Talking about things we could build."

"Can you build us another house? One for the gatherers to sort and store their harvest? A workplace to mix elixirs and make ointments? It's not too early to start thinking about what we will trade at the next festival. We will only get one chance a year to trade for all of the things we will need."

Putt-pay excitedly replied, "We could build spears for trade, Mother Valki. Those the hunters make may have wonderful spear points, but the wood shafts are poorly made. At least compared to what my master has already shown me how to make. Pumi could bring us spear points. My master and I could build the greatest spears in the world—longer—stronger—heavier—easier to handle. May we make these things, Mother Valki?"

Putt snapped, "Speak when spoken to, Apprentice."

"Yes, Master."

Putt continued, "Yes, Mother Valki. I will ask Palai where the gatherer's new house best be built, how large it should be, and what the women will do inside and when. I must know their every movement so that the house can be built to their needs rather than them adjusting what they do because that's what we built. Can I ask the hunters to assist in this project?"

Saparu, Palai, Moonman. Nanatan, Vivekamulla, Vaniyal, Littlestar. Irakka, Mari, Irul.

Valki answered, "That sounds wonderful, Putt. Tell me what I must provide you to do this thing. But, no, hunters are prideful of their manliness, and this would sound like women's work to them. It's best if only you and Putt-pay build it. If any of the children would be helpful, I am sure they would be thrilled to help. When Breathson is a little older, he can help. Oh, Putt, I was wondering. Nomi must use that crutch to walk around on. Is it possible to build a leg out of wood so that he can walk without a crutch?"

Putt's eyes widened. "A wooden leg!? Yes, Mother Valki. Today! I will wake Nomi and we will make a wooden leg for him today!"

Valki thought, *It's strange what excites them. Now, what will excite my once-great hunters?*

Pavett rose late. He sleepily greeted Valki, "The old are not as vigorous as the young, Chief Valki, but if you command me to rise at sunrise, I will."

She laughed. "The old have learned how to use their brains along with their brawn. They can do things faster, so they can sleep later. But Pavett, don't you think 'chief' is a bit presumptuous? Perhaps 'Pen Valki' would be closer to the truth. Now, I must ask you how to best use your talents and those of Nomi—and Moonman. Other men and young boys will someday come here to live. I am not a man and certainly not a chief. I can help the women and the builders and sometimes even the scholars from Tallstone, but I will need your wisdom in guiding the actions of men."

Pavett was silent for a moment. "Yes, I will think upon this, Great Mother Chief Pen-Valki. Now, may I join Nomi and the builders?"

"Most certainly, Hunter Pavett. But first, I was wondering if our women and children should be trained in the manly art of self-defense. There are certainly bears in the woods, and we have seen the damage a lion can do, and hunters passing through might wish to take advantage of our unprotected women gathering in the fields. And what else might be lurking in the woods? Moonman wanders off in there by himself. He will pass away soon enough but better in his sleep than in the death grip of some unknown creature in his woods."

"I will counsel with Nomi and the builders on these things, Great Mother Chief Pen-Valki. There may be much that we can do here. You are kind and merciful."

She nodded to him as she said, "You may join Nomi and the builders, Hunter Pavett."

After he departed, she giggled. *Great Mother Chief Pen-Valki. Mother, can you believe that!?*

Vanam, Kiya, Pumi, Valki, Putt, Putt-pay, Breathson, Littlerock.

And so the first day gave way to the second and then to the next. Pumi returned on the evening of the seventh day. He brought her a bouquet of wildflowers he had gathered. He listened to her every excited word—worried through every problem she had worried through—celebrated her every minor victory. He listened to her plans—the new building—the self-defense training for all residents.

She said, "Oh, and I will need spear points—many, good, wonderful spear points to make spears for trade and one for each resident—I don't have a lot to offer you in trade, but I will think of *something*. And the woods—there are many things in there—bees—bears—snakes—and the great river to the west, of course. Putt made Nomi a new wooden leg—he could walk without a crutch. He cried, Pumi. The first time he walked on it, he stood and cried. I didn't know hunters could cry. And then they all cleared out a trail for Moonman to walk safely to the river. Putt-pay made a chair especially for Moonman. He can sit in it and stare out over the river as long as he wishes."

Valki talked incessantly into the night. Suddenly—she stopped and stared at Pumi without expression. She rose, went to him, sat on his lap, wrapped herself in his arms, and asked, "And so, Pumi of Tallstone, from what great adventure do you return?"

He held her tightly for a long time, then whispered, "It is not the adventures that I return from that interest me. It is the ones that I return to."

< Sunrise >

Pumi took Breathson's hand and walked with him along the trail to the river.

On the way there, he met Pavett and Nomi. He was purposely submissive to both. Pumi wanted them to understand that he had no authority to command or direct them in any matter. He said, "Mother Valki has told me of your great accomplishments. Only a quarter moon and you have already done so much. Mother Valki has commanded me to supply you with many spearheads. She told me you wanted only the best that I could make. I will make it so. I have come to Urfa to visit my mate and her son. And you may know that I am interested in the work of the builders. Builders are scholars who can build useful things. Can you make any use of the builders?

Pavett launched into a monologue on how they were redesigning spears to be thrown longer distances with greater force. Spears could be thrown accurately but they sometimes bounced off the animal without slowing it down. "But yes, Master Pumi. You are correct. These builder people are quite clever. Allow me to show our new trail to you and your son."

Saparu, Palai, Moonman. Nanatan, Vivekamulla, Vaniyal, Littlestar. Irakka, Mari, Irul.

< >

That afternoon, Elder Woman Palai returned from the gathering field to show Pumi the location of the gatherer's new house. She told him, "The spears in the ground mark where the four corners will be. It will face east, the direction the women will leave and return from. And it will have an open, covered porch. I can sit on the porch in my chair and see everyone in the fields. Putt will make my chair so that it can be made to rock back and forth. And he said that he can attach long, narrow tables to the wall. He calls them 'shelves.' They will be perfect for setting bags and urns in a neat, orderly way. The women can leave their bags on the shelves, and I can sort and store the contents in the evening. Putt is so clever."

"So I understand," Pumi replied.

< >

Late in the day, Valki stood alone looking at the patch of einkorn. Neither she nor Palai harvested grain from it, nor would they until they understood why it grew in such thick profusion only in this place. Valki heard the footsteps behind her, but she did not turn toward them. Pumi wrapped his arms around her waist.

She gently leaned backward, pressing her body and head against him. "Is it already time to leave me?" she whispered.

He did not speak but continued to embrace her. Quiet intimacy was heretofore unknown. 'Intimacy' was always to the point and quick. Valki relished the moment, but eventually asked, "Do you have a new project?"

Pumi replied, "Yes," as he continued to hold her. "The skywatchers are upset that children play around the tall stone, especially during the festival. They destroy the careful markings showing the shadows cast as the sun progresses through the seasons. Patterns are emerging, but children's playing feet obliterate much of the work. Littlerock and I agreed to find a way to place the hill off-limits to everyone except the invited. We will surround the hill with twelve large stone guardians, with the face of a fierce hunter carved into each one. We believe this will intimidate the children and warn adults they should not enter. The twelve shapes have been freed from the rock. Each is the width of a hunter and twice the height. Littlerock is at the site cutting a hunter's face into each stone."

"And now you have yet another task," laughed Valki. She turned, took him by the hand, and led him into the field of einkorn. "You must renew me before you leave. A man's work is never done."

Vanam, Kiya, Pumi, Valki, Putt, Putt-pay, Breathson, Littlerock.

19. Urfa and Its People

Valki sat on her front porch with Breathson sleeping on her lap.

Palai, Moonman, Putt, Putt-pay, and the other residents had retired for the night. Pumi and his new skywatcher-builder apprentice, Starrock, were a day and a half to the north, working on Pumi's latest rock project. She stared at Stillhunter, ten seasons along with its yearly rotation around the night sky. In two seasons, it would return to its standing position and the second Winter Solstice Festival would occur.

Valki hoped she would be prepared. *Mother, you would be so proud of me. I stayed alive. And I am mated to the grandest man a woman could desire. He treats me as his equal. As someone equal to an elder woman—even a chief. Can you believe that? Your daughter—a chief!? And he is not like the hunters—he comes to me often—and holds me in his arms through the night—I don't think he even visits other women—at least that I have heard of—only me—your daughter. I will do anything he commands of me—without question—without judgment—I am Valki of Urfa, Mother—Can you believe that?*

Valki was close to Putt. Although not much older, Pumi had adopted the diminutive, self-assured, assertive boy as his son. The bond between the two was stronger than that of a master and his apprentice. Valki, too, considered Putt to be her own son. *I am at peace, Mother.*

She rose and retired to her sleeping blankets. The blankets lay on a "bed" that Putt had built for her. Breathson had his own bed nearby.

< >

The next day, Pumi returned to Valki. The evening meal was joyful. Palai and Moonman were always delighted to see Pumi. They told him about their daily adventures. Neither had expected to still be living, yet here they were, as full of life as they had ever been. Well, as full of life as they had recently been, anyway.

Putt and Putt-pay held their tongues. They knew Pumi was interested in their projects and would give them his full attention after the two elders retired for the evening.

As usual, Breathson remained silent. Valki had known that Breathson was weak, reclusive, non-talkative, and combative, but she had not hesitated to agree to become his mother. The chief wanted rid of the child—Valki wanted the child. Pumi thought she had agreed a little too quickly, but she seemed satisfied with the boy.

Book One. *The Beginning of Civilization: Mythologies Told True*

The seating arrangements were new to Pumi. Each person had a chair. The chairs circled a table of wood. The food was set on the table and the women sat with the men. Even the children sat nearby. No such arrangement could exist in the mobile camps from which they all had come.

Putt and Putt-pay had taken an aggressive, inventive liking to their new craft.

Toward the end of the meal, Pumi proclaimed, "Putt-pay, go to Tallstone tomorrow and invite Starrock and his apprentices to join us for tomorrow's meal. I will take the rest of the boys and men on a training hunt. Maybe we will be fortunate enough to add meat to our evening meals. Break out the spears!"

Everyone looked at Mother Valki.

Valki froze. "My mate sometimes forgets his place, *don't* you, Pumi?"

She stared at him without expression. Everyone waited in silence.

Pumi looked around in embarrassment. "What did I say? I meant to ask you if you would invite Starrock and his friends at Tallstone to the evening meal tomorrow. If you decide to do so, I will be happy to join the men on a hunt so we can add meat to the meal. They seldom have meat at Tallstone."

Valki said, "What a delightful idea! Palai, send one of your older children to Tallstone and invite them here—no, send three children. They may need to help each other find their way. Make sure they each have their spear made especially for them. Pavett and Nomi have been so busy assisting the builders that I have been remiss in not asking them to bring in some game. Pavett, would you lead a hunt tomorrow? Ask whoever you wish to go with you. Ask any young boys who might not be too much trouble—and maybe Pumi—he might be of some use."

She had just put great pressure on Pavett and Nomi to be successful. She should not have done that, but she was furious at Pumi for his oblivious attempt to usurp her leadership.

After dinner, Valki and Palai were alone planning the next day's activities.

Pavett came to Valki, knelt on one knee, and kissed her hand. "You are wise and merciful, Great Mother Chief Pen-Valki."

He then left to join Nomi to discuss the upcoming hunt.

When she joined Pumi in their bed late that night, Pumi asked, "Great and powerful chief, I request permission to mate with Valki of Urfa!"

She giggled.

Vanam, Kiya, Pumi, Valki, Putt, Putt-pay, Breathson, Littlerock.

< >

The next afternoon, Valki was relieved when the hunters returned with a small antelope.

Nomi laughed. "Did you think we might fail, Mother Valki? I wasn't worried. I will teach the children how to butcher an antelope. We will have just enough time to prepare it for this evening's meal."

Littlestar and two apprentice skywatchers arrived at Urfa late in the day. The men visited on the front porch of the main house before the evening meal. The conversation was animated. Even the two hunters appeared interested in the conversations, especially when the skywatchers began asking them about their hunting techniques.

The skywatchers were fascinated by the two houses and the wooden benches and chairs. Such concepts had never occurred to them, but they understood that the inhabitants no longer moved from camp to camp, and so these would be useful constructions. Although not of the builder class, skywatchers were inquisitive by nature and were interested in the reasons that led to these innovations. Putt and Putt-pay were excited someone other than themselves and Pumi could discuss these things.

Pumi said, "Littlestar told me a tribe passed through after the last Festival. He told them about our celebration and invited them to attend. Littlestar told their skywatcher how to identify Stillhunter, and how to determine which was the season of Stillhunter. He gave him a stone with Stillhunter engraved symbols. The skywatcher appeared to understand. Maybe they will attend the upcoming Festival."

Littlestar added, "In the future, I will also direct passing tribes to Urfa. They can trade grains and herbs for meat." He laughed. "Perhaps tribal elders close to making their last camp might decide that Urfa would be a wonderful place to do it. Palai and Moonman appear to be growing stronger, not weaker—and certainly not dying."

Everyone but Moonman joined in the laughter. He appeared to be listening but, in his mind, he was sitting in his chair looking out over his river.

The women finally called the men into the house for dinner.

The skywatchers were confused by the new protocols they saw—women mingling with men to eat at a wooden table with all manner of food, including meat. They had not had meat since last year's festival. The mention of meat led Pumi into a discussion of how none of them had

Saparu, Palai, Moonman. Nanatan, Vivekamulla, Vaniyal, Littlestar. Irakka, Mari, Irul.

spears with which to kill game or even to protect themselves. The skywatchers admitted to having had one scare when a bear wandered into Tallstone. The three had scattered in different directions. The bear, not interested in them, simply scavenged for food and then, not finding any, left.

"Well …" began Pumi.

He was interrupted by Valki as she continued, "Well, Urfa has strong spears and knives for everyone; women and children included. Tomorrow morning, Pavett and Nomi will train you in their use and how to protect yourselves. If training goes well, I am told that Pavett knows how to throw a spear and hit an antelope. Maybe if a skywatcher found a dozing rabbit, and could throw a spear straight, the rabbit might provide an evening meal." Her pronouncement was not met with the enthusiasm that she had expected. The skywatchers all let out small groans.

Valki invited the skywatchers to return to enjoy a meal whenever they could. The skywatchers decided that when their tasks were completed after each phase of the moon would be a convenient time to leave Tallstone for a day.

"By the way, Pumi," asked Littlestar, "how will we move the twelve Guardianstones from Rockplace to Tallstone?"

Pumi groaned and shrugged his shoulders.

"Oh," Putt blithely replied, "Pumi will simply find a passing auroch and ask him to move the Guardianstones. In return, Pumi will carve the aurochs' image onto one of them." The table howled with laughter.

Except for Valki—who knew nothing of aurochs but everything about Pumi.

< Sunrise >

Pavett taught basic spear and knife techniques to the skywatchers. The results were mixed. But they learned enough to work together to fight off a bear. Getting a rabbit was more problematic.

The skywatchers set off to return to Tallstone in the early afternoon, with a spear in their hand and a knife in their belt. The women retired to the gatherer's house to make bread and elixirs for the coming festival. They took the children with them. The builders and hunters went with Moonman to study the river and scout what wood was available along the way.

< >

After the evening meal, Valki said to Pumi, "Come. I will show you my quiet place near the einkorn field where I sit and think about things."

Vanam, Kiya, Pumi, Valki, Putt, Putt-pay, Breathson, Littlerock.

Holding hands, they walked to the einkorn patch.

As they sat down, Valki asked, "Do you remember this place, Pumi? I put pebbles in the exact place where I lay in your arms while the rain fell on us. You were so upset. I wanted to comfort you, but I didn't dare move because you might change your mind and drive me away. So, I just lay there. As happy as I had ever been."

He laughed. "This place still concerns you, doesn't it? Why einkorn grows so profusely in this one place and no other."

"Yes, my life has been too full to dedicate a great deal of time to think about it, but after this Winter Solstice Festival, I shall find the time. Palai grows stronger, not weaker. Between the two of us, maybe we can learn about einkorn."

She paused. "I need to thank you for helping my two hunters bring in the game. I would have been devastated had you failed."

"Well—about that. I was more in their way than I was helpful. They moved together as a team to ambush the young antelope. I am somewhat embarrassed at my loss of hunting skills. I was thinking about going out by myself tomorrow just to try to get back into the rhythm of a hunt. Do you think that might be possible?"

She leaned against him. "I don't know, Pumi. You are useful to me here. I suppose my decision will depend on how well you please me."

He rolled her onto the ground. She did not even feel the pebbles pressing into her back.

After they were sated, he lay exhausted, cradling her in his arms. Valki contentedly stared up at the night sky. She did not yet want to bear a child; she would take precautions. She thought of that which he had just placed inside her body. Her body could make a baby. She half thought and half dreamed of Pumi's discharge inside her—*like the stream of water that had flowed over me and the einkorn so many seasons ago. The water that had taken my einkorn with it. The einkorn that had ...*

She sat straight up.

Pumi mumbled, "Are you all right?"

Without speaking, she wrapped herself in her clothing and stood to stare out over the field of einkorn, her mind churning. Pumi rose and stood beside her.

Saparu, Palai, Moonman. Nanatan, Vivekamulla, Vaniyal, Littlestar. Irakka, Mari, Irul.

Looking across the dense field, she told Pumi with finality, "That seed that is you has been spilled into my body. That seed that is einkorn has been spilled into this ground. It is so obvious. How did I not understand? It has always been so obvious. It has been obvious since the beginning of time. How could I not understand?"

Pumi agreed and led her to their bed.

< Sunrise >

Valki roused Palai and explained why there was a field of einkorn—and what they must do.

Elsewhere, Pumi set out eastward at a fast trot. It was still early morning when he heard a rumble coming from his right—a herd of antelope pursued by predators. He ran to a stand of trees that the herd would pass nearby. He watched the approach carefully and picked his target, a smaller animal running at the edge of the main herd. Pumi timed his move precisely and exploded from the grove to bury the butt of his spear into the dirt with the tip pointed at the beast's chest. The animal tried to sidestep, but there was neither time nor space. The spear buried deep into its chest, flipping it onto its back. Pumi removed his stone knife and mercifully cut the animal's throat.

The herd continued its stampede, closely followed by their hunters—a pack of wolves. He picked up the spear and threw it blindly toward the herd. It found a mark, not killing the creature but making it stumble so that the wolves were able to close in and, with savage bites, bring it down. With mindless abandon, Pumi joined the fray to retrieve his spear and cut the animal's throat. The wolves were too intent on their prey to turn on him.

Pumi returned to *his* kill and began field-dressing it. The wolves would likely be sated and disinterested in his kill. Still, prudence would be advisable.

He bound his kill to two spears to drag it back to camp. He would be defenseless if the wolves turned on him, but he took the chance. As he passed the feasting wolves, he saw the matriarch sitting and monitoring her pack. She would stroll in and eat her fill once her pack had eaten sufficiently. He was sure that she had seen him throw, and retrieve, the spear that had slowed the antelope.

She had a white circle around her left eye.

Pumi had once gifted her a treat of entrails. *Do you remember?*

He stopped and cut a slab of meat from the carcass he was dragging and approached her in the same manner as he had long ago. She watched his

Vanam, Kiya, Pumi, Valki, Putt, Putt-pay, Breathson, Littlerock.

approach. He was sure he was much closer than he had been before when she finally stood. He repeated the same presentation gestures as last time, then turned his back and walked away. When he retrieved his kill, he turned to look at her once more. She was watching him without fear.

< >

This would be the skywatcher's last meal at Urfa before the festival.

Littlestar announced, "We have positioned the guardian stones to protect the hill where the tall stone stands. We could not find an auroch, but we begged a passing tribe to help us move them. If the guardian stones don't keep the children out of our field, I don't know what else to do."

Putt offered, "Let us builders look at the area. Maybe we can help."

Littlestar replied, "Any help would be appreciated but remember, we have nothing to trade. The only thing we have is our knowledge of the sky, which we share freely with all who will listen."

Valki said, "Knowledge is more valuable than you think, Littlestar."

Pumi had done much work at Rockplace during the year. The two builders at Urfa had described designs that would allow them to make finer and more exact cuts for their building efforts. Pumi had made cutting tools for them plus many spear points and cutting tools for Urfa to trade. He saved back the especially fine spearheads. The spear shafts the hunters had helped the builders learn to fashion were as fine a shaft that could be created. Pumi's best spear points attached to these new shafts would create a spear demonstratively better than any spears currently in use. They would command a great deal in trade.

Valki took control. She said, "Take the two finest shafts and engrave a Serpent into one and a Lion into the other. Tallstone can present these gifts to Chief Nanatan and Chief Vanam in an opening ceremony recognizing the greatness of their two tribes and as a tribute to hosting the festival. Pumi, have you made more sitting stones in case additional tribes show up for this year's festival? And Littlestar, are there any patterns in the sky of a serpent and lion to go along with Stillhunter? That would be such fun if there were. Maybe find a pattern in the sky for each new tribe."

Littlestar had never considered such a thing but said it was something that the skywatchers would certainly investigate. And finding such patterns would be useful; not "fun."

The time for the festival grew closer.

Saparu, Palai, Moonman. Nanatan, Vivekamulla, Vaniyal, Littlestar. Irakka, Mari, Irul.

20. Winter Solstice II

The next year in Year 28; ages 28, 24, 18, 15.

The season of Stillhunter arrived.

The Clan of the Serpent and the Clan of the Lion arrived on the same day and set up camps. A day later, a tribe that had been encountered and invited by the Clan of the Lion earlier in the year arrived, as did the tribe whose scout had been informed of the event at Tallstone by the skywatchers. Never before had four tribes converged onto one site at the same time. The chaos was impressive.

The twelve Guardianstones had been erected to guard the tall stone. Their significance was explained to all who ventured near. Dire punishment awaited anyone who dared enter the circle uninvited. The Guardianstones would undoubtedly eat the trespasser. It seemed to work.

There was a sitting rock for each of the twelve Guardianstones. The two new tribes chose their symbols, an Auroch and a Scorpion. These images were carved into the chief's sitting rocks and into a Guardianstone. Perhaps the skywatchers could find these patterns in the lights in the sky.

Littlestar fell to his knees when he found his master, Vaniyal. He excitedly escorted the older skywatcher and his entourage of apprentices to the tall stone, to explain their field of measurements. Vaniyal was impressed and complimentary of the work. He congratulated himself for having the foresight to leave his apprentice at Tallstone in the first place. The results had more than paid for his investment. Over the following days, Littlestar gathered all skywatchers, along with interested hunters and children, and took them to Pumi's rock table to discuss and share their knowledge of the lights in the sky.

< >

The residents of Urfa arrived at Tallstone.

Putt and Putt-pay searched for possible candidates who might be interested in their builder's craft. Pumi presented Palai and Moonman to Great Chief Saparu and Chief Vanam. Disbelief swept over Pumi's father and brother. They had assumed they would never see the two elders again. Saparu rambled on and on reminiscing with the two old ones.

Vanam listened in troubled silence. *What has my little brother created?*

Vanam, Kiya, Pumi, Valki, Putt, Putt-pay, Breathson, Littlerock.

Littlestar and Valki told the two chiefs that they wished to make a presentation to officially start the celebration.

Nanatan said to Vanam, "Well, Chief Vanam, start it."

Vanam bellowed for everyone to come stand before him. The crowd gathered.

Littlestar and Valki stood in front of the two chiefs. Littlestar raised his arms for silence. Valki's voice rode out over the crowd. She welcomed them all and thanked the two chiefs for all they had done. She welcomed the two new chiefs and their tribes. She introduced Littlestar, who wished to present a gift to each of the two great chiefs standing here before them. Littlestar held up the two spears but was at a loss for proper words. Valki shouted out over the crowd, "The two greatest spears ever created for the two greatest chiefs to ever live!"

The crowd cheered wildly. Valki screamed over them, "And it has their symbol engraved on it!" Both chiefs held their spear high over their heads for the crowd to see.

Pandemonium.

Chief Nanatan laughed and said to Valki, "Well, Mother Valki of Urfa, I suppose you should announce that the festival begins now."

Over the pandemonium, a woman's voice could be heard screaming, "The second Winter Solstice Festival begins—NOW!"

Pumi watched from the crowd. He realized that his sweet innocent mate had somehow nudged him completely out of the picture and was innocently doing the same to the two great chiefs. *Is this to become YOUR festival, Valki? Will Vanam even notice? Will ANYONE even notice? I have met my match, Woman. It is you.*

Pumi laughed to himself and went to congratulate Valki on her outstanding performance.

The great festival had begun.

Valki visited each of the four chiefs plus Great ex-Chief Saparu. She told them how well Palai and Moonman were doing. "Palai grows more robust and Moonman is still enjoying life. I would be thrilled to give a tour to any elder women who would like to learn about Urfa, either for themselves or for their older tribesmen. It is less than a half-day run from here. We could go, tour, and return in one day, but an overnight visit would be more informative. Please tell your elder women to stop by and see me at our trading area in the south. I would love to get to meet the ones I don't know

Saparu, Palai, Moonman. Nanatan, Vivekamulla, Vaniyal, Littlestar. Irakka, Mari, Irul.

and to see Vivekamulla again. I have so much gossip to share with her. And aren't those spears magnificent? It makes me almost want to be a man so I could have one."

The chiefs were delighted to chat with Valki, even Vanam. *You did all right for yourself, little brother. You have met your match. She is more powerful than you.*

She bid them goodbye. "Now, all of you be sure to visit me at my trading table. I'll be looking for you." She turned and waved back to them as she left.

Pumi strode up next to her when they were gone from the sight of the chiefs and asked, "Shall I say anything or just keep my mouth shut?"

"Did I do all right?" she asked timidly.

"Valki, you were wonderful! I'm not going to attempt to tell you how well you did. Anything I say would be an understatement."

She replied, "Thank you, Pumi, but I need some kind of a loud sound to attract everyone's attention to get things started."

They arrived at Urfa's trading table. Palai was there with the hunters and Breathson. Moonman had wandered off.

Valki asked Palai, "Will you watch Breathson a little longer? While I have time, I would like to take my protector and ask him to celebrate with me."

They found a secluded spot but did not "celebrate." Valki merely sat on his lap and quietly, tightly embraced him for a long time.

Vivekamulla was waiting when Valki returned to her trading table. Valki saw her and ran to her with outstretched arms. "Mother, Mother, Mother." The two women embraced. "I have so much to tell you. No woman could be happier with a protector than I am with Pumi. I'm so glad you made that happen. And little Breathson has come out of his shell—at least a little. He lets me hold him and sing to him. He will hold Pumi's hand when they walk. He will make some little sounds now and then and Urfa is a wonderful place." She stopped talking, paused, and said, "Listen to me, going on like a gossip girl. How are you, Mother Vivekamulla? You are looking well."

They visited, gossiped, and caught up. Pumi excused himself and wandered off to maybe find some scholars.

The elder woman from one of the new tribes arrived at Valki's trading table. "I am Elder Woman Tirma, from the Clan of the Auroch. I extend the friendship of my tribe." The three women chatted in newfound friendship.

Vanam, Kiya, Pumi, Valki, Putt, Putt-pay, Breathson, Littlerock.

But Valki was now a celebrity—"that woman in charge of starting the festival." Both elder women and common women, especially the younger women, wanted to introduce themselves to one such as Valki of Urfa—"that woman getting everyone excited."

The crowd of women admirers was gathered around the table awaiting their turn to meet Valki when a hunter strode toward the table. The women deferentially parted to make way for him. He was a chief. *The* chief. Vanam, chief of the Clan of the Serpent. He came to the table and, without preamble, said, "I was impressed with your performance at the opening ceremony. You took control away from all of them—from Pumi—from Nanatan—from Littlestar. You were magnificent. You excite me greatly. Come. Walk with me!"

Several women exchanged knowing glances and smiles.

Valki replied, "My protector's brother is gracious. I shall tell Pumi of your flattery. He will be pleased."

"I did not come to please my little brother. I come to walk with an exciting, talented woman who can command the obedience and attention of all those around her. Now, come! Walk with me!"

She smiled a small smile at him. *What is going on here? You are commanding me to "walk" with you? What, exactly, do you mean by "walk," Vanam? You may be a chief but "walk" with you? Really?*

"I would be honored to walk with you, Great Chief Vanam, but I expect my beloved Pumi to arrive at any moment. A woman must always be attentive to the expectations of her protector."

"Walk with me, Valki. Now!"

She rose. *This will not end well, Vanam. Proceed cautiously with me.*

She said, "Very well. But we must walk within sight of my tables."

"We will walk where I wish to walk!"

Pumi! Where are you? It is your brother! A chief! What do you want me to do?

She coldly said, "Very well, Chief Vanam. Let us walk into whatever darkness you seek."

The once giggling—now somber—women took notice that Valki's words were unabashedly threatening. *He is a chief, Great Valki. A powerful chief. You must do as he commands. You must walk with him. Your protector will understand.*

Saparu, Palai, Moonman. Nanatan, Vivekamulla, Vaniyal, Littlestar. Irakka, Mari, Irul.

She rose and walked to the end of the table.

He took her hand, which she tried to disengage, but his grip was unrelenting. He said, "We will walk into that grove of trees. As we walk, tell me when you decided to take over the opening ceremony. Did you feel the rush of power? I am excited by your presence!"

She started to respond but decided to say nothing.

They entered the grove. He commanded, "I am extremely aroused. Remove your tunic. Get on your hands and knees. I will mate with you!" He released her hand.

She turned to face him and pulled the hem of her tunic above her waist, exposing her genitals. "Is this what you want, Vanam? It's such a common thing. Every woman has one. Most women would love to share hers with you, but I don't, and I won't."

She lowered her tunic. "I share mine only with Pumi. I'm sure you understand. I'm also sure you will graciously accept my gracious refusal of your offer. Thank you for the compliment."

He was incensed. "I am a chief and I command you to mate with me!"

She demurely replied, "I, too, am a chief," and then coldly, "and I command *you* to accept my refusal."

Vanam grabbed to rip her tunic from her body. Her knee went to his groin, forcing him to his knees. She twirled, removed her hidden dagger, pulled his head back by his hair, placed the dagger to his throat, knelt, and whispered into his ear, "No, Chief Vanam. I will not mate with you."

He coldly stared at her with eyes of fury as he hissed, "I am a chief!"

She hissed back, "As am I!"

He hesitated, disengaged, stood, collected himself, and stormed into the coming night.

Valki rose and returned to her table. *I wonder if this will hurt my reputation. Oh, well.*

All the women were still there—waiting—with wide eyes. Valki felt an unknown emotion as if an inferior creature had tried to intimidate a superior creature. *Should I mention this to Pumi? His own brother!*

She smiled at the waiting women and said, "I'm so excited to see all of you here. Times are changing, don't you think?"

Vanam, Kiya, Pumi, Valki, Putt, Putt-pay, Breathson, Littlerock.

< Kiya >

Pumi found Kiya standing near the tall stone. "Elder Woman Kiya, greetings."

Kiya laughed. "Greetings, Elder Master of Everything Pumi. It is good to see you. Your mate put on quite a show. I hope you are proud."

"Very," he replied as he became serious. "Was Vanam pleased?"

"Very. I intend to visit Valki when things calm down. I will tell her everything you want to know. I believe that would be better for everyone—rather than you and me visiting together. What time would be convenient for her? You may visit Vanam while I visit Valki."

"Wait until after the evening meal. She usually plays with Breathson for a while and then she is free of everyone—except me—and I will be trying to visit my brother. You two can have an entire evening to yourselves."

"It was good to see you, Pumi. I expect to see you again—this time next year."

"You have not aged since the day I first saw you, Kiya."

"Thank you, Pumi—Goodbye."

She turned and disappeared into the crowd.

< Pumi >

Pumi and his son, Putt, approached the four chiefs and respected elders sitting at the base of the hill preparing for their evening meal.

Vaniyal called out, "Ah, young Stonecutter, join us for our meal."

Pumi noticed Vanam's sudden frown at the suggestion, so replied, "Thank you, Master Vaniyal. But I have promised Putt that I would personally show him the wonders that the tall stone is revealing to you and the skywatchers. Putt is extremely clever. He will appreciate the work that the skywatchers do at this place. Could we join you after you have eaten? Chief Vanam, will you have time to receive me after your evening meal?"

"Of course, little brother. I will make time for you. You can tell me about your triumphs since I released you from my tribe."

Pumi laughed. "That would be a short conversation, Brother. But I will find you later in the evening." He smiled at the assembly and walked with Putt up the hill toward the tall stone.

Beyond the tall stone lay an entire year's history of the passage of the sun. Five small rocks recorded the arc of Tallstone's Highsun. One could

Saparu, Palai, Moonman. Nanatan, Vivekamulla, Vaniyal, Littlestar. Irakka, Mari, Irul.

visualize each day's change in the sun's position in the heaven. This season, the season of Stillhunter, marked the farthest distance the arc would make on the field. Each new day would bring the arc back toward the tall stone.

Pumi told Putt, "This is why we placed the Guardianstones around the hill. Children naturally climb the hill and, in their innocence, will move the stones. The Guardians appear to do their work. The rocks are not disturbed, except by rain. I have made smaller stones for the scholars to make more precise measurements in the coming year. When they mark the day's position, they want to make a more precise recording to compare with last year's measurements. My problem is that if the stone is too small, the rain will move it from its position. We are experimenting with different sizes and shapes of marking stones. It's an interesting problem."

Putt stood silent for a moment looking at the field. "Would not small wooden stakes placed into the ground be a better solution? Rain would not move them, and mischievous children would be less of a problem. A stake would be smaller than a rock so the recording would be more accurate."

Pumi was taken aback. "Yes. Of course. Wooden stakes will solve many problems. I will tell Vaniyal about your idea. I was blind to never think of this. The skywatchers never thought of this. It is so obvious. I must think about why we were all so unthinking." Pumi embraced Putt and laughed.

Pumi found Vaniyal and Littlestar talking together. Pumi said, "Skywatcher Vaniyal, may I introduce my son, Builder Putt? He is more clever than I and has some thoughts you might find interesting."

Vaniyal had grown mellow with age. He would be delighted to meet Putt. Pumi left the three talking about the possible advantages of stakes over stones in the measuring field.

Pumi found Vanam talking with the three chiefs and walked over to join them. But Vanam rose, excused himself from the conversation, and walked over to join Pumi, thereby excluding Pumi from joining the chiefs. Vanam made no mention of his confrontation with Valki. He said, "Come, little brother. We can talk as we walk through the remains of today's activities. Tell me of your great achievements this year."

Pumi lamented, "I have none. The scholars have taken over Tallstone. I do Valki's bidding at Urfa. I stay at Rockplace quite a bit, making spearheads and cutting tools for the builders. I went hunting recently and almost killed myself. That's about it. What about you? Your tribe looks wealthy—a bit larger."

Vanam, Kiya, Pumi, Valki, Putt, Putt-pay, Breathson, Littlerock.

Vanam coldly warmed. He had no one to share his victories with. Kiya had once filled that need but, for whatever reason, Vanam no longer cared to confide in her or his random women. His father reveled in Vanam's triumphs, but Vanam had long ago passed his father's capabilities and felt no need to impress him. He no longer felt camaraderie with his hunters. They were to be used to increase the wealth of the tribe. Pushed whenever possible. Fear, not camaraderie, was the better motivator. *You wish to know of power, little brother. I shall tell you of power.*

Vanam said, "It's hard making hunters perform as well as they should and Kiya is far too soft on the gatherers. I make progress slowly. I have a son, you know. At least Kiya says it's mine." He stared at Pumi to see how he responded.

Pumi offered, "Congratulations."

Vanam continued. "I commanded Kiya to take a new daughter each Winter Solstice. I will choose her tribe carefully. It must be a tribe that brings the Clan of the Serpent greater power. Last year, I took, I think her name is Themis, from Nanatan. He inquired about her well-being. I am pleased. This year, I must choose between the Clan of the Auroch and the other one. I don't know which tribe would be better."

Pumi replied, "You already have relations with most of the tribes who hunt north of this place like the Clan of the Scorpion. I understand that the Clan of the Auroch hunts in more southwestern lands. This is as far to their north as they generally travel. Have you seen what goods they trade? The Clan of the Auroch seems to have more unusual merchandise. Their auroch hides look desirable to me. Build up your inventory of unusual items. It will increase interest from the other tribes you encounter. Palai told me the Clan of the Scorpion appeared to be a poorer tribe."

"Excellent suggestion. I will command Kiya to inspect possible girls to adopt from the Clan of the Auroch, tomorrow. I would want one that will have good trade potential when it comes time to trade her. Kiya has a good eye for that sort of thing. The auroch tribe looks like a healthy group. You were never anything but a stonecutter, little brother. But I must admit, an extremely clever stonecutter. I might have made a hunter out of you."

Pumi replied, "Better an excellent stonecutter than a poor hunter. Sorry to be a disappointment, big brother."

"Not at all. I am still proud of you. I often tell the chief of encountered tribes that Pumi of Tallstone is my young stonecutter brother."

Saparu, Palai, Moonman. Nanatan, Vivekamulla, Vaniyal, Littlestar. Irakka, Mari, Irul.

"You are gracious and merciful, Chief Vanam." They talked for a while and then Pumi left to return to his camp. *Today went well. No problems at all.*

< Kiya and Valki >

Kiya had arrived at Urfa's trading tables soon after the evening meal. She was accompanied by Assistant Elder Woman Panti and Kiya's toddler daughter, Themis. Panti carried Kiya's three-season-old son, Firstson.

The old hunter rose as they approached.

"Good evening. I am Elder Woman Kiya of the Clan of the Serpent. This is my assistant, Panti, and my two children. I request an audience with Mother Valki if she will see me."

Pavett replied, "Elder Woman Kiya, Great Mother Chief Pen-Valki commanded me to bring you to her as soon as you arrive. She has a drink and sweetbread waiting for you. This way, please."

He escorted them toward the west, away from the main Urfa encampment to a wooded area containing a small clearing. "This is Great Mother Chief Pen-Valki and Pumi's private area," he announced and then returned to his greeting table.

There was a small fire burning. Around the fire, blankets and sitting cushions had been spread. There were several portable chairs. Valki sat on a cushion playing with Breathson.

Valki saw Kiya approach, rose, and hurried to embrace Kiya. Valki made no mention of her confrontation with Vanam. "Sister Kiya. I am so glad to see you. So much has happened. And, I see so much has happened to you," she exclaimed, as she reached to take the infant from Kiya. Here, let us sit. There are more chairs over there. It is good to see you, too, Panti. And who is this?" Valki asked as she knelt on one knee holding the baby, to face the young child.

Kiya said, "This is my daughter, Themis, from the Clan of the Lion. Themis accepted me as her new mother this time last year. I am so pleased that she accepted me. I have always wanted a wonderful daughter like Themis."

"I am Valki, Themis. I am so pleased to meet you."

Themis rushed to Valki and hugged her around her neck. Valki returned the hug. "Do you help Mother Kiya with your brother?"

Themis nodded, "Yes."

Valki asked, "Well, I have a little boy your age. Would you like to meet him?"

Again, "Yes."

Vanam, Kiya, Pumi, Valki, Putt, Putt-pay, Breathson, Littlerock.

Valki told her, "Be careful. He is not as developed and caring as you. He may not meet well."

She led Themis to where Breathson sat throwing round stones into an urn and said, "Breathson, this is my new friend, Themis."

Breathson did not look up. He continued his play.

Valki advised, "Stand in front of him, dear. If he sees you, he may do better."

Themis walked to stand in front of Breathson. He saw her feet and looked up at her. He stared and then picked up a stone and held it out to her. "Play!"

She took the stone and then hugged him.

Valki was horrified. *Breathson—she is a friend—don't hit her—please!*

Breathson accepted the hug. Themis stepped back. Breathson looked at her and again said, "Play!"

She sat down with him and tossed her rock into the urn. He handed her another rock.

Valki looked at Kiya with extreme relief.

Kiya told her, "You have done well with him, Valki, extremely well."

Panti asked, "May I take the children back to camp now, Elder Woman Kiya?"

"Please not here, Panti."

"I'm sorry, Kiya. But Great Mother Valki is here, and I did not want to appear disrespectful."

"I understand, Panti. You are the perfect woman, but you cannot read my mind. Yes, please. Valki and I have so much to share. Thank you for being so helpful."

"Yes, Kiya," Panti replied as she took Firstson from Valki and then held out her hand to Themis.

Themis stood and hugged Breathson goodbye.

He continued his play.

After Panti and the children were gone, Valki asked, "Well, Sister Kiya, where do we begin?"

"Let's begin with the sad and end with the happy."

"You are wise, Kiya. What is your sadness?"

Saparu, Palai, Moonman. Nanatan, Vivekamulla, Vaniyal, Littlestar. Irakka, Mari, Irul.

Kiya laughed. "I am so happy you asked. I have no one else to share this with—Vanam made me elder woman after I begged him not to. Panti worked her entire life assisting Palai. It is Panti who should be our elder woman, not me. I told Vanam that I needed time to raise his children—that 'I can do well as the mother to your children or do well as the elder woman to your tribe but if I do both, I will not do well at either.' He laughed at me and commanded, 'Don't whine. Do it!' and walked off. Panti is so gracious to do everything she can to assist me in both duties. Thank you for listening, Valki. What is your biggest problem?"

Valki shook her head in sympathy but offered no words of wisdom. Instead, she answered Kiya's question. "I'm not sure. It's complicated. I corrected Pumi at an evening meal—like he was a child—in front of everyone. Everyone!—hunters—women—children. I corrected him and glared at him until he said words to my liking. I commanded him! And I was not afraid—or embarrassed—or sorry. He had commanded Putt-pay to go on an errand in the name of Urfa and then he dared to assume command of my hunters. I could not tolerate either action. I was so angry. I didn't think. I commanded a male—my mate—I don't think either has ever been done before. But Pumi recovered as only Pumi can. He accepted my command without question. He rephrased his words in a way that brought me greater respect—my hunters refer to me as Chief Valki. I told them not to do that, but both of them still do—and some of the children do. I think they need to do it—for their sense of well-being—so that they don't have to think. They don't see me as a woman but as a chief. Is this possible? I did all that and then proceeded to take over Pumi's natural right to present the ceremonial spears to the chiefs. I gave the honor of the presentation to Littlestar. It was I who commanded the festival to begin—not Nanatan or Vanam or Pumi or Littlestar. Pumi never admonished me about any of this. I think he may be a little bit proud. Am I upsetting the natural order of things, Kiya?—changing the way things should be?—have always been?—making things for the worse? I'm a little frightened."

"Sister Valki, you have given me a great deal to think about. The hunters see you as a chief? Not as a woman? You commanded Pumi?—reprimanded him? And, yes, you were in complete control of the start of the festival—Vanam certainly noticed that Pumi was in no way associated with it. I had thought it was Pumi's doing—putting you in charge—a way of reducing Vanam's jealousy toward Pumi and Pumi's successes."

Vanam, Kiya, Pumi, Valki, Putt, Putt-pay, Breathson, Littlerock.

Kiya hesitated, then said, "Did you see what I just did? I assumed Pumi put you in charge; not that you took charge—we both need to think about that way of thinking. You have an exciting life, Sister. You have left the path women have always traveled and entered onto a new path—one that a woman has never traveled before. Where will it lead you? Where will it lead us ALL? Don't be frightened. What is the worst that can happen? All Urfa will starve to death because of you? Your children will be eaten by wolves? You will single-handedly create a great flood that will destroy the world? Maybe—maybe not. But no matter where your path leads, I am excited for you. You have done so much in one year. What are your plans for the coming year?"

Valki answered, "I was wondering. Do you think Vanam would let you come with me to spend time in Urfa this time next year? I have an idea and your knowledge would help me a great deal. Do you still experiment with what different plants can be used for?"

"Yes, as often as I have time for. It is rewarding when I find a new use for one. Do you have new plants in Urfa?"

Valki answered, "No. Just an old one—einkorn. Kiya, I may be able to make einkorn grow wherever I want it to grow and in thick profusion—to the exclusion of all other plants. It will take many seasons to explore what must be done, but by this time next year, I hope to have a lot more knowledge. Your wisdom would mean a great deal to me."

Kiya considered, "Hmm. I will think about that. I wonder what could be done with that knowledge When Vanam tires of me, perhaps I can come to Urfa and be your elder woman."

Valki laughed. "No, no, no. Urfa will have enough elder women soon enough. Come be my friend. I will let you command Pumi if you like."

Kiya's eyes glazed over for an imperceptible moment and then she laughed.

Valki suggested, "Could you simply ask Vanam to make Panti his elder woman? For your sake and the sake of the tribe? Find a reason Panti would make your tribe more powerful."

Kiya replied, "Vanam does not care about my concerns and, no, he knows that my being his elder woman makes his tribe more powerful. There is no way to do that."

Saparu, Palai, Moonman. Nanatan, Vivekamulla, Vaniyal, Littlestar. Irakka, Mari, Irul.

They continued the discussion and gossiped into the night. It was late when Kiya left. "Stop at our tables. Pavett will be there—sleeping probably. Tell him I command him to walk you back to your camp. Pavett likes for me to command him to do things."

Pavett happily escorted Kiya back to her camp. Vanam woke when she slipped into their bed.

"Where have you been?" he demanded.

"Visiting," was her reply.

He stood and commanded her, "Tomorrow we will go to the Clan of the Auroch, and you will select me another daughter. Tonight, you will conceive my second son."

"Yes, Vanam. Thank you for your attention. I look forward to our new daughter and son. And think how mighty your sons would become if I dedicated all my time to teaching them the skills of the wise and powerful."

< Mnemosyne >

The next afternoon, Chief Vanam took Kiya and Themis to meet the chief and the elder woman of the Clan of the Auroch. Vanam asked the chief, "Have you selected a daughter for me? One that would create a strong bond between our two great tribes?"

The four exchanged pleasantries. "You may leave us, now, if you wish," the elder woman finally suggested to the two chiefs. The two women then talked about possibilities. "Yes, I have a girl, a precocious girl. Her father has begged me to find her a new mother. His mate died giving birth. The woman I assigned his daughter to does not give Mnemosyne the attention the father wants for his daughter. He has begged me to find her a mother who will love the child and raise her as her own. Will you see her?"

"Yes, of course," Kiya replied.

The elder woman took Kiya and Themis to an area where a hunter sat on the ground with his young daughter. Upon seeing the two elder women and child approach, the hunter stood, leaving the child sitting alone on the ground.

Kiya walked over and sat down cross-legged to face the child. Kiya motioned for Themis to come and sit on her lap. "Mnemosyne, my name is Kiya. This is my daughter Themis. We sing songs when we go to bed each night. Themis would like a sister to sing with her. I want another daughter to take care of and come and live with us. I would be so happy if

Vanam, Kiya, Pumi, Valki, Putt, Putt-pay, Breathson, Littlerock.

you would agree to become my daughter and sing songs with us at night. Will you be my daughter?"

Mnemosyne stared at Kiya and then at Themis. She then turned her head to look up at the man standing behind her. He shook his head, "Yes." The child rose and ran to Kiya. She hugged Kiya and then hugged Themis. She then sat beside her new sister on the lap of her new mother.

< >

The festival continued in full force for the entire season.

Contests were held. Garlands were given.

Eligible females were taken by accepting hunters. Goods were traded. Ceremonies performed.

Each new tribe assigned two older boys to each of the two local camps. There would be four more apprentice builders for Urfa, and four more apprentice skywatchers for Tallstone.

Valki visited each of the tribes. She took them each a gift of sweetbread with nuts in it, courtesy of the citizens of Urfa. She took many loaves to the Clan of the Scorpion.

Pumi and Kiya did not meet a second time.

Saparu, Palai, Moonman. Nanatan, Vivekamulla, Vaniyal, Littlestar. Irakka, Mari, Irul.

21. Valki's Great Experiment

They returned to Urfa from their successful Winter Solstice Festival.

Another elder woman, Tirma from the Clan of the Auroch, along with a half dozen people wanting to make a Last Camp at Urfa, had joined their little settlement. Valki had the two new builder boys clear vegetation from a large plot of land near the einkorn patch, and then dig twelve long trenches parallel to one another.

In the first trench, she laid einkorn harvested from her precious patch. This had been soaked in water for a full day. She made sure that water flowed from the urn, carrying with it the einkorn. In the third row, she placed only soaked einkorn, without pouring the water. In the second trench, between the other two, she poured only the water in which the third row had been soaked. She covered half of each row with dirt, leaving the other half exposed to the sun.

Valki was sure that at least one of these six plantings would yield a solid growth of einkorn. Which, she did not know. That which gave birth to the best einkorn would set her on her path of understanding how and when to allow the earth to grow her grain. *A woman can only become with child at a certain time of the season. Maybe the earth is the same way. Must einkorn be covered with earth, or does it need the sun shining on it to grow? How can I ensure that which was einkorn becomes part of the stream of water? I don't understand any of this, but I will keep trying until I do. Do the earth and the einkorn care where the moon stands? This was a night with a full moon. I will repeat all of this under the next new moon. I will keep planting until I understand what the einkorn and earth require of me.*

Silently, she looked at her handiwork. She was pleased. She was sure.

< The Next Season >

Valki inspected the einkorn every day. Nothing yet grew. She was not discouraged. It took a woman nine seasons to produce a baby. It might well take the earth nine seasons to produce einkorn.

She repeated her planting for the third time. She and Palai inspected for growth, and when it began, they would decide on the best planting times and conditions.

Palai was excited about the einkorn. She was an expert in harvesting, and to think she could control what grew was amazing. It filled her with a sense of immense power. Of course, she had not yet caused anything to grow, but Valki's optimism and self-assurance infused the same feelings in Palai.

Vanam, Kiya, Pumi, Valki, Putt, Putt-pay, Breathson, Littlerock.

Besides, she constantly felt joyful. She was still alive a full year after making her Last Camp. She would continue to live for a while, if for no other reason than to take care of the doddering skywatcher, and, of course, be part of Valki's great experiment. Life was good in Urfa. She was proud of her new tribe.

Moonman called out, to no one in particular, "Where is my porridge?"

< >

Halfway through the season, just after Valki had planted her fourth round of einkorn, sprouts appeared in the first and third rows of the covered portion of the first planting. She and Palai stared, unblinking, at the growth. It certainly appeared to be einkorn. There was a scattering of other growth in the field, and they knew not what was important and what was not. But if this growth was einkorn, this was the beginning of knowledge.

Valki thought, *Pumi will want to know. He thinks that all things are connected—the hunting seasons, the lights in the sky, the moon, and what plants grow on the land.*

He had once told her, as they lay together, "Something new is happening. Putt and Putt-pay are changing something basic about life. The two elders have not died at their last camp. Urfa has kept them alive. And grain is so plentiful that it's no longer a last resort against hunger. Urfa provides enough grain not only to keep the inhabitants of Urfa and Tallstone well-fed, but it has great excess for trade. Meat is needed only for variation. For the first time, we can live without hunting. And Tallstone Camp—the tall stone is producing new insights into the night sky all the time—it has become the place of all skywatcher knowledge. Knowledge shared with any interested tribe. Tallstone's fame is spreading. Urfa's fame is spreading—where an elder's last camp does not mean imminent death. We live in interesting times, Valki."

< >

The skywatchers attended their evening dinner. Another table had been added to the eating hut to accommodate the children. The conversation, as always, was animated.

Valki spoke of her einkorn field. "All but the last two plantings are producing einkorn. The covered rows are taller than the uncovered ones. The first and third rows produce greater abundance than the second rows. I believe it takes a season and a half for the earth to produce. Covering the rows with earth helps it grow. I am going to harvest the best einkorn and only use that for the next plantings and see if that produces better einkorn. This is so exciting!"

Saparu, Palai, Moonman. Nanatan, Vivekamulla, Vaniyal, Littlestar. Irakka, Mari, Irul.

She went on in great detail. The skywatchers listened intently. Urfa would produce a great quantity of einkorn in time for the next festival.

After dinner, everyone retired with their colleagues for further discussions.

Valki and Palai walked to their einkorn field. Valki said, "We will have so much einkorn, Palai. How do we best use this at our next festival?"

Palai answered, "I will counsel with Elder Woman Tirma. And Putt—he is clever—and Pavett—we will come up with a plan. You will be pleased."

"The Festival Council" developed an excellent plan.

Vanam, Kiya, Pumi, Valki, Putt, Putt-pay, Breathson, Littlerock.

22. Breathson and Wolfchief

Pumi returned to Rockplace to manufacture cutting tools to trade at the upcoming festival. Elder Woman Palai and Hunter Pavett had done quite well trading cutting stones at the last festival. The cutting tools were more in demand than even his spear points. Everyone could make a spear point; not a good one, perhaps, but still ... Cutting blades were difficult to make and Pumi was a master.

He escorted the skywatchers back to Tallstone. Along the way, he required them to practice their spear techniques. "Who knows," he laughed, "maybe between all of you, you can spear a passing rabbit."

At Tallstone, Pumi studied the markings recording the shadows cast by the tall stone. He listened with interest as the skywatchers enthusiastically explained the advantages of using small wooden spikes to mark the sun's daily progression rather than rocks. Having someone interested in and understanding their work was a pleasure.

< >

Before leaving for Rockplace, Pumi speared and carefully skinned a rabbit. He gave the meat to the skywatchers. He kept the pelt.

At Rockplace, he made many cutting blades for the elder women and Pavett to trade. They would be pleased. He also fashioned the rabbit pelt into a belt.

< >

After greeting Valki upon his return to Urfa, Pumi found Breathson. Pumi presented Breathson with the belt made from the pelt of the rabbit. Pumi explained what it was and where it came from. With wide eyes, the boy slowly accepted the gift and held it to his face. Stroking it, he murmured over and over, "Rabbit, rabbit, rabbit."

At the evening meal, Pumi asked Putt to fashion a special chair, one that would seat Pumi, Valki, and Breathson side by side. Putt promised the new "bench" before tomorrow's Highsun.

< >

The next day, the bench was delivered as promised. Soon after, Pumi handed Breathson a slab of meat to carry. Pumi and Valki carried the bench past the einkorn field and eventually arrived at the site where Pumi had his last encounter with the she-wolf. They set the bench on the ground. Valki and Breathson sat down on it. Pumi took his spear and slab of meat and

Saparu, Palai, Moonman. Nanatan, Vivekamulla, Vaniyal, Littlestar. Irakka, Mari, Irul.

walked fifty paces where he drove his spear deep into the ground and laid the slab of meat in front of it. He returned to the bench, sat down, and waited.

Soon enough, they saw movement on the horizon. The wolf appeared.

"This is a wolf," Pumi whispered to Breathson. "Her name is Wolfchief." He could feel the child trembling. Was it fear? Excitement? Whichever, Breathson was engaged. Pumi instructed Breathson and Valki to keep still, lest they frighten the animal. Breathson remained extremely still.

The wolf surveyed them and sniffed the air. She trotted to within a hundred paces of them and sat down on her haunches. Pumi was the focus of her scrutiny. She appeared to recognize him. Eventually, the wolf glanced at the piece of meat. She was hesitant but rose and tentatively approached the offering. Wary, she retrieved the meat and quickly retreated to her safe distance. Watching the three people in the chair, she devoured the slab.

Breathson's focus on Wolfchief never wavered.

After she had finished the offering, Pumi told Breathson and Valki that the spear and the chair would remain in place, but they would now rise and walk away in unison. After ten paces they would turn and face the wolf for five heartbeats, and then turn and walk toward Urfa—slowly.

Breathson followed the instructions perfectly.

Valki was thrilled.

This ceremony became a daily ritual. Pumi attended when he could. Valki usually attended but occasionally had Putt-pay or one of the new boys go in her stead. But always, Breathson was there. Protocol was observed. The child admonished any variation with "No. No. No." He always wore his belt made of rabbit.

Wolfchief attended more often than not.

Vanam, Kiya, Pumi, Valki, Putt, Putt-pay, Breathson, Littlerock.

23. Winter Solstice Festival III

The next year in Year 29; ages 29, 25, 19, 16.

Valki arrived at the festival site four days early to discuss her ideas for an opening ceremony with Littlestar. An opening that would follow a well-thought-out procedure rather than just being random events as it was the previous year.

She knew she could work with Nanatan to determine an official opening ceremony ritual, but that Vanam would reject any suggestion that a woman—especially Valki—would make. Valki must convince Nanatan to present the idea to Vanam as if it were his own.

As expected, the Clan of the Lion arrived a day early.

Valki gained an audience with Chief Nanatan and presented her proposal. The chief was concerned that Pumi, who had started all of this, would not be involved. Valki countered that it was really begun only by himself and his skywatcher. And maybe Vaniyal should have a prominent role befitting his rank and influence in establishing the festival. It was understandable, wasn't it, that the Clan of the Serpent should play an important role. But as for Pumi, it was best if his contributions were minimized. As for Valki, she sought no active role but would be delighted to provide whatever support the chiefs commanded. Chief Nanatan did understand, did he not, that this plan must be developed and implemented only by Chief Nanatan and Chief Vanam. That neither her name nor Pumi's should be mentioned."

The old chief laughed. "Trained by Master Pumi, were we? Of course, Chief Valki, this is the plan Chief Vanam and I will develop."

Valki returned to her trading area.

The builders had already set up twelve tables. Hunter Pavett would trade cutting blades and extra-fine spear points from one table. Elder Woman Palai would trade potions, elixirs, salves, and ointments from the second table. Elder Woman Tirma would trade linens, ropes, cords, and baskets from another table. Builder Putt would have a table from which to trade high-quality wooden spear shafts, sleds for pulling heavy loads across great distances, spinning tops for children's play, colorful pieces of wood that a child could place on a board containing colorful posts, and boards for moving blocks of wood depending on what the child rolled in a six-sided square of wood with dots on it. He had fashioned many other novelty items made of wood.

Saparu, Palai, Moonman. Nanatan, Vivekamulla, Vaniyal, Littlestar. Irakka, Mari, Irul.

Separate from the other tables, Valki had two tables with many chairs set around them where she would receive anyone interested in making a last camp or, with her chief's permission, a woman giving up her child because the woman was not capable of continuing to care for the child and no one else in the tribe would accept it. Every tribe had at least one boy who was not good material for a hunter. A chief would usually trade such boys for anything of value.

Six other tables were set apart. These contained loaves of already baked bread; sweetbreads, hard bread, soft bread, every bread imaginable. And urns of nuts, and roots, and every kind of plant, and einkorn—unbelievable amounts of einkorn.

Behind these tables, baking ovens had been built. Bread would be made continually throughout the festival. Bread free for the taking by anyone—contributions accepted.

A tall sign stood beside each table engraved with an icon of what could be found at that table.

And behind this, farther to the south, the most novel innovation of all time. One with which Pumi himself was impressed.

The innovation had come from a complaint by one of last year's boy apprentices assigned to Urfa. The boy had grown tired of stepping into human waste. Waste left by men too lazy to go far enough in the woods to relieve themselves. Although, there were so many people in one place that it was rather difficult to find a fresh open space to relieve oneself. He took his complaint to Putt. Putt had recognized the problem. But it had now been formally submitted to him as a problem in need of a solution. Putt solved problems. It was what he did.

And so, farther to the south lay a great open, flat field. Long trenches had been dug across this field. A small, movable hut had been placed over each of these trenches. The hut had a door on it. Inside the hut was a chair with a hole in the center and open to the trench. One could enter the hut, close the door, raise one's tunic, sit on the chair, and relieve oneself in the trench. There were even plant leaves available appropriate for cleaning oneself. After several uses, a boy from Urfa would pull the hut forward a small distance and cover the used portion of the trench with dirt. Water was available nearby for washing one's hands. The attendants instructed everyone who came on proper usage, ending with, "After you have finished using the hut, wash your hands, and pick up your free sample of sweetbread at the nearby table."

Vanam, Kiya, Pumi, Valki, Putt, Putt-pay, Breathson, Littlerock.

A tall sign, with the icon of a person relieving themself, identified the area. The young members of Urfa were tasked with carrying replicas of the sign throughout the crowd explaining what these structures were actually for—and reminding them to be sure to remember their sweetbread. Some pieces contained delicious nuts.

In the expectation that Valki's plan for an opening ceremony would be accepted, Putt had constructed a raised wooden stage at the base of the hill where the tall stone stood. Many colorful flags flew.

At an evening dinner, a long time before, Valki had explained her desire for something to make a great sound—loud enough to attract everyone's attention at the raucous festival. After the meal, Nonti brought his prized possession, a ram's horn. Everyone in Urfa heard the sound that a ram's horn makes if you blow into it. All the young ones wanted to be taught how to make the great sound.

< >

The day came. Highsun approached. A crowd was beginning to gather in front of the stage.

Littlestar busied himself in the center of the stage while surrounded by several apprentices. Valki prepared herself for her entrance. An older boy nervously stood at the back of the stage holding a ram's horn.

At Highsun, the ram's horn was blown with deafening sound. All the people heard, and a crowd grew quickly.

Valki strode upon the stage, both hands high in the air. She shouted, "Are you ready to have a festival?"

Many in the crowd replied, "Yes!"

This time she yelled, "I said—are you ready to have a festival?!"

The response this time was much louder—much more animated."

Valki looked disgusted. She put her hands on her hips, tapped her foot with great exaggeration, turned to look at Littlerock, turned back to look at the crowd, held her hands cupped to her ears, reared back, and in a voice louder than one might think possible, roared, "I said—ARE YOU READY TO HAVE A FESTIVAL?!!!"

The crowd erupted. She held both fists high, pumped the air, walked back and forth on the stage, and taunted the crowd. She made a show of stopping to talk to Littlestar. Then she walked to the front of the stage and held up

Saparu, Palai, Moonman. Nanatan, Vivekamulla, Vaniyal, Littlestar. Irakka, Mari, Irul.

her hands for silence. The crowd quieted significantly but not completely. She looked disgusted, put her hands on her hips, tapped her foot, turned toward Littlerock, turned to face the crowd again, held her arms high in the air, palms down, and slowly lowered her arms while slowly bouncing her body down until the silence was total. She shouted, "That's much better. You will all have to be quiet so you can hear my tiny little voice."

Laughter. She looked at them sternly—then silence.

"I wish to introduce Master Skywatcher Littlestar, once of the Clan of the Lion, now of Tallstone."

Littlestar stepped forward. Valki clapped her hands together, indicating the crowd should do the same, which most did.

Valki continued, "It is at Tallstone that Master Littlerock's scholars do such wonderful work with their studies of the sky. They share this knowledge with all who will listen. If any of you chiefs out there have any young boys—or, I suppose, young girls—interested in learning the mysteries of the heavens, speak to Master Littlerock. For a small donation, you can leave these boys and girls at Tallstone for a full year. They will learn much about the Heavens and other things. Perhaps they would become outstanding skywatchers."

She paused, then held up her arm toward the dignitaries waiting at the base of the stage. "And now, please recognize the two great chiefs who began this extraordinary festival—the Great Chief Nanatan of the Clan of the Lion and the Great Chief Vanam of the Clan of the Serpent."

The two men walked onto the stage and faced the crowd. Valki, with hand motions, encouraged polite applause, and then, with more forceful motions, greater applause, and then even more applause. She let the applause build upon itself and, with the flip of her hand, brought the crowd to complete silence.

She continued, "And, too, none of this would have happened had it not been for the knowledge, dedication, and effort of the greatest skywatcher to ever live—the great Master Skywatcher Vaniyal of the Clan of the Lion." She pointed toward Vaniyal as he mounted the stage. The crowd, now trained in what was expected, erupted in applause. She milked it and then abruptly motioned for silence. There was silence.

Valki said, "Chiefs, do either of you have any words for your admirers?"

Nanatan stepped forward and proclaimed, "This is the season that we should all clean our minds of the bad things that have happened throughout the year and embrace the good things. We should rededicate ourselves to

Vanam, Kiya, Pumi, Valki, Putt, Putt-pay, Breathson, Littlerock.

being the best person we can be. Make new friends and visit old friends. Test our strength. Exchange wisdom. And have some fun. Chief Vanam?"

Chief Vanam stepped forward and said, "I will meet you on the playing fields. We can test our strength and speed."

Valki took over. "I am Valki of Urfa. Our trading tables are to the south. Be sure to check out our toilet facilities and remember to wash your hands and get your sweetbread with nuts in it. Littlestar?" She motioned toward Littlestar who shouted in his loudest voice, "The third Winter Solstice Festival now begins!"

The great horn blew. Valki screamed, "LET'S GO HAVE OURSELVES A FESTIVAL!!!" There was pandemonium.

The dignitaries gathered on the stage to congratulate themselves on a successful opening. Six tribes were already there and several more were expected in the next few days.

Littlestar was beside himself. He said, "Girls as skywatchers, Mother Valki? Where did that come from? And—apprentice for a year and then pick them up after that? And a donation? We have never requested a donation in exchange for knowledge, Valki."

Valki was contrite. "I just made up some stuff, Littlestar. It sounded good at the time. But let's talk about it. It still sounds good. And, yes, girls! Get used to it!" She laughed.

Vaniyal looked like he should have thought of these things. Nanatan looked amused. Littlestar didn't look amused. Vanam didn't laugh. Pumi wasn't around. The festival had begun. Valki happily returned to her trading tables.

Pumi was already there, waiting with open arms. "You were incredible, Valki. We need a new field of study for whatever it is you did up there."

Vaniyal stood with Littlestar in front of the tall stone, basking in the glory of the day. Littlestar was lost in thought. *Girls? Teaching a child for only a year and then stopping? Trading goods for knowledge? We DO need food and materials, though. Knowledge is the only thing in which we are rich.*

People were beginning to understand and appreciate the toilets in the southern field. They remembered to wash their hands and get their sweetbread—with nuts in it.

Later in the day, Kiya adopted Phoebe from the Clan of the Eagle. After evening meal, Vanam impregnated Kiya with their third son.

The festival raged on.

Saparu, Palai, Moonman. Nanatan, Vivekamulla, Vaniyal, Littlestar. Irakka, Mari, Irul.

24. Valki and Kiya Go to Urfa

Vanam gave Kiya permission to go with Valki to Urfa. He required her to go toward the end of the festival when he knew Pumi would be busy with the scholars talking to chiefs about the advantages of educating their children for a year at Tallstone.

Valki and Kiya walked the path to Urfa behind Pavett and Nonti. Each hunter shouldered a long wooden pole of the running sled. The sled contained supplies, equipment, and trade items to be returned to Urfa after the festival. Valki took this opportunity to get a head start in returning things. On top of the packed merchandise, the three children rode, facing backward, laughing, watching their mothers. What a wonderful treat for Kiya's daughters; they had never even seen a running sled before and here they were—riding on one. They were going someplace and didn't even have to run to get there. It was wonderful."

Breathson took it all in stride.

"You show my children a new world, Valki. They are going to get spoiled."

Valki replied, "That is one of the things I'm afraid of—getting spoiled. Look at us—we are walking to Urfa—not even running. And two hunters are transporting things a hunter would never think of having—things too heavy or too bulky to carry from camp to camp, and this is only the first trip of many. We are collecting—'things.' It's not natural, Kiya. But we continue to do it. Are your daughters better off riding instead of running? I don't know, but I am fearful of it. Whether it makes life better or worse."

"How interesting, sister. The one making the biggest change is the one most fearful of change. But I see only the good that comes from it."

"Yes, Kiya, much good comes from Urfa, but is there not also bad? How do I measure the good versus the bad especially when I don't see all of either? Pumi laughs at me. But still—I am fearful."

"Look at the faces of our children, Valki. How happy they are. All we have is this moment. What has been is gone—what will come is not yet here—this moment is all that we truly have. This moment exists because of Urfa. I rejoice in this moment. Share it with me."

Valki pensively replied, "The past is never over, Sister. It is always with us."
I must do all that can be done to—to do what, Mother? Prevent the past from happening

Vanam, Kiya, Pumi, Valki, Putt, Putt-pay, Breathson, Littlerock.

to someone else? Remove all hunger and pain and injustice from the world? What would you have me do, Mother? What?

Valki continued, "I do rejoice in this moment, Sister Kiya—and in my family. Now, would you like to ride on the running sled?"

< >

In the late afternoon, they arrived at Urfa.

The two hunters began unloading the running sled. They taught the two girls how to help.

Valki took Kiya directly to show her the growing fields. Even after the recent harvest, much einkorn remained. Kiya looked out over the massive fields in awe. "This is unbelievable, Valki. Only good can come from this place."

They both silently stared out over the endless fields where the einkorn grew. Valki thought, *I hope you are right, my sister. I hope you are right.*

They walked back to the main house, where they were met by Breathson and Pavett. Breathson wore his rabbit belt.

Pavett said, "Master Breathson wishes to meet with Wolfchief, Great Mother Chief Pen-Valki. Is that satisfactory?"

Valki considered the request. "It's getting late in the day, Pavett, but Breathson has missed his daily meetings. He hasn't met with Wolfchief in a long time. Yes, take him there, be careful."

The old man and the boy slowly trotted off to the Wolfchief meeting place. Breathson carried a slab of meat.

Valki told Kiya the story of Breathson and Wolfchief.

< >

Breathson and Pavett returned long after sunset. Breathson went directly to his waiting evening meal and joined Kiya's two young daughters, already eating.

Breathson sat down without speaking and began to eat. The two girls looked at him with concern. Themis reached over and touched Breathson on his arm. He told her, "Wolfchief did not come," and continued eating. Themis patted his arm and returned to her meal.

Pavett said, "I told Master Breathson that we would return mid-morning and try again. Great Mother Chief Pen-Valki."

"Very good, Pavett. Tomorrow, she will come."

Saparu, Palai, Moonman. Nanatan, Vivekamulla, Vaniyal, Littlestar. Irakka, Mari, Irul.

< >

The next day, Wolfchief did not come.

They set off to return to Tallstone after Highsun. Kiya's visit had been a wonderful change in pace for both women. They had discussed complex concepts and issues that would concern only the two of them. They said words no one else would be interested in hearing.

Kiya said, "Let's do this again next year."

Valki agreed, "Yes, let's."

They returned to Tallstone and reality as the festival was closing down.

A wonderful time had been had by all.

Vanam, Kiya, Pumi, Valki, Putt, Putt-pay, Breathson, Littlerock.

25. Wolves

The residents of Urfa returned from the festival. They were excited about their trades and their new friends. A dozen people wishing to make their Last Camp along with several children with questionable capabilities were added to Urfa's citizens. All were put to work.

Breathson went immediately to the ceremonial meeting place. Wolfchief did not come. Breathson returned each day thereafter. Wolfchief did not come.

Valki, Pavett, and Putt-pay counseled Breathson that the wolf may have moved to new territory, had died, or simply was no longer interested in humans. After a while, Valki allowed him to go alone.

Breathson never wavered. He went every afternoon.

< >

A season passed.

Eventually, as Breathson scanned the horizon, the wolf reappeared and trotted to her sitting place. Three small shapes followed. They all sat.

Wolfchief saw the offering lying by the spear. She rose and trotted to it; her three cubs followed. She allowed them to smell, then taste, and then devour the piece of meat as she monitored Breathson. Her cubs finished the meat, sat back on their haunches, and looked around.

The female cub, and then the two males, saw Breathson. The female cub's eyes widened as she studied him. She suddenly raised her rear high in the air, leaving her chest and front legs on the ground. She jerked toward him. Breathson rose and fell to the ground with front arms down, rear high in the air. With his right arm, he slapped the ground and imitated her fake lunge.

The cub rose and ran full speed at Breathson. The two males reluctantly followed. Their mother rose and focused on the four creatures in front of her. The two males thought better of it and stopped halfway, but the female continued full force and collided with the boy. He took the impact, grabbed the cub in his arms, and rolled over on his back, tousling her the whole time. The cub escaped, retreated, bounced around, and charged again. Wolfchief strained forward, teeth exposed in warning, but did not charge to protect her cub. Breathson and the cub continued their play-fight until the cub was exhausted. The two males watched with interest but were not ready to challenge such a large creature.

The mother slowly relaxed and sat back on her haunches.

Saparu, Palai, Moonman. Nanatan, Vivekamulla, Vaniyal, Littlestar. Irakka, Mari, Irul.

Breathson held out his hand to the cub. She rose, sniffed the hand, and imprinted him into her memory. He told her, "Your name will be Wolffriend. We will take care of each other. Come here every day and I will have food for you."

He then rose, looked at Wolfchief, then turned his back, and walked away. The cub, Wolffriend, took a few steps with him, but then turned and looked at her mother, who signaled her to return. Her cubs were learning the way of the world, the female more so than her brothers.

Breathson told no one of this adventure. They would not understand.

< Wolfchief >

Wolfchief tolerated Breathson touching her female cub. The two had play-fought many times. Now the two sat resting together, Breathson's hand scratching Wolffriend's head.

A movement in the distant brush attracted his attention, as well as Wolfchief's. The boy slowly rose to a crouch to face the movement. Wolffriend did not know what was happening, but she knew something was. She, too, rose into a crouch. They both waited, motionless. There was another movement, and Breathson took off running, the cub keeping pace. A rabbit burst out of the brush. There was no way the two would ever catch such a creature, but then Wolfchief ambushed the rabbit, rolled it over, and knocked the wind from it. The pursuing cub caught up and sank her teeth into the rabbit's neck. She ripped it to pieces, devouring its flesh. The panting mother retreated and watched approvingly.

Breathson also watched—with slow understanding.

The rabbit had been a living, breathing creature who wished no harm to him or Wolffriend. Yet here was the rabbit; dead, ripped apart, being consumed. Breathson realized that his belt, too, had once been a living creature, its life ended, its skin—a belt around his waist.

Neither animal had wished for death. They had undoubtedly done all they could to avoid death. And yet ...

Without rancor or pity, Breathson watched Wolffriend strip and consume the rabbit's flesh. The wolf was a wolf, the rabbit was a rabbit. So it is.

He waited until the cub was sated and then reached to retrieve the remains of the rabbit. Wolffriend nipped at the boy. Without thought or hesitation, Breathson slapped her nose. "No! The rabbit is mine!"

Vanam, Kiya, Pumi, Valki, Putt, Putt-pay, Breathson, Littlerock.

The cub stepped back and stared at Breathson, waiting. Breathson turned and, with the remains of the rabbit, started back toward his bench. The wolf cub trotted obediently behind. Wolfchief looked on with satisfaction.

Her cubs, the female at least, were learning.

< >

The evening meal at Urfa was, as usual, animated.

Breathson arrived late. He walked to Valki. "Mother?" he asked.

Valki was pleased. "Yes, Son?"

"I made something. I want to give it to you."

Valki leaned over and said, "That would mean a great deal to me, Breathson."

Breathson held out a belt made of a rabbit pelt. "It is like mine," he said. "I made it from a dead rabbit."

She reached and took the gift. "It's beautiful—I will wear it every day." *Where did Breathson get a rabbit pelt? Did he catch it or find it?*

She said, "This was a fine rabbit. Where did you find it?"

Breathson replied, "Wolffriend and I caught it except Wolfchief slowed the rabbit down enough for Wolffriend to kill it and eat it and then would not let me have it but she had eaten all she wanted so I hit her nose and now she obeys me and Wolfchief isn't mad at me."

"Oh, I see," Valki calmly replied, her mind racing. She asked, "Has Wolfchief started coming back? Is Wolffriend someone you met at the feeding place?"

"Yes. She comes back every day now and she has three babies and the girl is my friend but the boys won't come and play with me but Wolffriend is my friend and we run and play together and at first Wolfchief watched us a lot and I thought she might bite me but now she is happy when Wolffriend and I play-fight and they come every day."

Valki laughed. "Well, that must be where the meat has been disappearing to. And this is a wonderful belt that I shall cherish forever."

"Thank you, Mother," Breathson said as he left to sit at the eating table.

Valki turned to Palai and said, "He has been dealing with a she-wolf and her cubs by himself without protection of any kind! Oh, Palai, I have been remiss in my duties. I have been so careless. Pumi will be mad with me."

Saparu, Palai, Moonman. Nanatan, Vivekamulla, Vaniyal, Littlestar. Irakka, Mari, Irul.

"Breathson gave no indication, Mother Valki," replied Palai. "No hint."

< >

After eating, Breathson looked for Pumi, who was with the builders discussing possible new construction for Tallstone. Breathson did not politely wait for a break. He interrupted Putt in mid-sentence and blurted out, "Father, can something come back to life after it is dead?"

Putt was annoyed that the little brat would dare interrupt his conversation, but Pumi held up his hand to cut off the coming admonishment. He turned to Breathson and said, "I know of nothing that has returned to life after it dies. That is a good question. I shall ask those wiser than myself. I will tell you if I find out. Why do you ask?"

Breathson repeated what he had told Valki, but ended with, "I would bring the rabbit back to life if I could, but I don't know how."

"I will speak to your mother about the rabbit and the wolves, and I will think about your question," Pumi answered. "I have found that thinking on such questions while watching the night sky in solitude is often useful. And remember not to interrupt other people while they are talking."

"Yes, Father," said Breathson, who then left.

Pumi thought, *Valki, we must talk. What's going on here? And the boy was more gracious than he had ever been.*

"Now," he continued, to an annoyed Putt, "what were you saying?"

26. The Scout

The scout came upon Urfa from the south as dusk approached. "What manner of place is this?" he asked Moonman, unfamiliar with a permanent camp and thinking that the old man was the tribal chief.

"A wonderful place! A place of greatness! A place I shall never leave," Moonman muttered as he wandered off.

"Greetings, friend," Valki said from behind the scout. "We shall eat soon. Will you join us? We have a little meat and are rich in bread."

He replied, "Yes. I will join you. Are there hunters or skywatchers here that I can discuss the lay of the land with?"

"You have met our skywatcher. He is beyond old, as you see. But I can direct you to a place within a half-day slow run where expert skywatchers reside. Our two hunters are with the builders, but they will return for the evening meal. I'm sure they will share what knowledge they have."

The scout asked, "Your tribe has only two hunters? How do you live?"

"We live well enough," Valki laughed. "This place is named Urfa. We live here year-round and have only a few hunters and skywatchers. Our men build structures, and we women harvest grains and herbs, enough to feed all of us without the need for meat. The skywatchers of which I spoke live year-round in Tallstone, toward the northeast. Pumi is their chief, although he has never taken that title. He shares his time between Urfa, Tallstone, and Rockplace, which is north of Tallstone. He is in Tallstone now. You will meet him if you choose to visit there."

"Oh, visit I shall," said the scout. *These arrangements are unnatural. I must know about these things.*

He continued, "So, it is you who commands this tribe?"

She laughed again. "We have little need for a chief in this place. Each of us has our responsibilities. If a problem arises, we are good at resolving it."

"I understand—I think. So, I may speak to anyone without first receiving your permission?"

"Yes. But to make you comfortable, I give you permission to do as you will while you are in Urfa."

"I look forward to evening's meal," the scout said. He nodded to Valki and walked away to explore this strange place.

Saparu, Palai, Moonman. Nanatan, Vivekamulla, Vaniyal, Littlestar. Irakka, Mari, Irul.

Book One. The Beginning of Civilization: Mythologies Told True

The scout noticed the einkorn field. It was of no interest other than something to keep the gatherers busy if his chief chose to camp here. He then found the builders at work, with their entourage of children helping. They explained their occupation with excitement. He nodded continually but had no concept of what they were telling him nor why they would do those things.

Soon, Palai called for all to come to evening meal. The scout felt he had entered an impossible world. None of the arrangements were familiar. Men and women sat and talked without rank or division. Children were permitted to sit near the adults.

He sat down at an almost inconceivable construction but mimicked what he saw others doing. The conversation turned to trade between Urfa and the scout's tribe.

"Yes, trade might be possible," the scout offered. "But other than some possible herbs and grain, there is little here of interest to my tribe."

Palai rose and returned with a basket of spearheads and cutting tools. "Might these be of interest?"

The scout examined them. *These are exquisite, the finest I have ever seen.*

He answered, "Why, yes. These might be of some small value to my tribe."

"Good," she replied. "This is a small portion of what we have available for trade. I have kept the finer pieces in reserve. The price of those pieces would be more than a smaller tribe could afford."

"I understand." The scout laughed. "I will convey this to my chief."

Midway through the meal, a boy walked in and went to the child's table, where he sat and started eating, without words or ceremony.

"Breathson," said Valki, "we have a visitor."

The boy continued eating.

Valki tried again. "Breathson, did your friends come today?"

Breathson replied, "They all came and we saw another rabbit and it ran away and we chased it but it was too fast and Wolfchief did not help and the rabbit did not die but Wolffriend did not eat either."

The scout observed that everyone listened with respect. He had no idea what the boy was talking about, but he heard words such as "wolf" and "chief" and "a rabbit got away." *The boy is obviously afflicted—probably because he has no exposure*

Vanam, Kiya, Pumi, Valki, Putt, Putt-pay, Breathson, Littlerock.

to normal men. A boy could not possibly grow normally surrounded by people such as these.

The room was silent until the scout spoke directly to the boy. He said, "There are two rules in hunting. The first is to know yourself. The second is to know your prey. You must know everything about yourself—your strengths, your weaknesses, your equipment, and the limitations of your equipment. You must know everything about your prey—their defenses, what they are likely to do, how fast they are, how strong. You must know everything. And knowing everything, the rabbit will never again escape."

Breathson stared at the scout with an odd intensity. He appeared to absorb every word, searing each into his brain. He continued to stare and repeated, "Know yourself—know your prey—know everything—I will do these things." He then turned and continued eating.

Everyone looked at the scout with admiration. He was almost embarrassed.

After evening meal, the scout retired outside, and everyone but Valki went into some type of "sleeping house." The scout was again incredulous. *What kind of people are these?*

Later that night, the scout's sharp ears heard the almost imperceptible distant sound of someone walking away from the huts. He rose, took his spear, and in complete silence tracked the sound to its source. Valki was standing in the bright moonlight, staring over a patch of grain. He stalked her from behind, grabbed her hair, and forced her to the ground. "Out in the night alone, good-looking. We have unfinished business," he said as he began pulling at her clothes.

He felt something sharp push against his scrotum and heard a sweet voice say, "Pumi has told me that a man without testicles has little interest in women. With a twist of my wrist, I can make this happen. Shall we see if this is true?"

She jabbed the blade to the cutting point.

"Another day, maybe," the scout responded quickly. "Tonight, let us instead discuss the wisdom of Pumi and the wonder of Urfa." He released her hair and pulled his body away from hers, noticing, with great relief, that the stone knife was no longer in his groin.

Valki rose and said, "I was wrong to allow this to happen. I thought I would not be heard. I hope this will not put a strain between our tribes."

Saparu, Palai, Moonman. Nanatan, Vivekamulla, Vaniyal, Littlestar. Irakka, Mari, Irul.

The scout laughed. "You must know that you are a strange people with different customs. But I am a scout. I must learn everything about you."

"Know your prey?" asked Valki.

Again, the scout laughed. "Very strange indeed. Let me repay you for my insolence. I leave at sunrise for this Tallstone camp. Let me take the boy—the strange one—with me. He appears interested in the ways of animals. In all the world, I know more about animals than anyone else. I will share this knowledge with him. A hunter cares little of an animal's nature beyond 'there it is, let's go kill it.' Maybe the boy will appreciate the things I know."

Valki replied, "Wisdom is difficult to find. Breathson does not show emotion, but he will hear and remember every word you say. He is extremely smart; just not social. He has made friends with wolves, and he continuously tries to capture a living rabbit. He collects scorpions and creatures from under logs. The builders have made enclosures to keep these creatures in so that he can study them. He has constructed what he believes to be a proper enclosure for a rabbit. Pumi and the others at Tallstone study many things, but what they really do is collect and share knowledge. What you know of animals will be listened to with rapt attention. They admire knowledge more than life itself. Of course, Breathson may go with you. It is my joy that you will take him."

The scout laughed. *A strange people, indeed.*

< >

Before sunrise, Valki woke Breathson and said, "The scout wants you to accompany him to Tallstone. He can tell you about animals and their habits. You may go with him and return with Pumi or one of the skywatchers."

"I cannot miss my meeting with Wolffriend. She will be there after Highsun, waiting on me."

"I will go in your stead. It is time I met this new friend of yours. Besides, I know her mother well."

Breathson was unsure of this, but the scout appeared to know a great deal about animals. Besides, his mother would be good to his friends. "Very well," he said. "I will go."

< >

The scout and Breathson trotted at a modest pace. The scout began talking about animals and how which types of animals lived in an area depended on several things. It began with the vegetation. Was there enough to feed

Vanam, Kiya, Pumi, Valki, Putt, Putt-pay, Breathson, Littlerock.

large herds? If so, the antelopes came, and with them the larger predators. Lions. Tigers. Bears. It depended on the density of the vegetation and the type of trees the area supported. He had seen one land, far away, where gigantic lizards lurked in the water waiting for prey. They were large enough to take down a full-grown auroch. And so vicious that few predators, including men, would attack one. The scout talked on and on. "Animals are most dangerous when hungry and when threatened. Learn to recognize these conditions. Watch them, listen to them."

Breathson was enthralled and memorized every word, especially about aurochs. He demanded, "Aurochs. More."

They reached Tallstone and were greeted enthusiastically by Pumi and the skywatchers. The skywatchers, too, were interested in the scout's stories.

Breathson followed the scout everywhere. He stayed quiet and out of the way, but Breathson had begun talking to the scout. At first only in single words and grunts, but after several days Breathson asked the scout, "My name is Breathson. What is your name?"

"My name is Mustakshaf. I am a scout for the tribe of Chief Eazim-Rayiys from far southwest of here."

Breathson said, "Stay in Urfa with me. Teach me about animals."

The scout was strangely moved. He replied, "I must return to my tribe at the end of this season. I have much to tell my chief—Stillhunter—Winter Solstice Festival—Urfa—Tallstone—scholars. Men who are different than hunters but who still command respect. You may return with me if your people will allow this."

"No. I must stay with Wolffriend. She likes me. I want her to like me more. I want her to be a real friend. Not a wolf-friend."

"I should have met this wolf friend of yours. There may be something about the nature of wolves to be learned. If I return, then I will find you and I can learn more about wolves."

"Tell your chief to come to the festival. We can counsel together. When I am a man, we will make friends with aurochs."

Mustakshaf laughed. "Maybe we shall. A scout doesn't have many friends. An auroch friend might be nice."

Breathson said, "I will make friends with Wolffriend. Then I will have a friend."

The man looked at the boy without expression. "Yes, Breathson. I will return."

Saparu, Palai, Moonman. Nanatan, Vivekamulla, Vaniyal, Littlestar. Irakka, Mari, Irul.

27. Winter Solstice Festival 11

Eight years later; ages 37, 33, 27, 24.

The years passed. Another Winter's Solstice came.

To the sound of the great horn, Valki strode upon the stage, both hands high in the air. She shouted, "Are you ready to have a festival?!" The well-trained crowd roared back, "Yes!"

Valki continued her traditional performance.

At the fourth festival, one of the new tribes had introduced the concept of drums. She now used three drummers in her performance. Drums were an instant success. One of the drummers was released to Tallstone as a "scholar" to teach this new art form to anyone who might be interested. Valki instantly capitalized on her drummers to add frenzy to her opening ceremony and throughout the festival. After the frenzy died down, she introduced the two founding chiefs and asked each to speak to the mass of people. She then introduced the twelve chiefs who had previously attended a festival and had adopted an identifying totem. She then introduced the chief of the two new attending tribes. Each chief announced their identifying totem, which would be carved into a Guardian stone in the second ring, and then, to the sound of cheers, recognized the members of their tribes.

She ended her performance with her usual, "LET'S GO HAVE OURSELVES A FESTIVAL!"

The sixteen chiefs and guests gathered at the base of Tallstone Hill to visit and to be seen.

Vaniyal and Pumi joined Littlestar at the tall stone to greet the tribal skywatchers with their apprentices. They discussed boys and girls who might want to make a permanent residence at Tallstone or who might want a year of training in the sciences—for a small stipend to Tallstone. Masters and apprentices were also available to travel with a tribe for a year, sharing their expertise with the tribe—for a small stipend to Tallstone.

In the early afternoon, Mustakshaf found Breathson and went with him to the boy's area to compete in games of strength, speed, and agility. Breathson excelled in all events.

But not so during the earlier festivals. Breathson had performed poorly. Pavett and Nonti had taken him in those days. Breathson did not understand the reason for useless games.

Vanam, Kiya, Pumi, Valki, Putt, Putt-pay, Breathson, Littlerock.

The tribe of Chief Eazim-Rayiys had finally attended a festival—the seventh. Scout Mustakshaf had sought out his little friend. By then, Pavett was dead. He had died during a training hunt he and Nonti had taken Breathson on. Mustakshaf replaced Pavett as the boys' mentor, at least for the month of the festival.

During the seventh festival, Mustakshaf said to Breathson, "You do not compete to triumph over other boys. You compete so that when you and I someday scout the great plains, you will be prepared to overcome all things that may occur preventing us from making friends with aurochs."

Breathson understood. He relentlessly excelled at all games from that moment forward. The other boys now remembered the "strange one."

Chief Eazim-Rayiys of the Clan of the Crocodile now attended all festivals. Mustakshaf and Breathson were inseparable for this season and exchanged knowledge of animals and their habits, including Breathson's continued friendship with Wolffriend and her offspring.

And now, Valki returned to Urfa's large presence in the southern fields after visiting with the chiefs. The people wishing to join Valki's village of Urfa continued to grow each year and they would now begin arriving at Urfa's trading tables. Valki had formed a Council of Elder Women to manage the everyday affairs of Urfa. It was they who effectively managed Urfa. Valki was the symbolic leader who greeted newcomers and would visit each tribe during the festival. She gifted each chief and elder woman a large loaf of sweetbread with nuts plus a gift for the tribe—many small portions of a lesser sweetbread—but still containing nuts.

Putt had a trading table within the Urfa trading complex. He did a brisk business with his transport sleds. A tribe only owned what they could easily move from camp to camp. Putt's sleds came in four models. Small—which a gatherer could pull with the two sturdy wooden poles hoisted over her shoulder with shoulder padding for comfort and easier pulling. Medium—which a hunter could pull. It was longer and wider and could carry more equipment. Large—which was designed to be transported completely off the ground, carried on the shoulders of four strong hunters. Extra-large—which could transport a chief from camp to camp, or elders who could no longer keep pace but were not yet ready for their Last Camp.

An almost woman, with her little sister, approached Putt at his table. "I am Themis from the Clan of the Serpent. This is my sister Theia. Theia is young and shy, but may she speak with you, Master Builder?"

Saparu, Palai, Moonman. Nanatan, Vivekamulla, Vaniyal, Littlestar. Irakka, Mari, Irul.

"Of course you may, Theia. I am Putt of Urfa, once from the Clan of the Lion. How may I help you? Do you need a sled but have nothing to trade?"

Theia haltingly said, "No, I have things to trade—but I have seen your sleds—they are good. They are good for mothers with babies. But I thought—it is probably a silly thing—but I thought that if you added little pegs down each side of your poles then she could take her gathering and traveling bags off her neck and waist and hang them on the pegs—it would make her travel easier—her older children could hang their bags from the peg, too—I don't know—but Mother has so much to carry—sometimes she has to carry my little sister Rhea when Rhea gets tired—I thought maybe your sled might make it easier."

Putt did not speak. He was lost in thought over the implications of such a simple upgrade.

Themis continued, "We are going to bring everything we have of value to trade for one of these as a gift for Mother. She is an elder woman. She can make other women share her load, but still—she has much to transport."

"Yes, yes—I mean—no—I mean—what a wonderful idea. I will make a sled with the upgrades of the pegs on the sides, especially for your mother. Whatever you have to trade will be more than acceptable. Come back at the quarter moon. I will have it ready then—but tell me about your mother— what she transports—what other ideas do you have?"

Themis beamed down with pride at Theia.

Theia stared at the ground in confused happiness.

< First Nightfall >

The chiefs held their traditional opening night evening meal at the chief's fire at the base of the hill. Valki had arranged for drummers.

Chief Nanatan announced that Vaniyal would make his Last Camp at Tallstone. He praised the contributions Vaniyal had made both to his tribe and to the world at large. It was, after all, Vaniyal who had discovered the secret knowledge held by the tall stone. He had been the force behind laying the stones and interpreting what knowledge they revealed.

Vaniyal listened with arrogant pride.

Littlestar stood beside Vaniyal, reveling in his master's reflected glory.

Vanam, Kiya, Pumi, Valki, Putt, Putt-pay, Breathson, Littlerock.

Pumi was happy for the old skywatcher. No one remembered that it was Pumi who had placed the tall stone and had encouraged Vaniyal to leave Littlestar for a year to track the shadows.

This was Vaniyal's well-deserved moment of recognition.

< Second Nightfall >

On the second night of the festival, each chief would hold a council with their tribe to conduct the usual tribal business.

As was her tradition, after this evening meal Kiya would find Pumi sitting on his flat rock table positioned due south of the tall stone. She would bring her sons and join him.

He rose and said, "Look who comes to see me! Clan of the Serpent Elder Woman Kiya and all her fine young sons." He nodded slightly to Kiya and struck his heart with his fist toward the boys. "And what fine young boys we have. Firstson, Secondson, Thirdson, Fourthson, and Fifthson, I believe," he said as he glanced at each boy.

Kiya smiled. "Hello, Pumi of Tallstone. Yes, you remember well. All my sons are inquisitive, smart, quick, and strong. Vanam often says they are more like their Uncle Pumi than they are like him. Firstson and Secondson are almost old enough to go on training hunts. Vanam will see then how much they are like their father."

Pumi asked Firstson, "Do you do well in the festival games?"

But it was Secondson who replied. "Firstson and I mostly stay around the tall stone and listen to the scholars. They are all so interesting and know so many interesting things. I am told that if Father will give Littlestar a small donation, Firstson and I could stay here learning for an entire year. That would be wonderful if we could do that. We are going to ask Father—if we ever find him in a good mood. He is so busy making our tribe richer that he is usually in a bad mood, and we don't like to interrupt him ..."

Kiya touched Secondson on the shoulder and held her finger to her lips.

Pumi laughed. The group continued their banter for a while and then Kiya dismissed her sons to the evening's activities. Drums could be heard from the playing fields.

Pumi and Kiya were left alone. They talked about life. Finally, Pumi said, "Littlerock is etching new totems into two Guardian stones. I see his torch burning from here. Would you like to watch him work?"

Saparu, Palai, Moonman. Nanatan, Vivekamulla, Vaniyal, Littlestar. Irakka, Mari, Irul.

"Yes, Pumi. I would like that a great deal."

They rose and walked toward the other side of the hill.

As was his nature, Vanam watched them visit from the shadows until they crossed over the hill.

And out of his sight.

< First Quartermoon >

Valki and Kiya set off for Urfa. Kiya's daughters were thrilled to go on this grand adventure.

Valki said, "You girls may be interested to know that Urfa has two women skywatchers."

Themis: "No!"
Mnemosyne: "Is that even possible?"
Phoebe: "They would let a girl be a skywatcher?"
Tethysis: "I want to be one!"
Theia: "What do they do?"

Valki laughed and said, "They are not master skywatchers, but they *did* each have a year's training in the art. They are both handicapped—crippled—one from birth, the other by a beating from her father. Littlestar accepted them into their school as young girls—for a full year—for a sizeable contribution of bread, of course. They took to their teaching well. I asked them if the heaven plays a role in the growth of our crops. Some crops are much more fruitful than others. And, yes, it appears to be so. They still study the skies and compare the yield of the crops. We have been planting every quarter moon but soon we will be planting fewer seeds less often and getting more and larger crops. There is so much to learn about growing things. It's so exciting."

Tethysis: "Mother, can I be a skywatcher? That would be such fun."
Themis: "Can I grow plants?"
Phoebe: "The only thing you will ever grow are babies!"

There was laughter. Their talk went on.

Breathson also brought Mustakshaf on these excursions. He was excited to show off his animal friends and their living facilities. On the next afternoon, they would go to the Wolffriend meeting place. Wolfchief no longer came but Wolffriend usually did. Several of Wolffriend's pack were also coming. None were as friendly as Wolffriend, but all grew more tolerant of Breathson and his friends and of the nice cuts of meat they were offered.

Vanam, Kiya, Pumi, Valki, Putt, Putt-pay, Breathson, Littlerock.

28. Winter Solstice Festival 17

Six years later; ages 43, 39, 33, 30.

The years passed.

A builder apprentice escorted two young men into Valki's kitchen where she stood kneading bread for the imminent festival. "Mother Valki, these two scouts came across us as we were harvesting trees."

"Welcome," Valki said. "We gather for dinner at sunset. Join us and tell us your stories. For what tribe do you scout?"

"We are from Chief Vanam's Clan of the Serpent," Rivermaster replied. "Our names are Rivermaster and Sagacity."

She stopped her work, turned, and stared at him. "You will know Chief Vanam and Elder Woman Kiya!"

Rivermaster responded, "They are our parents."

She went to them and embraced them. "You are Kiya's sons! How wonderful! I met you many years ago at Tallstone when you were still children. Now you are scouts. Come sit on the front porch and let me catch up on the Clan of the Serpent."

She called a young woman to take over her task and led the two scouts to the porch where they all sat in "chairs." Another young woman brought food and drink to them.

Rivermaster told Valki, "My name was Firstson until Mother gave me my man's name. Sagacity's name was Secondson. Our mother respects you more than any other person. I wish you to know our story. Sagacity can tell it with words better than I."

Sagacity told Valki of Kiya's problems including more than he should; things Phoebe had told him about words between their parents. Valki listened intently, shaking her head in understanding, and asking delicate questions that led to even more explanations. When he had finished, Valki knew more than Rivermaster about Vanam and Kiya.

Valki replied, "Well, Kiya is a wise and determined woman. Good things shall come to pass from this. And, she is proud of her two sons, 'the scouts,' I know."

Rivermaster feared unforeseen complications arising from Valki's knowledge of sensitive internal family affairs. He asked her not to repeat any of these words to anyone for any reason until all had come to pass, one way or the other. She agreed that it would be bad if any word of this conversation made it back to anyone in the Clan of the Serpent.

Valki agreed to total secrecy until she knew that all decisions had been made. *Kiya—My sister!—My friend!*

The two young men enjoyed their first real meal since they had begun their adventure. The next morning, they departed, with gifts from Urfa, to meet their destiny at Tallstone.

< >

The day of the festival came. Valki stood waiting at the base of the stage. She had mixed emotions about the upcoming days.

She was thrilled that the Clan of the Serpent had set up their camp. They had not attended in six years. She looked forward to seeing her old friends, especially Kiya and her children. But there were also the difficulties that Kiya and Vanam were having. *Vanam replaced Kiya as elder woman and might banish her and their children from his tribe. They would be outcasts whom no one could even look upon. Oh, Kiya, if anyone can resolve these problems, it is you.*

And, too, this would be Valki's last year to host the opening of the festival. She was growing too old. There was no longer joy in it. She had auditioned young women of Urfa to be her replacement. There were so many candidates; all so eager to replace the great Valki of Urfa as the host introducing the great festival. She had selected three to assist her this year. They each had specific responsibilities. They were all bright, outgoing, and full of life. Next year one of them would become the new face of Urfa.

But for now? The great horn sounded. Valki strode upon the stage, both hands high in the air. She shouted, "ARE YOU READY TO HAVE A FESTIVAL?!" The opening ceremony was magnificent!

The festival began.

The strange one, Breathson, was the instant, overwhelming center of attention. He walked around looking for his old friend Mustakshaf. Breathson's new best friend, Nay, walked obediently beside him. Nay was a full-blooded wolf. The crowd parted as they approached and watched them pass with wide-eyed disbelief.

Boys in the crowd shouted:
"Look! A wolf!"
"The strange boy is walking with a wolf!"

Vanam, Kiya, Pumi, Valki, Putt, Putt-pay, Breathson, Littlerock.

"Look at that, will you? That man walks with a wolf!"
"Will it bite me? Should I run away?"
"Hey, Master. How do you do that?"

An emotion formed in Breathson he had never before experienced—pride?—arrogance?—joy? No matter. Nay was being looked upon with wonder.

From the distance, Mustakshaf saw a great commotion. *Breathson? Is it you causing this excitement? Did you bring a friend?*

The crowd parted and the two men saw each other. Mustakshaf put his hands on his hips and waited with a wide stance as the man and his wolf approached. The scout then fell to his knees and held out his hand for the wolf to inspect.

After sniffing, Nay licked the hand with her big, wet tongue.

Breathson said, "This is Nay. She was a wolf but now she is my friend. I call her a Wolfdog. She likes humans better than she likes wolves. She had six babies. They all like people best. Nay likes you. You are her friend."

"May I touch her?" the scout asked.

"Yes, she likes for you to scratch her head. She will obey you if you know how to tell her what to do."

The crowd looked and listened to the unbelievable scene. A small boy called out, "Master, can I touch her?"

Many hunters witnessed the scene. They were unsure of what—but this that knew—something had changed.

What had changed was this. That which Valki had done for farming and Putt had done for building, so had Breathson done for animals. Urfa now grew rabbits for fur and food. Serpents and scorpions seemed not to be trainable, but fish and turtles were happy enough to be in Breathson's charge.

Nay, the Wolfdog, had been the culmination of Breathson's deep friendships with Wolfchief, with Wolffriend, and with Wolffriend's pups. Not all Wolffriend's pups became friends with Breathson, but those that did accepted him as one of them. Several from their litters identified as much with him as they did their brethren. Then one day, a pup followed Breathson back to Urfa rather than returning to her mother. Wolfdogs preferred living with humans to living with wolves. Nay was a faithful companion to Breathson, constantly by his side, learning to obey his every command. Breathson communicated with Nay better than with people.

Saparu, Palai, Moonman. Nanatan, Vivekamulla, Vaniyal, Littlestar. Irakka, Mari, Irul.

Book One. The Beginning of Civilization: Mythologies Told True

Nay was Breathson's friend. The litter of six pups she had weaned before leaving on this grand adventure had each already adopted a suitable master.

Nay was friendly and enjoyed the attention of humans. She was an expert huntress.

At the tall stone, Pumi, Littlestar, and the masters of the various guilds received the mass of males—and several females—waiting to see and speak to Pumi and Littlestar. They were both celebrities. They received each person in turn. They introduced those who wished to be apprenticed to one of the five guilds to the appropriate Guild Master, who then assigned those who might prove worthy to an apprentice within the guild for further, deeper discussions.

Eventually, a familiar stonecutter stood before Pumi. Neither spoke for a long time. The stonecutter fell to his knees and touched Pumi's feet with his forehead. Pumi drew the man to his feet and said simply, "Littlerock, my dear friend. I rejoice to see you. We will meet over a campfire as soon as all is calm."

"Yes, Master," Littlerock replied. "But allow me to introduce my apprentice to you." He pushed Piercer to face Pumi. "Piercer, this is my great master, Pumi. Pumi, this is my new apprentice, Piercer."

"You have an excellent master, Piercer. Littlerock is accomplished and a wonderful teacher. You have an interesting name. Is there a story there?"

"Yes, Master," Piercer replied. "I pierced holes into five colored rocks and made a necklace. I gave it to my mother. She gave me my man's name."

"Colored rocks? I have noticed such rocks near streams but have never studied them. Do they make better spear points than regular rocks?"

"I don't know, Master. I began only a season ago. I have much to learn but I like colored rocks."

"Well, keep me apprised of your progress. I need to know how colored rocks differ from regular rocks. I look forward to finding a woman wearing a pretty necklace of rocks."

"You already know her, Master," Littlerock said. "Piercer was once named Fifthson. He is Kiya's son."

Pumi's expression did not change. He stared at Littlerock. "Kiya?"

"Yes, Master. We need to talk. I will stay nearby. Before you leave to greet old friends—find me. We must talk."

Vanam, Kiya, Pumi, Valki, Putt, Putt-pay, Breathson, Littlerock.

Littlerock left, taking Piercer with him.

Pumi thought, *Kiya? Vanam? Talk? Yes, Littlerock, I shall find you.*

Kiya did not wish to meet with Valki, at least not yet. She and Valki had not visited in five years. Valki had risen to high rank and power. Kiya at fallen to the depths. But Urfa's great presence drew Kiya like a magnet to inspect the many tables of grains and bread, the many trading tables, and the people who traded there. She talked with several of the women to admire all they were doing and how efficiently they did it. To feed and care for this many people was impressive. She did not mention that she was the one-time mate of Chief Vanam of the Clan of the Serpent. She would be an embarrassment to her tribe soon enough.

An elder woman walked over and introduced herself. "I am Tirma, once elder woman of the Clan of the Auroch. I am now on Urfa's Council of Elders." She waited for Kiya to reciprocate.

"I am a common gatherer from the Clan of the Serpent."

The elder woman's face brightened. "Oh, then you must know their Elder Woman, Kiya, and her mate Chief Vanam!"

Kiya thought, *There we have it. There is no way past this. I was foolish to think that I could avoid this and the dishonor it brings.*

She answered, "I am Kiya."

Tima was elated. She said, "I am honored to meet you. Mother Valki has spoken highly of you many times. Have you not yet presented yourself? She will be insulted if you ignore her. Come, I will escort you to her."

Kiya could remain silent and go with Tirma, but hard, cold protocol demanded that she speak the truth; and clear all misconceptions of rank. "You are kind, but I am no longer the elder woman of my tribe." *Don't lie. Tell enough truth to maintain what honor I still have.*

She continued, "I requested Chief Vanam relieve me of the burden of leadership. The tribe's new elder woman is Panti. Panti was more accomplished than I in all things except the knowledge of plants. To transfer leadership from me to Panti was a joy to me, to Panti, and to our women. I cannot present myself to Valki as an elder woman. I must wait until she has finished her duties, and I can approach her as a common woman."

Tirma was unsure how to proceed with this information. She said, "Wait while I consult Mother Valki." Tirma scurried off to the large house built

Saparu, Palai, Moonman. Nanatan, Vivekamulla, Vaniyal, Littlestar. Irakka, Mari, Irul.

for Valki to use during the great festival and for the scholars to use during the remainder of the year.

Within moments, Valki burst from the house followed by Tirma. Valki hurried to Kiya with extended arms. "Sister, how can you neglect me so? It is a joy to see you after all these years. Come into the house. We have much to discuss!"

She took Kiya's hand and began pulling her toward the house."

Kiya followed, saying, "Valki, much has changed. Nothing is as it was."

"That's wonderful news," Valki responded. "Change is so interesting, don't you think?"

They entered the house. It was alive with newcomers. Urfa's elder women busied themselves acclimating the newcomers to the new, unfamiliar environment. Valki took Kiya through the large main room to a small room in the back, which could be closed off for privacy. They sat down in facing chairs.

Valki said, "Putt insisted that he make me a place away from the people. Unnecessary, but nice for gossip. Now, let us gossip." Valki leaned forward and looked expectantly at Kiya—waiting.

Kiya was silent for a while; then the words burst forth.

< >

The first day of the festival roared on. The chief's ceremonial opening evening meal was held at the foot of the tall stone hill. There were many fires surrounded by hunters and gatherers and children from many tribes. Old friends visited and gossiped. Copious amounts of meat and bread were consumed. Drums beat. Most things were good.

The second day of the festival proceeded much as the first. The evening meals, however, were limited to individual tribes to conduct tribal business.

< Clan of the Crocodile >

Breathson and Nay were invited to observe the evening council of Chief Eazim-Rayiys. The chief announced, "Master Scout Mustakshaf wishes to make his last camp at Tallstone and form a new order of scholars. He wishes to share his knowledge of animals and the lands in which they live. Master Scout Mustakshaf is an honored member of our tribe and has served us well. I hereby release you from my tribe, Scout Mustakshaf. Live long and with good health!"

Vanam, Kiya, Pumi, Valki, Putt, Putt-pay, Breathson, Littlerock.

His tribe stood and shouted warm words to the old scout. After they quieted, the chief commanded, "Great Scout Mustakshaf, tell us about your strange friends."

Mustakshaf called Breathson to join him and his chief at the fire.

Breathson had become more accomplished at handling the attention of people. Nay attracted their attention, but it was Breathson who needed to respond to that attention. Mustakshaf had helped Breathson a great deal when he had observed, "Just consider people to be another animal. One you must deal with. Know their strengths, weaknesses, and expectations."

Breathson and Nay walked to join the scout and his chief. Breathson knew that he must tell the story of his best friend, Nay the Wolfdog.

He told it as best he could.

< Clan of the Serpent >

Sitting in the darkness on his flat rock table, Pumi could hear the Council of the Clan of the Serpent in the distance. The banishment of Kiya and her daughters from the tribe was straightforward. The banishment of her sons took more discussion but, in the end, the command was simple, not appealable, not revocable—Kiya and her children were banished. No member of any tribe could ever look upon their faces again.

Pumi watched in silence as Elder Woman Panti self-righteously led Kiya and her children out of the camp into the dark unknown toward the West.

In the dark of night, Pumi found Valki.

He asked her, "You knew?"

"I suspected. The gossip was different. I had thought—hoped—he would just release them from his tribe. They could settle in Urfa. It might be a good thing. But—banishment?! What can she do?—What can I do? I would ignore her banishment, but Pumi—my elder women would not hear of it. A Proclamation of Banishment must be honored by all members of all tribes. I gave a survival package to two of her sons in case this happened. But if my elder women even saw me talk to her—there would be fury in all of Urfa. I can't help her, Pumi. I can't help my friend. I have never felt so helpless in my life. Why do we do the things we do to each other? What is wrong with us?" She ran for him to embrace her; to hold her close. In his arms, Valki cried.

After a while, she whispered, "Your name was brought up."

Saparu, Palai, Moonman. Nanatan, Vivekamulla, Vaniyal, Littlestar. Irakka, Mari, Irul.

Pumi asked, "My name? What did I do?"

"Kiya told me Vanam thought that you fathered her sons—the two older ones, anyway. They did not take to the hunt. They stayed to themselves and were not interested in manly pursuits—like you. She believes Vanam is jealous of you."

"If they were mine, I would have told him—and you. Honor requires it. He has a right to know whose child he raises. No. They are not mine. Kiya and I never mated. I never asked her to. If for no other reason than she is my brother's mate. A normal man would not even ask such a thing from his brother's mate."

"Your brother did—on the afternoon of the second festival. He found me after the evening meal and asked—commanded—me to walk with him. He told me how impressed he was that I had taken over the opening of your festival. It aroused him greatly. He told me he would mate with me—then and there. I wasn't sure what to do. It was acceptable if I mated with him, but it was my right as a woman to refuse. I wasn't sure about refusing a chief, but I decided that I was as much a chief as he was, and I did not want to mate with him. I politely refused. He wasn't accustomed to refusal in any matter, especially, I'm sure, from a woman. He became furious with me—and physical. It did not go well. The matter ended poorly for him. Now I am afraid that banishing Kiya may have been revenge on me. Oh, Pumi. What have I done?"

Pumi was lost in thought as he replied, "Perfectly, Valki. You have done everything perfectly. The question is what have *I* done—or not done."

They sat together in the stillness of the night.

< >

The third day of the festival continued in full force. Pumi and Valki walked together back to Urfa. Valki wished to be away from the crowds. Pumi needed time away to come to terms with his older brother's actions. *Vanam was within his right to command Valki to mate, but still ...*

Their night at Urfa restored their emotions and made the world once more a world of hope and promise. Pumi promised Valki that he would address the issue of Kiya and her children and that all would be well—eventually. Valki was happy enough—for a while.

But Valki's sadness was not yet done.

Vanam, Kiya, Pumi, Valki, Putt, Putt-pay, Breathson, Littlerock.

< Quarter Moon >

Pumi and Valki returned to Tallstone toward the end of the festival.

They ate their evening meal inside her house at Tallstone. The meal was festive and animated and attended by the many soon-to-be new residents of Urfa. Valki was slowly regaining her positive attitude. Nay lay at the feet of Breathson as he and Mustakshaf sat at one of the far tables, lost in deep conversation. Valki had never seen Breathson stay focused for such a long time. This was good—she hoped.

After the meal was finished, Pumi and Valki sat talking. From the corner of her eye, she saw Breathson rise and motion Nay to "stay." Breathson walked to Valki and said, "Mother, may I talk with you?"

"Of course, Breathson. Sit. Join us."

"Just you and me, Mother. Alone."

"Yes, Breathson. The meeting tables in the front of our house are empty now. That will be a good place for us to talk." She glanced at Pumi, concern in her voice, concern in her glance.

Pumi acknowledged the glance and then stared at Mustakshaf still sitting at the table with Nay. Mustakshaf returned the stare, then clasped his hands, closed his eyes, and bowed his head.

Breathson replied, "Yes, Mother. We can talk at a meeting table."

Breathson and Valki rose and walked outside to a meeting table. They sat. Breathson began, "Mother, I don't know good words to tell people things."

Valki remained silent. Waiting.

"Mother, I am going to leave you."

Her heart went cold. She was terrified. "Oh?"

"I am going away with Nay and Mustakshaf."

"Oh?"

"Mustakshaf has been released from his tribe. He can go with me to make friends with aurochs. Nay will go with us."

"That's interesting, Breathson. Will I ever see you again?"

"Yes. When I make friends with aurochs."

"And how long do you think that will be?"

Saparu, Palai, Moonman. Nanatan, Vivekamulla, Vaniyal, Littlestar. Irakka, Mari, Irul.

"Mustakshaf told me it would take at least one full year. Maybe two."

"But you intend to return to me, someday?"

"Yes. When I make friends with aurochs. All my animal friends are here. You are here. Father is here. I will return as soon as I make friends with aurochs, and they will come to live with me."

Valki exhaled a great sigh. "So, you will be gone just for a little while? Probably less than two years? You and your best friends are going on a grand adventure. How exciting, Breathson."

"You are my best friend, Mother. I will miss you. I did not know how to tell you that I was leaving you."

She rose and embraced him. "You told me just fine, my son. But you are not leaving me. We just won't get to see each other for a long time. But you aren't leaving me," she sobbed.

With an insight of inspiration, she asked, "How do you make friends with an auroch?"

Breathson began. He talked and talked and talked.

Pumi had already joined Mustakshaf and had received the more detailed version of their plans to capture and tame aurochs and return them to Urfa. Pumi heard, with a degree of satisfaction, Mustakshaf say, "The boy dreaded telling his mother. He was afraid it would upset her. He was upset. It's the only time I have ever seen the boy upset. We want to leave as soon as the festival ends. It's a long run to where the aurochs are plentiful. The sooner we can start the better. We have all the supplies we need. All that remains are the goodbyes. You do approve, don't you? You do understand that the boy must do this? Must! Two full years maximum. We will return within two years—with aurochs. The boy is prepared and determined. He is a hunter on the hunt. It is what he must do. You can make this all right with his mother, can't you?"

< Half Moon >

Valki wanted to return to Urfa immediately after her son had departed on his great quest. Pumi walked with her.

Pumi walked in silence. Valki was not at peace.

She said, "I have given my last opening of the festival. I was good, wasn't I? Something came over me when I got up there. Life looked so rich from that stage—so full of joy. I will never have that experience again—but it was time to quit—don't you think, Pumi?"

They walked on.

"Banished—my friend and her children are banished—and I can't help her—you will find a way to help them, won't you, Pumi?—won't you?—was it my fault? What could I have done differently, Pumi?"

They walked on.

"My child will be gone for two years—in strange lands with strange beasts—he could die—I know that—that is the risk of living—I told him to stay alive one more day at a time—then he will come back to me with his auroch friends—he will come back to me—he will come back, won't he, Pumi?"

They walked on.

"I never bore you a child. I tried so many times. But I could not conceive a child. Are you angry with me, Pumi? I could not stand it if you were angry with me."

They walked on.

"Everyone at Urfa is not productive. Some refuse to contribute to the city. They only take and take and do not give back. Some are seriously overweight. There is no way they could run to Tallstone. They could not even walk without stopping to rest. Young women are having greater difficulty giving birth. There is one boy who went to a woman's room and took all her personal belongings. What should I do? Where will it all end? I feel so alone sometimes, Pumi. Even when you are with me. I cannot see Mother's face anymore. I am losing my mother, Pumi."

They walked on.

Saparu, Palai, Moonman. Nanatan, Vivekamulla, Vaniyal, Littlestar. Irakka, Mari, Irul.

29. Pumi and Vanam

The seasons passed.

In Urfa, Valki settled into a semblance of normalcy, but her heart was with Breathson and her friend Kiya in faraway lands. Pumi could not help Breathson, but surely, he could help her friend.

So it was, Pumi set off to the north to find his brother Vanam. Each quarter moon of travel north of Tallstone, the less the fame of Pumi and the greater the fame of Vanam. And certainly, all knew the direction where Pumi would find the Great Chief Vanam and his powerful Clan of the Serpent.

At last, in the far north, as the sun fell into the horizon, Pumi stood on a hill watching fires being built in a distant camp. A large camp with many fires. And gathering around the largest fire would surely be the man with whom Pumi wished to reason; to ameliorate the problems of days past; to find common ground for Vanam and his once-mate Kiya; to salve the pain of jealousies, whatever they may have been; to reason man-to-man. *Vanam, my brother, let us find peace.*

Pumi walked into the darkness toward the fires of his brother's tribe.

He arrived.

Women danced to the beat of drums. Two large hunters, spear in hand, met Pumi at the edge of the camp. They did not speak but walked on either side of Pumi to face Vanam reclined on a heap of animal pelts. Vanam watched the festivities, the cooking of the meats, the women dancing for him. A well-fed, totally naked woman sat behind him massaging his shoulders. The curves of her oiled body glistened in the reflections of the fire.

Vanam looked up at Pumi standing before him and said, "The boy leaves the land of women to venture into the world of men. Are you frightened, little brother?"

"No, Chief Vanam. I have my spear in hand, and I was trained well in my youth. I come to counsel with you. Will you talk with me?"

"Let me consider, Pumi. You want something from me, or you would not be here. You have something to offer, I suppose. Although you have nothing I want. But you are my brother, and I would be ungracious to turn my brother away. Yes. We will talk. Sit!"

Vanam, Kiya, Pumi, Valki, Putt, Putt-pay, Breathson, Littlerock.

Vanam whispered to the oiled woman, who barked orders to two women standing nearby. "Bring food and drink to the boy!"

Pumi was impressed. *She picked up on Vanam's reference to "the boy." Nicely done. I will be wary of you.*

Vanam said, "Very well, Pumi. What do I have that you want?"

Pumi replied, "I don't know, Vanam. Love? Brotherhood? A friendly word? Something of that nature."

Vanam snapped his fingers and pointed toward Pumi. The two large hunters on either side of Pumi stepped forward and turned to face Pumi with their spears in a threatening position. Vanam said, "You do not amuse me, brother. What do you want?!"

Pumi returned the glare. He replied, "Truth. Knowledge. A better world. You have knowledge I wish to have. I am your brother. Will you share knowledge for no other reason than I am your brother?"

Vanam laughed. "I have knowledge that my meddling little brother does not have? What a glorious night! Of course, I shall share!" He whispered to the oiled woman, who directed the drummers to quicken the beat—for the women to line-dance through the camp and chant to the beat.

The women began snaking through the camp with the soft guttural chant of "Van-nam … Van-nam …Van-nam …"

More wood was thrown into the chief's fire. The flames rose higher.

Vanam asked, "So Pumi, what knowledge do I have that you want?"

Pumi's mind raced. *If the question is not framed to your liking, you will be enraged. How do you wish to hear her name spoken, Vanam? What will not enrage you?*

Pumi said, "I have not been formally introduced to your tribe, Chief Vanam. I do not see Elder Woman Panti at your side. Is the magnificent woman behind you your new elder woman?" The two large hunters' spears were still in the threatening position. Pumi looked at them and waved his hand in dismissal. The hunters looked at Vanam, who waved his hand to dismiss. The hunters lowered their spears and stood back.

The dancers chanted, "… Van-nam …Van-nam … Van-nam …"

Vanam replied, "No. Panti is in the women's area. She is old and ugly. I prefer to surround myself with beauty."

Saparu, Palai, Moonman. Nanatan, Vivekamulla, Vaniyal, Littlestar. Irakka, Mari, Irul.

"Well, that answers *that* question. I, myself, feel that I must promote tranquility and peace in Tallstone and Urfa, yet the old women there are in constant agitation over a presence that lives in the land west of Riverport. I tell them nothing west of Riverport should concern them, but they are afraid something will drift across the river into their world that in some way pollutes them. I wish to understand this abomination and their fear of it."

The dancers chanted, "... Van-nam ... Van-nam ... Van-nam ..."

Vanam asked, "And what is this abomination?"

Pumi replied, "Names I should not speak that are banished from your lands."

The dancers chanted, "... Van-nam ... Van-nam ... Van-nam ..." The fire roared higher.

Vanam asked, "The bitch still lives? Her bastard children still live? She did not watch them die one by one and their bodies rot? There is no justice in this world. No justice at all.

"... Van-nam ... Van-nam ... Van-nam ..."

Pumi said, "The scholars of Tallstone, of course, have no appreciation of their banishment. They would freely trade with them. The elder women in Urfa would burn Riverport and even Urfa itself if she or her children attempted to trade. What say you in this matter? Do your grievances against them remain?"

Vanam rose. He wore only his loincloth and he, too, was anointed with oils. His woman rose with him, retrieved his spear, and handed it to him. He pounded his spear into the ground and spat, "Tell the scholars this: If they trade with the bitch or her children—if they see the bitch or her children and do not kill them, then I, Chief Vanam of the Clan of the Serpent, shall burn Tallstone Camp to the ground with them in it! Am I clear in this matter, little brother?!"

Louder, faster. "... Van-nam ... Van-nam ... Van-nam ..."

Pumi, too, rose and calmly asked, "And why is this, Chief Vanam?"

"Because I command it!"

"... Van-nam ... Van-nam ... Van-nam ..."

Pumi calmly said, "Commands are commands only to those who accept your command. Kiya and her children live to the west of Riverport—far from your lands—far from your commands. Why *did* you banish her, Brother?"

Vanam, Kiya, Pumi, Valki, Putt, Putt-pay, Breathson, Littlerock.

Vanam stepped to within inches of Pumi, his face in Pumi's. "Your bitch whore slut is banished as are her worthless abominations of sons. I banished her. I need no reason. That is all you need know. I SEE IT NOW! You crawl on your belly into my camp to beg for mercy for your whore." He laughed. "There will be no mercy, little brother!"

Vanam spit into Pumi's face.

The oiled woman motioned to the drummers. Faster. Louder.

"… Van-nam … Van-nam … Van-nam …"

Pumi replied, "Nice talk, big brother. Now—so there is no misunderstanding—as long as Kiya and her children remain west of Riverport, I shall protect them. They may be banished in lands you command but not in lands I command. I will respect their banishment east of Riverport to maintain peace and good relations between our people. Live in peace, Great Chief Vanam. You achieved everything our Father commanded of you. You have excelled beyond any greatness a father could want for his son. As my parting gift, I give to you all the love our father may have had for me—and whatever respect—and whatever hope—it is all yours, Vanam. You have won!"

"… Van-nam … Van-nam … Van-nam …"

Pumi glanced into the sanctimonious face of the well-fed, curvaceous, naked woman by Vanam's side; her arm on his shoulder, the firelight reflecting off both their oiled bodies making them seem larger and more powerful than they really were.

"… Van-nam … Van-nam … Van-nam …"

Vanam glared and spat out, "You did not *give* it, girly boy. I *took* it!!!"

"… Van-nam … Van-nam … Van-nam …"

Pumi did not reply. He turned and began his long walk back to Urfa. Chants followed him into the night. *Valki will be sad.*

Saparu, Palai, Moonman. Nanatan, Vivekamulla, Vaniyal, Littlestar. Irakka, Mari, Irul.

30. Valki and the Oceanids

Valki was not sad. Valki was furious. She would not have it!

She commanded Pumi, "Send Littlerock into the west and find Kiya. Determine if trade can be established between her and the western bank across from Riverport. It can't be much or widely known but find a way for Kiya to trade without injuring her pride or enraging your dumb-butt brother or upsetting my elder women!"

More seasons passed as Littlerock made the journey and returned.

He reported, "Kiya has little need for our generosity. She and her children prosper. They established the city of Tartarus and Kiya gave four of her granddaughters' permission to trade at Urfa and Tallstone. She maintains that her granddaughters were not banished, and it is their right. The young women call themselves Oceanids and were originally girls who ran away from Urfa to join the Titans. They are a free-spirited group and will do well enough, but they will not needlessly mention their association with the Titans. They will be passing through soon. In the meantime, Queen Kiya invites you to Tartarus at the full moon in three seasons. You will find more there than you imagine."

Littlerock continued his report long into the night.

< Oceanids >

Soon after Littlerock's report, the Oceanids arrived in Urfa and presented themselves to Elder Woman Paravi and inquired into the possibility of trade.

They did not mention they were associated with the banished Titans. Paravi, oblivious of their background, graciously declined their offer to trade and suggested they might be more successful dealing with less wealthy tribes who often camped near Tallstone. The Oceanids were happy enough with the rebuff and set off to find someone else to trade with.

The Oceanids came back through Urfa within a quarter moon. The four young women appeared pleased with their trades. They were accompanied by a powerfully built man named Enceladus who carried their large chests, apparently filled with trade. The leader of the group, Metis, asked Paravi for an audience with Great Mother Valki. Paravi knew that Great Mother Valki would be highly displeased if anyone requesting an audience with her was refused. Paravi reluctantly led the Oceanids to Valki and announced Metis and her sisters, "They are traders from the Oceanid tribe, Mother Valki."

Vanam, Kiya, Pumi, Valki, Putt, Putt-pay, Breathson, Littlerock.

Valki feigned ignorance and asked Metis, "Oceanid tribe? I'm not familiar with that tribe. Are you from a distant land?"

Metis replied, "We are a new tribe formed from changing conditions. May we tell you our story in privacy so that we will not embarrass our people in front of your elder woman?"

"Of course, you may, Metis. Come with me to my hideaway." She led them to her private sitting room at the back of the building and called out, "These four delightful young women are telling me stories of distant lands and strange creatures. We will have our evening meal in my hideaway so that they can continue their stories. Bring us food and drink when it is time to eat."

With that, she closed the door, sat down, looked at them, and solemnly said, "Tell me your story!"

Metis said simply, "We are Queen Kiya's granddaughters."

Valki calmly asked, "Is Sister Kiya doing well? She is banished, you know. You should not be here. We must keep this meeting our secret."

Metis replied, "That's why we call ourselves Oceanids instead of Titans. We were not banished. Grandmother told us to tell you our story if we were able to have a private audience with you. Do you wish to hear it?"

Valki wished to hear it.

The four Oceanids took turns talking. They talked late into the evening.

Valki listened intently to every word. *Kiya is doing well!—Vanam will not be pleased—or any elder woman! Stay strong, my sister!*

Metis finally said, "There you have it. That's all there is to tell."

Tyche was increasingly drawn to Valki's warmth as her grandmother had told them they would—Valki's genuine concern—her way of converting weakness into strength. Unbidden, Tyche's long-festering concern blurt itself out—"Except that none of us want to mate!"

Everyone looked at Tyche with surprise.

Clymene said, "We should keep that to ourselves, sister."

Tyche was defensive, "Well—we don't. The thought of coupling with a male is disgusting. They simply want to use our bodies for their selfish relief. We don't get anything out of it except maybe a baby. I'm not ever going to let a man do that to me!"

Saparu, Palai, Moonman. Nanatan, Vivekamulla, Vaniyal, Littlestar. Irakka, Mari, Irul.

Valki asked, "Have you been properly instructed in such things, Tyche?"

Tyche said, "Mother has instructed us. 'Raise your tunic, fall to your hands and knees, show him your rear!' It's disgusting!"

Valki gently said, "Well, men must be trained in the art, you know. Would Sister Kiya be angry if I shared *my* experience? There is more to it if you are interested in such things."

Metis exclaimed, "Yes! Knowledge is power! Tell us!"

Valki was a caring, nurturing woman talking to inquisitive frustrated young women. As it turned out, Valki had significant knowledge of an interesting subject with an intensely interested audience.

Oceanids would share their newfound knowledge with all their sisters and sing Valki's Song forevermore.

Vanam, Kiya, Pumi, Valki, Putt, Putt-pay, Breathson, Littlerock.

31. Report from Tartarus

So it was that Pumi, Littlerock, and a party of volunteers traveled to Tartarus. Their adventures are songs from a different story but know that Valki patiently sat on her front porch swing each evening waiting for Pumi's return.

He finally appeared in the distance with his traveling bag on his back.

She smiled broadly, stood, and placed her hands on her hips. He arrived, climbed the stairs, dropped his backpack, and faced her. They stared at one another in silence for a long moment.

She threw her arms around him and whispered, "Come with me right now! You must entertain me! Many times! I demand it."

He answered, "I will entertain you many times for many days. But now, I wish to tell you about the trip."

"You want to talk when you could be entertaining? This is not the Pumi I know."

He led her to the swing, sat her in it, and sat beside her.

She rang a bell; a young girl came. Valki said to her, "A Bitter for myself and one for my talkative friend, please."

He put his arm around her shoulder and pulled her close. She tucked her legs beneath her. The Bitters came.

Pumi began. "My trade mission and private negotiations were either a huge success or a huge failure. I will tell you which after the upcoming festival when I find out. Our delegation was well received. I wish you had been with me. Kiya and her children know how to put on a reception. It was designed to impress us. Their future depends on my goodwill and yours. They went out of their way in trying to win the favor of Elder Woman Paravi. Kiya knows the elder women of Urfa will not consider ignoring their banishment, but Kiya tried to soften Palai's attitude toward them."

Pumi said, "Wait." He reached into his traveling bag and withdrew a small package. "I brought this for you," he said as he handed her a colorfully wrapped package.

She excitedly took it, opened it, and squealed with delight. "Oh, Pumi. They are beautiful. I shall wear them every day." She put on bracelets of polished stones and seashells and held them up to her wrists to admire. "You are trying to bribe me, aren't you?"

Saparu, Palai, Moonman. Nanatan, Vivekamulla, Vaniyal, Littlestar. Irakka, Mari, Irul.

He replied, "Not I—but perhaps Kiya is—she talked a long time about needing your support. He reached into his bag again, pulled out a large, elaborately wrapped package, and handed it to her.

She took it, felt its weight, looked at Pumi, looked again at the package, and slowly unwrapped it. She stared at the contents with wide eyes.

Pumi explained, "It's a walking stick, just like the one she gave to me, but mine has a blue geode in the handle. Yours is golden like einkorn tassels in the sun. She said to tell you of her deep love, respect, and admiration for you."

"It's beautiful, almost as beautiful as the bracelets you gave me. But I shall wear the bracelets every day. A walking stick, I'm not sure how useful it is, but it *is* gorgeous. We can place it on a wall as a decoration to remind us of Kiya. Now—tell me about your negotiations, which were either a huge failure or a huge success—which was it?"

Pumi became reserved. "She wants Tallstone's permission—my permission—to set up trading tables at Riverport. No banished Titan will cross the river; only followers who were never banished. I told her candidly about Vanam's growing hatred of her. She and her children were supposed to die a desolate death on barren plains. Instead, they prosper. Vanam wants her to suffer—greatly. I told her that Urfa would not receive her because she and her children had been banished. No proper tribesman will even look upon them. She insisted that her trading people were not outcasts, and they would not leave the Riverport docks, anyway. She demanded that I either forbid it or NOT forbid it—that she would address any issues with Vanam—that this was her duty and hers alone. We talked for a long time. I could not dissuade her."

He paused, sipped his Bitter, and said, "I did not forbid it and I fear the worst. We will know early into the Festival if I chose well or failed."

Valki asked, "What did she wear?"

Pumi responded, "What?"

She repeated, "What did she wear during your long, private negotiations? How long did she remain dressed? Was she pretty?"

He was silent for a while and then replied, "The dress was red with a deep cut down the front. It had a long slit up the side, exposing her leg. She was beyond beautiful—like a painted work of art. She told me she would bear me a son. His name will be Cronus. We coupled five times."

Vanam, Kiya, Pumi, Valki, Putt, Putt-pay, Breathson, Littlerock.

Valki replied, "I see."

Pumi quietly said, "You are a beautiful sunrise on a spring morning—like golden tops of golden einkorn reflecting golden sun—like the heavens above on a crisp, clear evening. To mate with you one time brings me more joy than mating with Kiya five times. You are my love—my life."

She sat for a moment, stood, looked down at him, and said, "Liar! Come—let's have our evening meal. Then you will couple with me in every position that you did with her—and then in one position of my choosing. If you please me, I will consider allowing you to leave my bed."

32. Valki Goes to Tartarus

The next year in Year 44; ages 0, 40, 34, 31.

The seasons went on as did life.

In Tartarus, Kiya gave birth to Cronus.

Pumi was invited to come and meet his son. It was natural that Pumi would invite Valki to go with him. Valki accepted his invitation without hesitation.

She said to Pumi, "I'm so excited! Are you sure my dress looks exactly like the one she wore? I love this color. I should tell my Festival Girls to wear red when they start the festival. Should I take my walking stick like yours or would that be too much? It *is* a visit to meet your son, after all. I don't want to overdo it—like I'm threatened or something. Do you think the baby will like the mobile? It hangs from the ceiling and a breeze turns it continuously. The little animal figures are so cute, aren't they? Should I take a gift to Kiya, too? Some sweetbreads with nuts or something? Will the baby look like you? You are both so tall! I've never been that far west. It's a long journey, isn't it? Kiya is much older than I am, you know. But she never seems to age at all. She will look so much younger and prettier than me. Will you be ashamed of me? Should I wear makeup, maybe? I am not as well-traveled as I should be. You are *so* well-traveled, Pumi. Do you think I will do all right when I see Kiya and your baby? But really, you should know that I am happy about this. I could never bear you a child. I have always felt guilty about that. I'm glad Kiya did. I really am!"

< >

They traveled west to Tartarus to meet Pumi's infant son, Cronus.

And where Valki met Cronus and everyone else.

Kiya's family was as infatuated with their Great Aunt Valki of Urfa as she was with the Titans and what they had done. After the official activities, introductions, laughter, and all-around good times were complete, Valki and Kiya finally found time to become two women, long parted, rich in experience. The two important, powerful, accomplished women retired to Kiya's private chambers, where they fell into each other's arms and cried.

Finally, they sat back in Kiya's comfortable chairs and stared at one another. Drinking cups were raised and gossip was shared.

Vanam, Kiya, Pumi, Valki, Putt, Putt-pay, Breathson, Littlerock.

They giggled as Kiya told of Pumi's unfulfilled boyhood attraction to her and how she finally faced her desire to bed Pumi. Kiya listened in disgust of Vanam's attempt to enter Valki and with wonder hearing of Valki's seduction under the tall stone. They shared the tribulations of the powerful and the impossibility of doing the right thing because every action gave bad results along with the good. They talked of power and management techniques and change and success and failure and the sadness of the poor in spirit.

Valki talked of cabbages, Kiya of kings. They agreed that in the long arc of time, cabbages would prevail.

The two women from the Clan of the Serpent slowly began to realize what it really meant to be Kiya of Tartarus and Valki of Urfa and that they had changed the world.

For better or for worse.

The next day, Valki and Pumi said goodbyes and departed Tartarus.

Saparu, Palai, Moonman. Nanatan, Vivekamulla, Vaniyal, Littlestar. Irakka, Mari, Irul.

33. Breathson's Return and Parting

Two years later; ages 0, 42, 36, 33.

Several years passed.

Valki inspected her great fields of einkorn. The work of the two astronomy-trained women had brought significant improvements. Planting times were targeted. Crop yields increased dramatically. Valki played less and less of a role in the operation of Urfa. It had grown so large. So many buildings were being added. She had several councils dedicated to directing different operations of her community. One of the female dogs from Nay's first litter had given birth to her own litter.

The second season of the year was coming to an end. A full-scale planting would take place in two more seasons. It had been over three years since Breathson had left. "No more than two years" is what Pumi had told her. *Liars. All men are liars. He will never come back. He is dead, or some young woman enchanted him, or they just kept walking. Liars. All of them. They just tell you what you want to hear.*

Still, she continually scanned the horizon. Just in case.

She scanned the horizon.

A strange beast walked her way. Then another. A wolfdog ran beside them—herding them—toward Urfa. Two more beasts appeared and then two more. The beasts obeyed the commands of the wolfdog. She stared—and waited—then *they* appeared.

She did not fall to her knees. She did not run toward them. She stood motionless and watched them draw closer.

Breathson saw her and broke into a run. "Mother. Mother. I am home. I have brought my auroch friends home with me."

He came to her. She took him by his shoulders and stared at him without expression. Nay herded his auroch subjects onward. Mustakshaf nodded his head in salute as he walked past the woman and her son.

Valki then violently embraced Breathson and held him close. She said, "Yes, Son. You have. I am so happy to see you. I am so proud of you. You did what you set out to do. You are a man. I am so pleased. Welcome home, Breathson."

Breathson did not try to express himself. He merely accepted the intense embrace of his mother.

Vanam, Kiya, Pumi, Valki, Putt, Putt-pay, Breathson, Littlerock.

The evening meal was crowded.

Valki stood and introduced their guests of honor. She said, "Now tell us everything, Breathson. Everything that you did."

Breathson stood and looked over the eating area. He said, "I went to where the aurochs live. Nay went with me. Mustakshaf went with me. We made friends with aurochs. Some aurochs came home to live with me." He sat down.

Valki said, "I see. Nicely told, Breathson. Mustakshaf, do you have anything you could add?"

Mustakshaf stood. "A few details, I suppose. Aurochs are all over, but the great herds are in the south. We needed a large herd that didn't move around too much. We traveled a long time before Breathson found the herd he was looking for. We studied the herd for many seasons. Then we studied individuals. We moved among them, letting them grow accustomed to us. Breathson began touching them, talking to them. Most bolted at his touch; some didn't. He began offering favorite foods to the females that didn't flinch at his touch. They would finally eat from his hands. We made a dedicated feeding place for the most accepting females. They began to depend on Breathson. When Breathson decided that eight were his friends, we had to wait until they became pregnant. It took six seasons to bring them back to Urfa because we had to wait until the calves they gave birth to along the way were strong enough to travel. Nay was a great help. She learned to command them to go in the direction Breathson wanted them to go. Once, she alerted us to predators stalking us. We kept our spears ready. We built fires at night. The fires and Nay's barking kept the predators away. With unceasing effort, all the aurochs survived. Wild aurochs are difficult to control but Breathson has brought us tame aurochs. Their worth to Urfa is unlimited—they produce raw power, milk we can drink, meat, hides. It is glorious."

Mustakshaf became embarrassed and sat down.

Everyone at the evening meal stood and applauded the returning explorers.

Valki felt happiness return to her. *Where have you been, happiness? Oh, yes, I remember—in the land where the aurochs are.*

< Leaving >

The enclosure Putt had built for the eventuality of a captured auroch was not sufficient. It needed to be much larger and with access to the stream.

Breathson went to Putt and explained.

Saparu, Palai, Moonman. Nanatan, Vivekamulla, Vaniyal, Littlestar. Irakka, Mari, Irul.

Book One. *The Beginning of Civilization: Mythologies Told True*

Putt told Breathson that it would be done, but that first he had to travel to Tallstone, to meet with the skywatchers. He would build the enclosure when he returned.

Breathson was emphatic. "No. Build it now. You will build it now before you leave. The aurochs must have a larger home now!"

"When I return, Breathson," Putt told him. "This meeting has been planned and must be accomplished before the full moon. I don't have time to build your enclosure now. I will do it as soon as I return."

Fury built within Breathson. Old, imagined slights loomed larger. His inability to articulate his needs frustrated him. "No. Build it now. You will build it now before you leave. It must be built now!"

"No," Putt said and turned to walk away.

Breathson, much larger and stronger than Putt, brutally grabbed Putt's shoulder and spun him back around. "No! Build it now! I will tell Pumi to command you to build it. Pumi will command you to build it because I will tell him to. Pumi loves me more than he loves you. He has always loved me more. Pumi will command you to build it! Now!"

Putt's face turned red; his breath came rapidly. "No!" said Putt. He turned again and began walking away.

Breathson spun him around again and put his face inches away from his brother's. Spittle flew into Putt's face as Breathson screamed, "He loves me more! They both do! They always have! They will MAKE you do as I command."

Putt's cutting blade slipped gently into Breathson's heart. Blood gushed easily from his body and flowed to fertilize the earth beneath their feet. Putt held his brother's dying body tightly to his own. "Yes," Putt whispered. "Yes, they always have."

Nay lay down at the feet of her master as her master's rich, warm blood seeped into the fertile earth beneath.

Putt carried his brother's body in his arms to the front of the porch of the main building. He faced the building and sank to his knees, still holding his brother's bloodied body.

An elder woman saw them first. She screamed.

All ran through the open door and stood to look at the unimaginable.

Vanam, Kiya, Pumi, Valki, Putt, Putt-pay, Breathson, Littlerock.

They parted as Valki walked through the gathered women. She cleaned the dust of ground einkorn from her hands. She did not scream. She walked to her sons and fell to her knees. The dagger was still in Breathson's chest, a statement of what had happened. Valki looked at Putt. He would not return her gaze. She held out her arms and took Breathson's body from Putt. She lowered her head to Breathson's bloody chest. She did not scream.

< >

She buried her son in the original einkorn field, beside Palai and Moonman.

After the other mourners had left the grave, Valki turned to Pumi and violently ripped his tunic from his body. She stared at him with fury. "I never bore you a child. I am not a woman—not a person—I WILL bear you a child—I WILL!" She shoved him to the ground and mounted him. "I WILL—I WILL!"

Her thrusts eventually caused the uninterested Pumi to respond to her demand.

Her fury—her despair—her anguish—her hatred—her love—washed through and over their bodies.

Like torrential, unending rain.

< The Wanderer >

At sunrise the next morning, Pumi walked to the pastures and found Putt standing inside the freshly enlarged auroch enclosure absent-mindedly stroking the forehead of an auroch.

Putt walked and placed his arms over the auroch.

The two men stood in silence for a long time.

Finally, Pumi said, "What will you do? Where will you go?"

Putt replied, "Away—far away—I suppose. I can wander the eastern lands. Maybe do some good for people I find there. Maybe not. I have already packed. Should I speak to Mother or simply go?"

"Your mother's mind is somewhere else. When it returns, I will tell her you bid her farewell. She loves you both, you know. But this is difficult for her. You had your reasons. He had a difficult life. He was difficult to talk with. But he is at peace now. I hope you can find peace in your travels. You have my love. You have, in her way, your mother's love. I will not see you again, son. Be well."

Pumi turned and left his son absent-mindedly stroking the forehead of an auroch.

Saparu, Palai, Moonman. Nanatan, Vivekamulla, Vaniyal, Littlestar. Irakka, Mari, Irul.

34. Winter Solstice Festival 34

Fourteen years later; ages 0, 56, 50, 47.

Years became years became years.

The great horn sounded. Three young, vibrant women dressed in identical red dresses with a slit up the side ran onto the stage below the tall stone. Hands held high in the air, they shouted in unison, "ARE YOU READY TO HAVE A FESTIVAL?"

The original chiefs were now dead, but their clans lived on. Their clans still gathered each year for their festival and even more tribes joined them.

Pumi now watched from the crowd rather than with Littlestar at the tall stone. He watched their performance with admiration. They introduced the chiefs, sang songs, danced to the drumbeat, and drew the crowd into a frenzy. Just like Valki did—better—she would be proud.

The horn sounded again. The three women dismissed the raucous crowd with the scream, "LET'S GO HAVE OURSELVES A FESTIVAL!"

Pumi said to his young son, "We should have made her come, Replaceson."

"My leaving is difficult enough for her, Father. Watching this would simply add to her despair."

"You are right, of course. I'm proud of you, son. I wish your mother could share my joy. I wish it so much."

"I would fly to the heavens and touch the lights if wishes were fulfilled, Father. She will be happy enough. After the first year, I can return to Urfa every full moon. You and Mother should have had more children. Being a child would have been more fun with someone younger to command."

Pumi laughed. "We did try. Many times. You were the only attempt that took. That's why you mean so much to your mother. When my son murdered her son—I mean—when our older son murdered our younger son, it was beyond her bearing. She poured all her love into you. She doesn't care about the festival anymore. Urfa runs well enough without her guidance every minute. You should have seen her back in the day, Replaceson. Neither you nor I—nor anybody else—could keep up with her. She was a force of nature."

He paused and then continued, "Well, are you ready to formally meet your soon-to-be master, the great Littlestar? We are honored that he demanded

Vanam, Kiya, Pumi, Valki, Putt, Putt-pay, Breathson, Littlerock.

you be his apprentice. He doesn't do that anymore, you know. He has Masters of Masters who bow before him. Don't worry if you don't live up to expectations. Nobody could. You are the son of Pumi of Tallstone and Valki of Urfa. I'm sorry—it will be a heavy burden. Do the best you can. Your mother and I will be proud of you no matter what happens."

The boy laughed as he said, "More demanding than myself? Maybe."

They walked side by side to stand in the long line waiting to meet Littlestar and the scholars. All the masters recognized Pumi and would have happily escorted him and his son to the head of the line. But they had strict instructions. Pumi wished to be treated equally with all others. He and his son would wait in line with everyone else to meet Master-of-Masters Littlestar of Tallstone.

The two were finally received by Littlestar. He said, "Master Pumi and young Replaceson. This is a wonderful moment in my life! Welcome, Pumi! Welcome, Replaceson! I shall take good care of him, Pumi. I shall teach him all there is to know of Astronomy. He will become the great skywatcher you never were. He will be taught the arts of all of our scholars."

Pumi replied, "Replaceson is an eager and interested student of all things, Great Master Littlestar. He can fashion rock better than me, build as well as Putt could, and knows as much about planting and crops as his esteemed mother. His mind may run out of places to store all of the information."

"Ah, he will be the first to know everything there is! But can he hunt?"

Replaceson answered without irony, "Great Master, I have hunted and killed an antelope and dressed it. It was interesting enough but being in the growing fields at sunrise with my mother is more rewarding."

Littlestar laughed again as he said, "Return at the half-moon. We will begin your familiarization then. You will be initiated into our order under the new moon after the festival has ended. I will allow your father to observe. He has participated in enough of them. I look forward to our new life together, Replaceson. Now, go with your father and enjoy the festival that your father began but which no one remembers."

The three exchanged smiles. The father and son then moved on to walk the grounds amid the people.

Replaceson asked, "*You* started the festival, Father?"

Saparu, Palai, Moonman. Nanatan, Vivekamulla, Vaniyal, Littlestar. Irakka, Mari, Irul.

"I had a hand in it, but it is your mother that the old ones remember—jumping on the stage, getting everyone excited. She took the thing over. It became as much Valki's festival as the chief's festival. It blurs together over the years. Do you want to try your skill at wrestling?"

"No, maybe javelin throwing. That seems more useful."

"Javelin throwing, it is!"

As they walked to the throwing fields Pumi said, "By the way—I did start these games—single-handedly—just so you know."

< Acceptance >

After Replaceson had been initiated into the Tallstone Society of Scholars, Pumi returned to Urfa.

He found Valki standing staring over her fields. He approached her from behind and put his arms around her. She did not turn. She leaned against him and asked, "Is it done?"

"It is done. Our son is on his way to becoming a scholar. All went well. They gave him a new name—'Seth.' You are to be pleased and proud—of both our son and your festival. Your three entertainers always exceed your hopes."

She asked, "He will be well? He wasn't nervous about leaving home?"

"We raised him to be self-confident and independent, Valki. You can't have it both ways. But he did express concern for you. He wants you to be happy—for him and for yourself. He will be out of your sight for only a year and then he will come home every full moon."

She said, "Breathson was gone for more than three years, and he came home, didn't he?"

"Yes. And life went on except for Breathson. Shall we cry?"

She twisted in his arms, hugged him, and stood back. "No. I have a better idea. Let's go try again."

He laughed. "Let's!"

< Renewal >

She lay contentedly in his arms. She whispered, "I'm going to be all right. I have been remiss in my duties at Urfa. My Council of Elder Women has a long list of things I should have been addressing all these years. They have

Vanam, Kiya, Pumi, Valki, Putt, Putt-pay, Breathson, Littlerock.

invented new words like 'corruption,' 'theft,' 'disease,' 'insolence,' and 'laziness.' A lot of new words that I don't want to know about. Words created for people who no longer hunt and gather. Words for problems I created with my little 'Last Camp.' I only wanted Moonman and Vivekamulla to have a place to die in peace. Something happened. There were unintended consequences. Should I be sad or happy with my little city? I must do all that I can do to help them, and it is past time that I address these issues. I am ready, Pumi. I release you from your self-imposed bondage to me. Go back out into your world of Tallstone and Rockplace and the lands beyond. Go change the world, again. Go create a new Earth. It's been a while."

"We could travel together."

"We could. But my heart is here—with my fields—my crops—my city—my people. Your heart is out there. The western lands grow more civilized. They could use your talents. Visit Kiya. She would like that. But I expect to see you at least once a year. More if you can. Less if you can't. You entertain me so. But when all is said—you are Pumi, and I am Valki.

Saparu, Palai, Moonman. Nanatan, Vivekamulla, Vaniyal, Littlestar. Irakka, Mari, Irul.

35. The City

Five years later; 0, 61, 55, 52.

Pumi visited Valki at least every change of season and each winter solstice. The years passed.

Valki dedicated herself to solving the problems of her city. Urfa's big day arrived.

Pumi sat on a stone fence surrounding the man-made lake facing the new building soon to be dedicated. The building would become Urfa's center. He had arrived early to ensure a good view. He stayed out of Valki and Putt-pay's way while they completed their preparations for the ceremony. Putt-pay had proposed a new, large building to house the ceremonial and administrative functions of the city. Pumi had proposed adding a lake to the front of the building. It would be decorative and functional. He had seen such a thing on his travels and helped Putt-pay in the design and construction. He also added stone obelisks on either side of the entrance of the road connecting Urfa to Tallstone. Seeing the completed complex impressed even Pumi.

Valki was thrilled with the result. Putt-pay, Pumi, and all concerned breathed a collective sigh of relief.

The ceremony would begin when the sun reached its highest point, and now, Highsun approached. The crowd grew. Everyone in Urfa and Tallstone would attend. They were overwhelmed by the size of the building. It was two levels tall. Putt-pay had used every building trick he knew in its construction. Porches surrounded all sides on both levels. Windows and doors allowed air to flow freely through the building. An atrium allowed light to flood both floors. The atrium could be covered if needed to keep out the rain. A fire could be built in a stone fire pit on either level, and the smoke would be discharged outside above the roof. A street circumnavigated the building where a flag representing each known tribe flew. Fragrant shrubs were planted to accent the building and grounds.

The Administrative Building, as did the other buildings, faced Urfa Street which ran due west from the einkorn fields.

The crowd grew restless. Pumi stood on the rock for a clear view of the front porch.

A great bell pealed.

Vanam, Kiya, Pumi, Valki, Putt, Putt-pay, Breathson, Littlerock.

Valki strode from the front door with hands high in the air, to face the crowd. She let the resulting chaos go on for a while, then lowered her hand to demand silence, and said, "Is not this a glorious day?!"

The crowd erupted again. She smiled at them, egged them on, and once again silenced them. "This is all for you, People of Urfa. This is the result of your hard, dedicated work throughout the years, the culmination of the vision and unending work of our Builders Guild, of its Master Putt-pay, of Urfa's Council of Elder Women, of our Council of Health and Sickness, of our farmers, our hunters, our traders, our programs of education and training of our children. This is the culmination of the vision of our Citizens."

The small interruptions by the crowd erupted into one large interruption. She could not quiet them. Eventually, she motioned Putt-pay to join her on the porch—then the masters of the Builders Guild—then the Council of Elder Women. The noise roared on. She then dismissed all but Putt-pay to go to their offices within the building.

She, at last, obtained the silence of the crowd.

She spoke. "A tribal chief demands absolute obedience of the tribe—or else. We do not demand absolute obedience. We, the people, will learn to make our own decisions with integrity and intelligence for the benefit of *all* people—everywhere. This must become our nature, or we will revert to our old ways of life. Change is hard and may not be possible. It is up to each of us. The name of the man standing on the box with the rope around his neck is Nungarra. The Council of Urfa commanded him to leave Urfa three times because he took from others what was not his to take. He would leave but then return and again take things not his to take. We have no chief to tell Nungarra what to think and what to do. It is my wish that he learns these things for himself. If not, he will remain unenlightened and can do as he wishes—just not in Urfa. Nungarra will remain gagged and standing there with the rope around his neck for two days. At the end of two days, if he still stands, he will be released and commanded to go away. If he does not leave or if he leaves and returns, he shall stand on the box for a quarter moon. If he cannot remain standing, then he will die. His body will be left hanging to rot. The hanging post is surrounded by fragrant and lovely shrubs. He will die surrounded by beauty he could not bring into his world. But now, let us celebrate our enlightened citizens who take us into our new future. Let us visit the rewards of civilization!"

Saparu, Palai, Moonman. Nanatan, Vivekamulla, Vaniyal, Littlestar. Irakka, Mari, Irul.

She held out an arm toward the great building and said, "Ceremonial and meeting rooms are on the first floor—offices for your councils and administrative leaders are on the upper floor. I am Valki of Urfa. My office is always open to you."

Valki then shouted, "Enter and see what you have built!"

The bell rang. Putt-pay stood at the door to control how many entered at one time. Valki left and walked through the crowd to join Pumi.

That evening a large fire was built outside the city gates. Tables were set up with meats, sweetbreads, and all manner of food. Drummers drummed. Everyone came. It was almost sunrise before Valki and Pumi returned to their home.

< Contentment >

Valki and Pumi were in no hurry to rise. They lay together in their bed until late morning.

She said, "Putt-pay is taking care of the offices today. We knew that I would be too tired. I have been feeling weak lately. He and Seth will join us for the evening meal. The little street festival was Seth's idea. He told me, 'We can't have a festival to last a season, but we can have one to last a night!' He was right, wasn't he? Everything went so well."

Pumi replied, "Yes, Seth is the best of both of us—better than either of us. Are you sure you aren't ready for the two of us to start walking toward the east and never stop? Our worlds will be left in good hands."

She laughed and snuggled closer to him. "Soon enough, my mate. I am content now. The problems Urfa creates have been addressed as well as I can address them. It's time for the Sweating Sickness to begin again, but my Council of Health and Sickness has made a lot of progress. They had Putt-pay construct a building dedicated to taking care of the sick. They keep detailed accounts of each person who becomes sick. They will learn from where it comes and who will get it. Most recover but not all, especially the old. I have done all that I can do, I think. It took a long time, but I am content."

"Shall we try to have another child?"

She laughed. "I am a little old for that, Pumi. But yes! Let's try!"

< Gossip >

At Highsun, she still lay in his arms. "That was nice. I shouldn't tell you this because it won't do either one of us any good."

Vanam, Kiya, Pumi, Valki, Putt, Putt-pay, Breathson, Littlerock.

"Tell me what?"

"I always gossip with the old women and the farmer girls. Did you know that hunters aren't that interested in mating or that accomplished in doing it? They seem to have a need they want to rid themselves of—the sooner the better. The women find the builders much more interesting to mate with. Builders treat the woman with respect like when they are crafting a piece of wood into something beautiful. The farmer girls said that a builder sometimes actually brings them pleasure. I blurted out, 'Pumi always brings me pleasure!' I was embarrassed that I had spoken so—but their eyes widened—they asked, 'Always? May he visit us in the fields when you don't want him?' I told them, 'Sorry girls, but I always want him.' I considered giving you as a prize to the woman who had the best farming record each season. Would you have liked that, Pumi? To be given away as a trophy?"

He laughed. "Had you commanded it, it would have been my duty. Anything for you."

She laughed as she embraced him. "Let them find their own pleasure."

< Closure >

As Valki prepared the evening meal, she saw Putt-pay, Mustakshaf, and Nay approach. Behind them were Seth and Littlestar. Valki's heart soared.

They ate the evening meal on the front porch of their house. The porch faced west; toward the sunsets, with a view of the original einkorn field where she now buried her dead and with Urfa in the distance. Pumi and Valki were the only inhabitants of Urfa to have their own personal home. Putt-pay had built it for them soon after Putt murdered Breathson.

Seth talked with great enthusiasm about the continuing work at Tallstone. "All tribes now send their skywatchers to be trained here. We have guilds for astronomers, stonemasons, shepherds, builders, farmers, and shamans. Littlestar and I need to talk with your Council on Health and Sickness. People seem to become sick more often. We may want to form a guild so that we can exchange health information with all tribes, although this does seem to be more prevalent in Urfa and the little villages beginning to form."

Putt-pay asked how Valki wanted to handle the incessant requests for personal homes from young, mated couples. "They see you and Pumi have your own house. They want to know why they and their children must live in communal buildings. It is beyond my imagination if we start building houses for individuals. The city would explode with new buildings. Already

Saparu, Palai, Moonman. Nanatan, Vivekamulla, Vaniyal, Littlestar. Irakka, Mari, Irul.

the best wood has been harvested from our nearby woodlands. Where would it end?"

Mustakshaf talked of his continued work with his animal friends—aurochs and dogs, especially. He said, "Mother Valki, you need to come to the ranch and select a puppy to live with you. They bring joy and protection. A new litter is being born as we speak. Come in two seasons and select a new friend. Maybe bring back a friendly auroch. I believe you could train it to work in your fields. Putt and Breathson would be pleased."

There was frozen silence at the table. Putt's name had not been spoken in front of Valki since he had murdered Breathson a lifetime ago.

Seth finally said, "It is time to speak of it, Mother. Are you ready?"

Valki stared into nothingness as she shook her head, "Yes."

Seth said, "Putt-pay told me the story many times. Of how Putt found Putt-pay at Tallstone and confessed that he had killed Breathson. Of endless things said. Of seeking forgiveness for the unforgivable. Putt-pay could tell of what was said far into the night. But in the end, what matters is this:"

Seth looked at Putt-pay, and said, "Builder Putt-pay, deliver Putt's message to his mother."

Putt-pay rose and leaned against the table. He looked into the moist eyes of Valki and said, "I am commanded by my master, Putt, when the time comes, to say these words to his mother, Valki: 'If time ever softens the horror of what I have done, then know this. I spend my life seeking atonement. I love my brother Breathson. If you can ever forgive me, face east and tell me so. I will hear you. I love you. Your son, Putt.'"

Putt-pay sat down.

Dumbly, Valki rose and walked to the east side of her house. Pumi followed behind.

With folded arms, she stared into the distance for a long time; moving her lips; saying words Pumi could not hear.

Finally, she turned, smiled at Pumi, and said, "I feel better, now."

They walked back and rejoined the others on the porch.

Valki: "Now, let us talk of children and dogs and parks where they play; of the pool we can wade in on hot days. Let us speak of the joy of life."
Pumi: "We need some drummers here. And a girl to sing songs."

Vanam, Kiya, Pumi, Valki, Putt, Putt-pay, Breathson, Littlerock.

Seth: "Yes. And a guild for drummers. Maybe drumming can be expanded into something useful!"

They all laughed.

Valki talked with Pumi, Seth, and her friends well into the night. Finally, she said, "I will leave the men to talk of manly things, but now I am tired."

< Fever >

Pumi came to their bed late in the night. He slipped in behind her and wrapped his arms around her without waking her. They slept for a while.

Her trembling woke him. He lay for a moment and then felt the heat coming from her body. He sat up and felt her. She was hot and covered with sweat. He rose and lit a lamp. Her face was flush, her breathing labored. He brought a wet cloth and washed her body.

She said, "Pumi, I don't feel well."

"I will get someone from the Council of Health to come and tend to you. They will know what to do. Don't be frightened. Rest until we return."

Pumi dressed and ran full speed to the building housing the women he sought. Three dressed and returned with him immediately. They brought their bags of liquids, potions, ointments, and healing herbs.

They found her incoherent. The women applied their formidable skills to their Great Mother Valki.

In the morning light, they came to Pumi. One said to him, "Our medicines have helped, but only a little. We will try new mixtures, but Pumi, she is old and weak. We will stay with her and minister to her, but the Sweating Sickness shows little mercy to the old or weak. I will call you if she regains consciousness."

Pumi said, "I will stay with her. She must know that I am with her."

She lay there for two days. Many people milled around outside her house but only Pumi and the three attendants saw her.

On the morning of the third day, she opened her eyes and reached out. "Pumi? Are you here? I can't see. Are you here?"

He took her hand. "I am here. You have been resting. Do you feel better?"

"Yes. I believe I am ready now. Did I please you, Pumi? I tried so hard to please you. Even if I did take over your festival. I remember the first time

Saparu, Palai, Moonman. Nanatan, Vivekamulla, Vaniyal, Littlestar. Irakka, Mari, Irul.

I saw you—walking past me—you were beautiful. Everyone thought you were wonderful. Do you remember holding me during that terrible rain when I trembled so? You thought I was scared and miserable. You were so silly. I trembled because it was the first time anyone had ever held me close. At least after Mother died. I did well at the festivals, didn't I? And learning to grow the einkorn? And Urfa? Did I please you, Pumi?"

Tears formed in his eyes. "You pleased me greatly, Valki. We were so good together. No man could be more pleased."

"Yes, we were so ..." She became silent. Her blind eyes widened as she looked beyond Pumi. *Mother? Is that you? Mother! I lived. Be proud of me. I lived! I still hear the songs you sang to me. Vivekamulla? I thought you were dead and yet there you stand. I remember when I asked you to be my mother. Do you remember that? ... And Moonman, you old moonwatcher, you ... There you all are ... Breathson! My son, how I have missed you. You were like me—different—no one wanted you around—they mocked you—but we both did well, didn't we? Everyone's here—Is it a festival?*

In her mind, they segued into one beautiful light—a light that looked like everyone she had ever lost—that looked like her talking to the man sitting on a trail, like her running after her tribe, like the first time she saw Pumi. Her when she first lay with him, her running onto a stage, a lifetime of hers—all at one time.

The light seemed to hold out its arms. It seemed to say, "I am Valki of Urfa and I have come for you."

< Next Day >

Her cleaned, perfumed body lay in the center of the great building for two days. All came and beheld her. From Urfa, from Tallstone, everyone who knew of her passing came. Pumi, Putt-pay, and Seth greeted and thanked each person.

He buried her next to Breathson—in the einkorn field.

At the foot of her grave, Pumi placed the bench on which she, Breathson, and he had sat when they visited Wolfchief.

At the head, he placed a carved stone. On it, he engraved the image of a woman. Beneath the woman were engraved three children. Beneath the children, an image of a large building. Beneath that, twenty-four smaller buildings. In the blank spaces that remained, he carved images of einkorn—endless einkorn.

Vanam, Kiya, Pumi, Valki, Putt, Putt-pay, Breathson, Littlerock.

36. Soliloquy

After it was done, Pumi asked Seth to travel with him for a few seasons.

They went to Pumi's old campsites. Pumi told of their history as he remembered days past. They encountered many tribes of hunter-gatherers but also found several small permanent settlements that grew einkorn and fished for their food. Wherever they encountered people, they were met with great respect and excitement. Everyone had heard of Seth of Tallstone. But to think that they now stood before Pumi, creator of Tallstone and the Winter Solstice Festival and all the knowledge that it generated, was an honor of unimaginable proportions.

Seth joked that Pumi was making this trip just to garner adulation.

His response was simply, "Perhaps."

Pumi did not dwell on the nostalgia of the old places but rather talked about what was now being done in all the different lands. He told Seth, "I'm free of all responsibility. I have done all I was meant to do. I'm going to travel to the east. I've never been there. Maybe that's where the dead live. Maybe I will find Valki there."

After three seasons of travel, they returned to Tallstone. Pumi embraced Seth and said, "I hope to see you again, my son—older and wiser."

Pumi returned to Urfa, where he sat on the great patio of the main office building and reflected on life. Late that night, Pumi slept in the house that Putt-pay had built. He spent the next day wandering the city—remembering every moment of its growth.

He ate his evening meal in the dining room, surrounded by Valki's people. They talked of Nungarra and if anyone had learned from his death by hanging. Of how difficult it was not to have a chief to tell you what to think, how to think, and when to think. Of how many in Urfa were uneasy when a strange and different person entered their city. Of what Valki had brought forth and if it could continue to grow without an all-controlling chief to destroy those who did not mindlessly obey his commands.

They talked of life. Of death. Of their new civilization.

Darkness came.

Pumi said his goodbyes and walked to sit on Wolfchief's bench facing Valki's grave.

Saparu, Palai, Moonman. Nanatan, Vivekamulla, Vaniyal, Littlestar. Irakka, Mari, Irul.

Book One. The Beginning of Civilization: Mythologies Told True

Good evening, Valki.

She wore black—at my son's wedding. The wedding was the last time I saw her, and I shall never see her again. She would, even now, accept me into her life—into her bed. But she is Kiya, and I am Pumi. My story is the story of Valki and Pumi. Kiya has her own story—a different story for a different time.

You wanted to hear every detail about the day but nothing of the night. Well, the night was as it should have been—and you were never threatened.

Seth and I have spent three seasons traveling and talking. I missed you. We talked of my retiring to Tallstone and training to become a shaman. But I remembered your words—"Go change the world, again."

He laughed out loud.

I doubt if I can change the world, but the world can change me. Tonight, I will sleep in our bed and undoubtedly reach out to touch you in my sleep.

At sunrise, I will begin walking due east until something stops me. I shall constantly be looking for you—in every plant—in every rock—in every tree. But I know that I will not find you. Within this body, I can only move into tomorrow. You still live, but only in yesterdays. I believe that every day that has ever existed—still exists. All things that lived in that day—still live in that day. But I cannot go to yesterday as long as I wear this body. I must shed it. Then I can travel to yesterdays. Then I will find you—and Breathson—and all whom I once knew.

I shall be patient and live each day as best I can.

I shall not come to this place again.

Aloud, he said, "You pleased me, greatly, Valki."

He rose and retired to their bed.

Vanam, Kiya, Pumi, Valki, Putt, Putt-pay, Breathson, Littlerock.

37. Tallstone

Twenty-two years later; ages 0, 83, 77, 0.

The years passed.

Cities grew. Many things changed but Tallstone remained the center of knowledge. After Littlestar died, Seth became Master-of-Masters.

On this day, a scout came to Tallstone out of the east riding a horse. With sign language and scattered words, he told the scholar that he sought Seth of Tallstone. Was this Tallstone? Was he Seth?

The scholar said, "Yes, this is Tallstone. No, I am not Seth. Wait here." The scholar hurried off and returned with Seth of Tallstone.

They exchanged greetings as best they could. Seth led him to a flat stone table, sat the visitor down, and ordered refreshments. Seth called for a scholar who understood the languages of the far east.

A scholar came and talked with the scout. The scholar—once he understood the scout's story—translated it for Seth.

Seth composed himself and asked, "When?"

The answer was at least two days, maybe three, but the scout would find the caravan and bring it to Tallstone as swiftly as he could because the old man barely lived. Every breath was labored—every breath perhaps his last.

The scout mounted his horse and left to find his people.

Seth prepared his people to welcome home Pumi of Tallstone. And to welcome and honor the people who brought him.

The caravan arrived in the early afternoon of the second day.

The scout led six men of rank followed by six strong men carrying a covered litter. Behind them were dozens of attendants, servants, and workers. Seth and his interpreter met the party and bowed in respect. Pleasantries were exchanged and ranks established.

The leader of the eastern delegation nodded to his litter carriers, who then sat the litter upon its six attached legs. The leader led Seth to the litter, paused, and said, "This is Vohu Manah, my friend and teacher."

He drew back the curtain on the litter. An old man lay there laboring for breath. He looked up, saw Seth, and said, "My son. I am home."

Saparu, Palai, Moonman. Nanatan, Vivekamulla, Vaniyal, Littlestar. Irakka, Mari, Irul.

The two talked for a while and then Pumi asked to be laid on his stone table. He requested a scribe come and record words he had spoken to Valki at her grave. He dictated, with labored breath, 'The Book of Pumi, thoughts on where the dead might live.'

He finished late in the day, asked for water, sipped it, held out his hand to his son, looked up toward the tall stone, closed his eyes, breathed deeply, and sighed, "Valki, is that you?"

< A New Heaven and Earth >

The next day was spent visiting, exchanging stories, exchanging knowledge, and preparing the body. That evening the scholars were ready for their ceremony.

Twelve scholars stood around the stone table in their auroch garments of knowledge. Facing the table sat rows of silent acolytes, heads bowed, wearing the necklaces that signified their guilds.

Logs and branches and twigs were piled on the table of stone. Over that, a bearskin robe signifying a chief had been laid. On the almost white bearskin, stems of einkorn had been strewn. On the einkorn on the almost-white bearskin robe on the logs and branches and twigs on the table of stone, lay the body of Pumi. He had lived 930 seasons—more than seventy-seven years—an impressive span of life.

The last sliver of the sun slid below the horizon. Master-of-Masters Seth walked up the hill to face the tall stone and place his hands upon it. He felt Pumi's presence in the stone. Seth looked skyward. "My Father, your name is honored by all people. Your work is everywhere. Your will is all around us. Bread is given to all who ask. Let us be worthy."

Seth walked to the ceremonial fire burning behind the tall stone and from it, lit a torch. He walked down the hill to stand before the stone table where Pumi the stonecutter lay.

He placed the torch upon the pyre.

Upon the table of stone—wood and flesh turned to fire and flame—fire and flame that, rising, saw the old heaven and earth pass away and become new once more.

Vanam, Kiya, Pumi, Valki, Putt, Putt-pay, Breathson, Littlerock.

Tallstone and the City: A New Heaven and Earth, Second Edition

< >

The Beginning of Civilization: Mythologies Told True

continues in

Book 2.
Kiya and Her Children: Rise and Fall of the Titans, Second Edition

which tells the story of
Vanam and Kiya in full.

And of the glory of her Titan children.

Available Fall 2024

Saparu, Palai, Moonman. Nanatan, Vivekamulla, Vaniyal, Littlestar. Irakka, Mari, Irul.

APPENDIX

Author's Notes

Gobekli Tepe is the world's oldest megalithic site. It was built by hunter-gatherers over ten thousand years ago and predates agriculture, animal domestication, and settlements.

It has no known reason to exist.

Wheat domestication is thought to have occurred within sixty miles of Gobekli Tepe.

Sanliurfa, in modern-day Turkey, lays claim to being the world's oldest city. It lies twelve miles from Gobekli Tepe.

This landscape provides the backdrop for my reimagining the tradition of the Garden of Eden and its people.

Glossary of Names and Places

Years are referenced from the birth of Vanam.
Dim = diminutive of a source name from the Akkadian, Sumerian, or Tamil languages.

Aman was mate to hunter Ramum and Vanam's biological mother by Chief Saparu. She was Pumi's adopted mother. {*dim of Sumerian "Ama + Vanam" or "Mother + Chief"*}

Aurochs were herd animals that Breathson domesticated into modern cattle.

Breathson was Valki's afflicted son whom she adopted from the Clan of the Lion. He was the first shepherd who domesticated wolves, aurochs, and other animals.

Banishment was a decree by a tribal chief that cast members out of his tribe. The banished were forbidden to approach or be approached by another person.

Bitter was a social drink made with various herbs.

Clan of the Auroch was the third clan to attend the Winter Solstice Festival.

Clan of the Crocodile was a tribe from the far southwestern lands. Notable members include Chief Eazim-Rayiys and Master Scout Mustakshaf.

Clan of the Eagle was a tribe encountered by the Clan of the Serpent from which Gatherer Kiya was obtained as mate to Vanam. Notable members include Chief Irakka, Elder Woman Sophia, Moonwatcher Irul, and Kiya.

Vanam, Kiya, Pumi, Valki, Putt, Putt-pay, Breathson, Littlerock.

Clan of the Lion was the first tribe to be designated "Clan" and was a founding tribe of the Winter Solstice Festival. Notable members include Chief Nanatan, Master Skywatcher Vaniyal, Skywatchers Littlestar and Voutch, and Elder Woman Vivekamulla. Notable members acquired include the foundling Valki.

Clan of the Serpent was the second tribe to be designated "Clan" and was a founding member of the Winter Solstice Festival. Notable members include Chief Saparu, Hunter/Chief Vanam, Moonwatchers Karan and Nilla, Elder Women Panti and Palai, Hunters Ramum, Valuvana, Maiyana, Master Stonecutters Pumi and Kattar, and Gatherer Amma. Notable members acquired from other tribes include Kiya, Valki, and Skywatcher Voutch. The tribe was originally Chief Saparu's and then Chief Vanam's.

Clan of the Scorpion was the fourth clan to attend the Winter Solstice Festival.

Cubit was one foot six inches in this narrative. See Measurements.

Eazim-Rayiys was chief of the Clan of the Crocodile.

Einkorn was a wild grain domesticated into wheat by Valki.

Encounter was a chance meeting between two tribes. Generally, the two tribes would agree to meet with one chief being selected as the host. The tribal elders would meet with their counterparts. The tribal elder women would negotiate to trade their eligible young women to eligible young hunters of the other tribe. Trade of skins, linens, food, spearheads, cutting instruments, baskets, and other necessary products would be negotiated. A feast would be held, and the members of the tribe would mingle. See Winter Solstice Festival.

Guardianstone was one of the twelve original monolith monuments placed to surround the tall stone to discourage children from disturbing the measurements being taken by astronomers. See Tallstone.

Guild was a collection of early scholars with similar interests. The first guild was the Skywatchers Guild, who wore necklaces of serpent skins to signify their guild. Then came the Stonemason Guild, identified by a necklace of stones. Then the Builder Guild, identified by a necklace of wood; the Agriculture Guild, identified by a necklace of wheat; and the Shepherd Guild, identified by a belt made from rabbit pelt. New disciplines would form thereafter as mutual interests were discovered. See scholars.

Saparu, Palai, Moonman. Nanatan, Vivekamulla, Vaniyal, Littlestar. Irakka, Mari, Irul.

Irakka was Clan of the Eagle chief. {*Dim of "Irakkamulla-Talaivar" or "compassionate leader."*}

Irul was Tribe of the Eagle moonwatcher. {*Dim of "Irul-Iravu" or "dark night."*}

Karan was the successor to Nilla as Clan of the Serpent moonwatcher. He was originally a hunter. {*Dim of "Palaiyatu-Vettaikkaran" or "Old Hunter."*}

Kattar was Clan of the Serpent stonecutter. {*Dim of "Kai-Kattar" or "Stonecutter."*}

Kiya was the daughter of Clan of the Eagle Chief Irakka and Eder Woman Sophia. She became mate to Vanam, Clan of the Serpent chief.

Kiya's adopted daughters were
1. Themis,
2. Mnemosyne,
3. Phoebe,
4. Tethys,
5. Theia,
6. Rhea.

Kiya's sons were
1. Firstson by Vanam, aka Rivermaster,
2. Secondson by Vanam, aka Sagacity,
3. Thirdson by Vanam,
4. Fourthson by Vanam,
5. Fifthson by Vanam, aka Piercer,
6. Cronus by Pumi.

Last Camp was a euphemism for "left to die." The elderly or disabled tribal member was given food, water, a spear, and tribal best wishes and was left behind at their "Last Camp."

Littlerock was Pumi's apprentice stonecutter and lifelong friend.

Littlestar was an apprentice to Vaniyal, Clan of the Lion skywatcher. He developed the concept of using shadows cast by the tall stone to better understand the motion of the constellations. He eventually became Master-of-Masters at Tallstone.

Maiyana was the second strongest hunter in the Clan of the Serpent. {*Dim of "Valimaiyana-Karam" or "Strong Arm."*}

Vanam, Kiya, Pumi, Valki, Putt, Putt-pay, Breathson, Littlerock.

Measurements:

Length: The most common unit of length was the cubit, which was equal to the distance from the elbow to the fingertips. The cubit was divided into smaller units, such as the palm and the finger.

Weight: The most common unit of weight was the shekel, which was equal to about eleven grams. The shekel was divided into smaller units, such as the half-shekel and the quarter-shekel.

Mnemosyne was the second adopted daughter of Kiya and Vanam.

Moonman was the elderly Clan of the Serpent moonwatcher and the second inhabitant of Urfa.

Moonwatcher was a less accomplished skywatcher. See Skywatcher.

Mustakshaf was the greatest scout of his time. Originally, the Clan of the Crocodiles scout, he retired to Tallstone and then immigrated to Urfa.

Nanatan was Clan of the Lion chief. {*Dim of "Nanamulla-Manitan" or "Wise Man."*}

Nay was the first dog; a fourth-generation wolf domesticated by Breathson.

Nilla was the original Clan of the Serpent moonwatcher. He was abandoned when he became useless to the chief. {*Dim of "Nila-Parvaivalar" or "Moonwatcher."*}

Nonti was a lame Clan of the Lion hunter who made his "Last Camp" at Urfa.

Nungarra was the thief hanged by the neck at Urfa. {*Sumerian for "foolish" or "disorderly."*}

Outcasts were tribal members banished from a tribe. No other people could look upon an Outcast. The group that Vanam banished from Clan of the Serpent were his mate, Kiya; his natural sons, Rivermaster, Sagacity, Thirdson, Fourthson, and Piercer; and his adopted daughters, Themis, Mnemosyne, Phoebe, Tethys, Theia, and Rhea.

Palai was the elderly Clan of the Serpent elder woman. She was the first inhabitant of Urfa. {*"Pen-Palaiyatu" or "Woman Old."*}

Palm was three inches in this narrative. See Measurements.

Panti was the successor to Palai as Clan of the Serpent Successor elder woman. {*Dim of "Pen-Pantittiyam" or "Woman Wise."*}

Saparu, Palai, Moonman. Nanatan, Vivekamulla, Vaniyal, Littlestar. Irakka, Mari, Irul.

Paravi was a senior elder woman of Urfa. When younger, she was Clan of the Auroch elder woman.

Pavett was a Clan of the Lion Hunter who made his Last Camp at Urfa.

Pen was a generic title for females. {*Tamil for "girl" and "woman."*}

Phoebe was the third adopted daughter of Kiya and Vanam.

Protector was the title given to a male who agreed to accept a female from another tribe to be under his protection. The protector would ensure the female was fed and clothed and was responsible for raising any children she might bear, either fathered by himself or by any other male. This was a tribal responsibility. Affection might, or might not, develop between the two. Generally, a female would never decline sexual requests from her protector or a higher-ranking male. Her acceptance of a male of her protector's rank or lower was her decision. A precursor to the concept of a mate and an arranged marriage.

Pumi was the Clan of the Serpent stonecutter and the premier stonecutter in the known lands. He founded the Tallstone Camp and Urfa Camp. He was the protector of Valki. He adopted Breathson and Putt as his sons. He was the biological father to Replaceson. {*Tamil for "Earth."*}

Putt was Pumi's adopted son from the Clan of the Lion. Putt mastered the art of building and was the first Builder. {*Dim of "Putticalli" or "Clever."*}

Putt-pay was Putt's apprentice builder obtained from the Clan of the Lion.

Ramum was Chief Saparu's second in command and was tasked with raising Vanam and Pumi as his sons. {*Dim of Akkadian "Rab Habrum" or "Best Hunter."*}

Replaceson was the only biological son of Pumi and Valki. He joined the Tallstone Skywatcher Guild and was renamed Seth.

Rhea was an adopted daughter of Kiya and Vanam.

Rockplace was a campsite favored by Pumi due to the great selection of rock available for him to carve premium spearheads and cutting tools. He eventually manipulated the tribal elders into moving their campsite farther south to Tallstone because the new site was more favorable for gatherers. Rockplace was the source of the stones used to construct Tallstone Camp.

Vanam, Kiya, Pumi, Valki, Putt, Putt-pay, Breathson, Littlerock.

Rock Table was the flat worktable that Pumi inadvertently carved from a massive rock at Rockplace. The hunters and gatherers discovered that it was useful for separating grains and butchering game. A tradition evolved that hunters would run their fingers over engravings it contained as they departed camp for a hunt. Pumi eventually found a way to move the table to the Tallstone Camp, where it was placed due south of the tall stone.

Seth, see Replaceson.

Scholars were students of a specific area of interest who met, shared knowledge, and dedicated themselves to developing the knowledge in their field. Their center of learning developed at Tallstone. See Guilds.

Season was one month beginning on the new moon and divided into quarter moons. Tribes would camp, hunt, and gather for one season and then migrate to a new campsite.

Skywatcher was the chief council, along with the elder woman, to a tribal chief. He was responsible for monitoring the moon and heavens and deciding when to break camp and which direction to travel to set up the next camp.

Sophia was Clan of the Eagle elder woman and mate to Chief Irakka. She was the mother of Kiya. {*Greek for "Wisdom."*}

Starrock was Pumi's cross-trained apprentice.

Stillhunter was a constellation used by Skywatcher Vaniyal to track the twelve seasons of the year and identify the winter solstice, the moment when daylight began increasing.

Stone Cutting Tools include hammerstones used for striking, anvil stones used as a hard surface against which to hammer a stone, burins with chisel-like edges for carving and engraving, plus grinders, flaking tools, and pressure flakers. Spearpoints were made from flint, chert, or obsidian. Tools could be made of appropriate stone, bone, antlers, or wood.

Sweet was a term of endearment plus a drink made with honey and various herbs.

Saparu was the chief of the Clan of Serpent. He was the biological father of Vanam and Pumi by different gatherers. {*Dim of "Nanru-Saparu" or "Great Chief."*}

Tall stone was the stone obelisk four times the height of a man that was placed on the hill marking the location of Tallstone Camp. The site could be easily seen from a distance.

Tallstone Camp was the camp surrounding the large rock referred to as the tall stone. The original site was on a hill marked by Pumi by driving a spear into the ground to identify a potential campsite favorable to his tribe's gatherers. Pumi manipulated his elders into accepting the site as a recurring camp. Pumi relocated his utilitarian Rock Table, containing engravings of hunters and antelopes, from his favorite source of stones—Rockplace Camp. He then erected the tall stone obelisk on the hill so the site could be easily seen from a distance. Circumstances caused him to surround the tall stone with Guardian Stones and personalize Sitting Stones for each chief who attended the eventual Winter Solstice Festival. The tall stone cast shadows that helped the skywatchers understand the motion of the sun and constellations.

Tethys was an adopted daughter of Kiya and Vanam.

Theia was an adopted daughter of Kiya and Vanam.

Themis was an adopted daughter of Kiya and Vanam.

Tirma was a Clan of the Auroch elder woman who made her Last Camp at Urfa.

Tribe was a collection of nomadic hunters, gatherers, and children who lived and traveled together as a unit under the direction of the tribal chief and his council. In this story, they hunted and gathered from a campsite for a season (i.e., a month) and then migrated to a new site for the next hunting season. The tribes were originally known by the name of their current chief but, with the influence of Winter Solstice Festivals, the names shifted to a "Clan of the (Totem)" designation.

Urfa was the first city. It was founded by Pumi as a campsite favoring Gatherers. It was grown into a city by Valki with endless construction projects by Putt with his apprentices. It was originally a "Last Camp" for elderly members of the Clan of the Serpent and tended by Valki. It was here that Valki domesticated einkorn. Notable inhabitants include Valki of the Clan of the Lion, Elder Woman Palai of the Clan of the Serpent, Moonwatcher Moonman of the Clan of the Serpent, Breathson of the Clan of the Lion, Putt of the Clan of the Lion, Putt-pay of the Clan of the Lion, old Hunter Pavett of Clan of the Lion, lame Hunter Nonti of the Clan of the Lion, and Elder Woman Tirma of the Clan of the Auroch, Scout Mustakshaf, and Replaceson.

Vanam, Kiya, Pumi, Valki, Putt, Putt-pay, Breathson, Littlerock.

Valki was a foundling by Vivekamulla, Clan of the Lion elder woman. She became mate to Pumi. She grew Urfa from a camp for the elderly and tribal misfits into the major city of its time. She domesticated einkorn into modern wheat. She developed the Winter Solstice Festival into a major yearly event. She adopted sons Breathson and Putt and was the biological mother to Replaceson. *{Dim of Tamil "Valkkai" or "life."}*

Valuvana was the strongest hunter in the Clan of the Serpent.

Vanam was the ambitious successor to the Clan of the Serpent Chief Saparu and the older brother to Pumi. He was the protector of Kiya. He fathered five sons by her and adopted six daughters. He eventually banished Kiya and her children from his tribe.

Vaniyal was the great Clan of the Lion skywatcher. He was the Father of Astronomy who proposed that the tall stone at the Tallstone Camp could quantify the motions of the lights in the night sky. He was the founding father of the Guild of Skywatchers, which was the prototype for the concept of scholars. *{Dim of "Vaniyal" or "Astronomer."}*

Vivekamulla was the Clan of the Lion elder woman. She was the adoptive mother of the foundling Valki. *{Dim of "Vivekamulla" or "Prudent."}*

Vohu Manah was the name given to Pumi in his last years of travels in the Far East. *{Dim of "Good Purpose."}*

Voutch was an apprentice Clan of the Lion skywatcher. He was eventually traded to the Clan of the Serpent.

Winter Solstice Festival was a festival held at Tallstone Camp each Winter's Solstice. The first Festival was the first planned encounter between the Clan of the Lion and the Clan of the Serpent. The festival grew each year as more tribes came to the planned encounter. It solidified the position of Tallstone and Urfa as the cultural and scientific center of the world and was the catalyst for the beginning of civilization.

Wolfchief was a wolf tolerant of Pumi and semi-bonded with Breathson.

Wolffriend was Wolfchief's female cub who bonded with Breathson.

Year eventually became one cycle of the heavens beginning with each Winter Solstice Festival. Tribes thought in terms of seasons. The concept of a year was not developed until the Winter Solstice Festival became fully developed. Within this work, a year is measured from the birth of Vanam and is not strongly associated with a Winter's Solstice Festival. See Season.

Saparu, Palai, Moonman. Nanatan, Vivekamulla, Vaniyal, Littlestar. Irakka, Mari, Irul.

Book One. The Beginning of Civilization: Mythologies Told True

Second Edition Changes

1. Updated sub-title.
2. Simplified birthnames for Kiya's sons: *Mutal to Firstson, Iran to Secondson, Manar to Thirdson, Nan to Fourthson, Ain to Fifthson.*
3. Changed derivation of several primary names to Akkadian and Sumerian instead of Tamil and Sanskrit: *Talaimai to Saparu, Amman to Aman, Cirantatu to Ramum.*
4. Added narrative of Pumi working at Rockplace with innocent sexual undercurrent as referenced in item 5.
5. Added Valki's first sexual union to infer "she invented sex."
6. Reimagined narrative of Putt as being self-banished.
7. Restructured Valki's final speech.
8. Shorter narrative for Pumi's death.
9. Expanded narrative detailing Vanam's descent into jealousy.
10. Expanded narrative for Vanam and Pumi's closure.
11. Expanded narrative for Valki and Kiya's closure.
12. Improved page design with a new cover and trim size.

Second Editions Publishing Schedule

Book 1. Tallstone and the City: A New Heaven and Earth, Second Edition.
June 4, 2024: Hardback ISBN 979-8-9860246-8-4, $32.00
July 8, 2024: eBook ISBN 979-8-9860246-7-7, $9.95
Summer, 2025: Paperback ISBN 979-8-9860246-6-0, 240 pages, $18.95
    75,500 words

Book 2. Kiya and Her Children: Rise and Fall of the Titans, Second Edition.
Fourth quarter, 2024.

Book 3. Dionysus and Hestia: Rise and Fall of the Olympians, Second Edition.
Fourth quarter, 2024.

Book One Publishing History

Tallstone and the City: Foundation is the first book in the series, *The Beginning of Civilization: Mythologies Told True*. It was first published as a short story, in digital format, entitled *Genesis: We Begin* on www.smashwords.com on 11/28/2018. The short story was digitally published in the anthology *Seeking Truth - Seeking Why* on Smashwords.com on 10/18/2019. *Seeking Truth - Seeking Why* was also published in paperback by DCW Press and printed by Rocky Heights Printing and Binding in March 2020 with limited copies available directly from the publisher.

The first edition of *Tallstone and the City*, ISBN 979-8-9860246-0-8, was published on September 1, 2021.

Saparu, Palai, Moonman. Nanatan, Vivekamulla, Vaniyal, Littlestar. Irakka, Mari, Irul.

Milton Keynes UK
Ingram Content Group UK Ltd.
UKHW020317070624
443692UK00011B/205/J

9 798986 024684